eXces

Happy Ever After © 2010 by Selena Kitt

All rights reserved under the International and Pan-American Copyright Conventions. No part of this book may be reproduced or transmitted in any form or by any means, electronic or mechanical, including photocopying, recording, or by any information storage and retrieval system, without permission in writing from the publisher.

This is a work of fiction. Names, places, characters and incidents are either the product of the author's imagination or are used fictitiously, and any resemblance to any actual persons, living or dead, organizations, events or locales is entirely coincidental. All sexually active characters in this work are 18 years of age or older.

This book is for sale to ADULT AUDIENCES ONLY. It contains substantial sexually explicit scenes and graphic language which may be considered offensive by some readers. Please store your files where they cannot be access by minors.

Excessica LLC
P.O. Box 127
Alpena MI 49707

To order additional copies of this book, contact:
books@excessica.com
www.excessica.com

Cover art © 2012 Alessia Brio
First Edition 2010

Warning: the unauthorized reproduction or distribution of this copyrighted work is illegal. Criminal copyright infringement, including infringement without monetary gain, is investigated by the FBI and is punishable by up to 5 years in prison and a fine of $250,000.

Table of Contents

Emet by Gabrielle Daemon	1
Red Smoke by Elise Hepner	40
The Goose Girl by Giselle Renarde	55
Black and Gold by Tessa Buxton	72
The Little Mermaid by Karenna Colcroft	83
Jack and the Beanstalk by Phineas Magnus	114
Annie and the Young Master by Bekki Lynn	135
Re-Write by Marshall Ian Key	172
The Lothian Farmer by Willsin Rowe	193
A Lover for Caché by Dakota Trace	224
The Sleeping Booty by Ava James	253

EMET
By Gabriel Daemon

Emet always dreaded the walk home from the train station. Aside from the perpetually chilling dampness and the constantly overcast sky—why he had been cursed to call this miserable coastal city home, he could not fathom—it was the human element that bothered him the most. To walk amongst these particular dregs made him lament the circumstance of his birth. The drugs, the poverty, the desperation sapped at him, ironically stealing the very humanity from his soul, bit by bit, like mosquitoes.

The Devil's Block, he often thought acidly. *An appropriate name for this place.*

Most ignored him, thankfully enough; he was no man of means, a fact revealed starkly by his clothing, so that made him target for neither beggars nor thieves, and even the pushers left him alone. But the women...

He snorted derisively when he saw them. They always came to mock him, to flaunt their bodies and display themselves as the tawdry whores they were. Whether it was the pale of the day or the pitch of the night, they wore only what they needed to preserve whatever it was they considered modesty. They reeked of sweat and cigarettes and whichever cheap perfume they could scavenge after purchasing their narcotic of choice. There was one in particular whose disgusting status was made even more tragic by the fact that she really could have been a very pretty woman. She was the worst, for her lack of shame was inversely proportionate to her physical charms.

"Well, hey sweetie!" she called, strutting from her usual perch at the corner. She always plied her trade from that same corner, beneath the leering eyes of a stone gargoyle seven stories directly above. Emet found that poetically just, for he saw the stony beast not as a protector of the dilapidated building, but as a watchdog for the Devil who oversaw the wretchedness of the world beneath.

Emet winced at the sound of the prostitute's salacious voice. It was only his personal etiquette that bade him pause and respond. "Dierdre," he rasped to the buxom redhead, both glaring at the woman while admiring the pale ripeness of her nearly-revealed breasts.

She stopped and leaned in, thrusting her cleavage toward the slightly-built man while peering within the large paper sack he carried. "What'cha got? Been to the market?"

He stiffened, wrinkling his nose at the acidic scent wafting from the woman. "If you must know, it is twenty-five pounds of clay I need to finish my latest sculpture."

She straightened, shaking her head and smacking her gum. The iridescent vermilion of her lips glowed in contrast to her pale, smooth face. Emet watched them move as she spoke again, wondering how many men she had serviced with that same mouth.

"You and your sculptures," she remarked. "Like you're some kind of fucking artist or something. What, you think you're gonna get rich some day? Move out of the Devil's Block?"

He sneered. "I don't need to be rich," he snapped. "But, yes, some day I will move out of this Dante-inspired place, and you know what?"

Dierdre planted her hands on her hips. "What."

"I would surely not return here to soil myself with a disgusting whore such as yourself."

For a brief moment, Dierdre looked insulted, but she covered it well, emitting a cackle as pale blue eyes drifted critically up and down Emet's lanky body. "I knew it," she said at last.

"Knew what?"

She passed a glistening tongue across her upper lip and allowed her eyes to drop momentarily to the sculptor's crotch. "You wanna fuck me."

He recoiled visibly, mouth agape in revulsion. "I would sooner perform cunnilingus on a goat," he declared.

She blinked, face blank. "Huh?"

Emet rolled his eyes. "Leave me alone," he growled, then resumed his march along the sidewalk.

She called after the shuffling man. "Always nice talking to you, Emet Lowe!"

* * * *

His foul mood did not dissipate upon arriving at the building wherein he lived. The aging edifice was unremarkable in that it resembled dozens of other such constructions within the Devil's Block. Made of brick and mortar, at one time it—like the others along the street—had been home to well-to-do families before the intrusion of poverty. Once-inspiring gables had sagged, shingles had slipped from the roofs, and the bricks themselves looked tired and haggard from the burden they bore.

Kicking away trash before the short stairwell to his basement abode, Emet stiffened at the shrill sound of his landlady's voice.

"Rent's due in a week, Mr. Lowe. You gonna be on time?"

He forced as amenable a smile as he could muster and looked up to the portly woman. She stood like a beggar queen at the head of the stairs before the door to the house proper. He could nearly smell the woman in her stained and wrinkled house dress. She glared back in expectation, dark little eyes almost concealed by the prolific chubbiness of her face.

"Of course, Mrs. Rudolf," he answered. "Haven't I always been on time?"

"So far," she retorted. "But I keep waiting. I don't much want to clean up that mess you've made down there."

Emet frowned. "What mess?"

"All that stuff you got lying around. It smells funny. And what is it you got under the sheet down there?"

Emet bristled. "You've been in my rooms?"

She stared back. "They're *my* rooms, Mr. Lowe. I can come and go whenever I want. You're just a *tenant*."

The slender man resisted the urge to snap back. "I assure you, I am not making a mess, as you may think. And I would like to remind you that I have, for seven months, been a good tenant."

Mrs. Rudolf's face soured as the little man scuffed his was down the steps to his door. "Nothing lasts forever," she muttered under her breath.

* * * *

"The nerve! The audacity! The sheer arrogance of that vile, malodorous woman! And those whores! Why must I be surrounded by the very worst of femininity?" Emet cried once his door was closed behind him and the heavy bag of clay had been deposited upon the only table in the spacious room. He nearly ripped his coat as he jerked his arms free of the sleeves and hurled it toward one of only two chairs. His rooms—the main one in which he stood was accompanied by a single small bathroom and closet—were cool and damp, perfect for the plying of his art. He possessed little in the way of furniture; a table, two chairs, a simple bed and a single dresser of drawers. Much of the space framed by cold, sweating bricks was devoted to his art.

Numerous clay sculptures lay along the wall beside the door, rendered as small animals or mythical creatures. They fetched fair enough prices at the various stores which deigned to sell them, enough for Emet to cover the costs of his impoverished life. But they were mere trinkets, carved to appease the children of the upper classes and those society madams who thought it "quaint" to indulge in a poor sculptor's offerings. They possessed little of Emet's spirit and desire...unlike the magnum opus which lay beneath the soiled white cloth in the center of the room.

He approached the linen-clad statue with reverence akin to a devoted worshiper entering a house of God, enjoying, for the moment, the sense of anticipation which always nibbled at his heart upon doing so. His hands—strong and firm from a lifetime of kneading and shaping—reached for the cloth, drawing it away like the sarong of a lover.

"But not you, my sweet," he whispered in awe, gazing upon the form he had crafted. Eyes which looked upon the world through a harsh veneer now softened, taking in the perfection before him. "You are not like any of those. You are my Aphrodite, my Calypso."

The statue was sublimely nude, seated upon a simple blocks of cheap, discarded cinder. The dampness of the air made her pale skin glisten, accentuating the lines of her arms and legs, the fullness of ripe breasts, the painstakingly detailed curls of sparse hair above the simple slit of her sex. Every bit of her body had been carefully and lovingly detailed, save for the round, featureless face. Emet had saved that for last, allowing his dreams to foment, over time, the vision of his personal goddess.

"The time has finally come, my dear," he announced to the statue. He took up the heavy bag from the table and tore it open, allowing blocks of moist clay to tumble to the floor. "Tonight, you shall finally have your face. Tonight, you shall be complete."

* * * *

The hours were spent in silence save for the wet smack of clay and the belabored breathing of a dutiful sculptor. As the world outside devolved into night, Emet remained with his creation, applying the clay slowly, systematically, as the vision in his head was rendered into immutable reality. First was the neck, extending strongly from its base, the line of a firm tendon leading to the edge of the jaw, then to the ear just above it. Emet took special care in shaping the lips and cheeks, wanting his perfect woman to possess the strength of Helen or Eleanor, but also the demure, innocent sweetness of Andromeda or Pandora.

The nose, first, then the eyes, were particularly challenging. He shaped and reshaped, wetting his hands with water from a bucket. The face in his dreams was hazy and vague, but as he continued, it coalesced slowly as each feature was rendered in clay.

He gave his perfect woman thick, luxurious locks, piled atop her head with a few Medusa-like curls settling upon her rounded cheeks and trailing the length of her neck. He envisioned the statue's hair as being of burnished copper, or perhaps the purest sun-kissed gold. Every curl, every lick, every tendril was maddeningly rendered until Emet was satisfied.

Once he finally stepped back to admire the beauty of his creation, even the Devil's Block, with its offensive music blaring from passing cars, the shouts and insulting cries and degenerate expletives, had grown quiet. The world, as far as Emet Lowe was concerned, had vanished. He was alone with his creation, which suited him just fine.

"Now to name you, my lovely," he said, flushed and tired. Thin lips stretched into a smile as his eyes wandered over the wet, hardening clay. "As if there were any other choice, really. I cannot name you anything but Galatea."

He stared into sightless eyes which glimmered wetly beneath carefully-formed lashes. *If only you could come to life*, he mused silently, then frowned with an afterthought. His eyes fell to the sculpted woman's left foot. *Ah, yes. My signature*, he thought, then dropped to his knees before the figure.

Every one of his creations bore a tiny inscription in the clay marking its creator, and this one could not suffer its absence. With a simple chisel and tiny hammer, he chipped into the clay just beneath the left ankle.

"Emet."

He sat up with a wrinkled brow, wondering why he did not simply carve his initials as he always did. But glancing up to the face of his goddess beyond the gentle swell of her belly and the upturned mounds of her exquisite breasts, he realized he could not have given her the same banal epitaph worn by so many meaningless creations. She deserved more.

Fatigue was finally encroaching upon him. With a groan, he rose and stumbled to the bathroom door. Dank, cracked tile and comparable mirror greeted him. The porcelain of the sink and toilet were stained to a shade of candlelight seen in dirty bordellos. Pipes protested behind the walls when he turned on the faucets to wash his hands. Bits of grayish clay swirled in the basin before slipping into the greasy blackness of the drain. A nail brush removed what little remained.

Drying his hands upon a tattered towel, Emet returned to the studio with the anticipation of gazing upon his personal Venus as he fell asleep. There would be no drape for her tonight.

The towel dropped to the floor, falling from shaking hands.

"Wh—where is she?"

His eyes fell to the rough stump upon which the statue had sat. In the pale, blue-white light streaming through his windows from the street lights above, it yet glistened as if from the moisture of a lover. Panic sliced through Emet with the precision of a surgeon's scalpel aiming for his heart.

Did someone steal her? How? I only turned away for a moment!

His gaze shot chaotically around the apartment, spying the still-closed door with its three bolt locks in place, the intact windows beside the door, even the sealed-up flue of what had once been the laundry chute for the old building. The obvious conclusion was that his statue had not been taken, yet...*where did she go?*

The sound of movement from his little kitchenette made Emet freeze.

Ssssmack. Ssssmack.

He turned his head slowly, seeing only her silhouette against the stark light of the windows: Voluptuous body, thick-locked hair dangling past a cherubic face. The erect points of her nipples stood out in stark relief against the background. One leg moved, planting a foot upon the ground, then another. The figure moved slowly.

Ssssmack. Ssssmack.

"Oh my God!" The exclamation burst from Emet's lips before he realized he was speaking.

The figure stopped, then pivoted, facing him. The simple light pouring forth from his bathroom allowed the faintest glimpse of her face. What the sculptor saw was an innocent, wide-eyed expression akin to wonder and confusion. The lush lips of a classically full mouth parted as if to speak, but no sound issued forth.

Emet stumbled back, staring in bewildered awe. The woman before him was clearly the selfsame statue he had just minutes before finished, yet, how could that be? She was a construct of clay, not flesh and blood. There was no heart to beat, no arteries to carry blood, no brain to think. There was no possible way, in heaven or on Earth, for this creation of clay and water to be alive.

Yet it was.

She reached for him hesitantly, as if not knowing what to do. Emet recoiled, but it seemed obvious to him that his creation was not about to attack. As if a newborn child, she was simply curious, unsure, confused. With that realization, Emet understood.

Tentatively, he approached, reaching to touch her hand. He tried not to focus upon the delicious nakedness of the woman before him, although he did notice the inhuman glow of perfectly golden hair upon her plump sex.

"It's okay," he cautioned, gracing her fingertips with his. "You're safe here. You're safe with me."

She seemed to acquiesce gingerly, allowing him to take her hand, touch her arm. Emet was surprised to find her warm to the touch, as any real woman would be. Carefully, he stepped closer, the features of her face becoming more clearer. She had soft, glimmering eyes the color of polished pennies, eyes which drank him in.

He led her to one of the chairs beside the table. "Here. Have a seat. Are you cold?"

She shook her head slowly, even as she settled onto her rump in the rickety chair. Her gaze remained fixed upon his face, as if seeking direction.

"So, you can understand me," he said, letting go of her hand and taking a step back. With new eyes, he appraised her nude body. *She is the most beautiful woman in the world*, he thought. A stirring within his loins made him feel a bit uncomfortable. He made an effort to quell the rush of desire. "Can you speak?"

She opened her mouth once again, pale pink lips parting with a hint of moisture, revealing a healthy tongue and fine teeth beyond. Her jaw and lips worked as if to make a sound, yet nothing issued forth. She frowned, then looked down as if in shame.

"It's all right, Galatea," Emet said quickly with all the sympathy of a father to a daughter. He took her hands once again. *She is like a child,* he thought. *Or, at least, a child in mind. Newly birthed, feeling the desires of life, but not yet knowing how to follow them.*

She looked up at the sound of the name he had given her, brow furrowing slightly.

He smiled. "Yes. Galatea. That is your name. That is who you are."

She sat up straight, clutching the sculptor's hands gently as she seemed to contemplate his words. While she did so, Emet's eyes roamed over the exquisite body he had given his creation. He was grateful for the detail he had applied to her crafting, for there was nothing about Galatea that did not conform to his fantasies. She was voluptuous without being Rubenesque, demure without being childish. The firm shape of her breasts defied gravity, pushing plump pink nipples up toward the ceiling, while the soft yet firm shape of her belly only accentuated the golden-haired treasure beneath.

Her eyes followed his, and fell to what her creator beheld. Still maintaining that expression of demure innocence, Galatea parted her thighs, allowing full access to Emet's questing gaze.

He swallowed thickly, feeling his heart hammering with arousal and anxiety. The plump lips of his creation's sex parted, allowing the glistening, sleek inner folds to play out like the petals of a blossoming rose. The bulbous head of her clitoris swelled and pushed outward, shining like a pearl above a bed of pure, pink silk.

Emet cleared his throat uncomfortably. "Y-you shouldn't do that," he stammered, attempting in vain to tear his gaze from that succulent vision of sexual loveliness.

Galatea's response was to spread her legs even more brazenly. She reclined in the chair, slipping her firm buttocks to the edge. Her labia flared, glistening as if with true womanly arousal.

Emet pulled his hands from hers and forced himself to meet her penny-colored eyes. "You don't know what you're doing--" he began, but caught his words in the back of his throat when she reached to cup the obvious bulge beneath his dirty pants. Her touch was firm yet soft, massaging and exploring. Her sweet round eyes quested within his.

"You...you cannot know what you are doing," he said, even as she lowered her gaze and brought up her other hand. Lips pouting and eyes glowing with what seemed to be interest, Galatea worked her fingers to undo Emet's pants, pushing them off his hips. He wore nothing beneath, and his erection jutted out firmly and fully, surrounded at the root by a thick patch of dark, sweat-dampened hair.

She smiled, then, cheeks bulging, and lifted her hands to caress the firmness of Emet's cock. The sculptor shivered, wavering on his feet. It had been years since he had been touched in this way. And never before had he felt the sweet, searing heat and luxurious wetness that now bathed him as Galatea bent and slid her soft, eager mouth around his shaft.

"Oh, god," he panted, light-headed, reflexively pushing forward. He watched in rapture as the full length of his penis disappeared into the accommodating mouth of his impossibly alive statue. He groaned when her nose pressed against his flat abdomen, her chin against his hairy testicles. She suckled him affectionately, pulling and caressing with lips and tongue. Her hands caressed up and down along the outsides of his thighs, then between to find and knead his swollen sacs.

This is not real, he thought even as he pumped into Galatea's mouth. *It cannot be. But, by God in Heaven, nothing has ever felt so delicious, so pure...surely no whore upon the* could face the door was a man who appeared to have aged not a day since Emet saw him last.

The younger man's words were timid. "Rabbi?"

Rabbi Rausch glanced up from the newspaper he had been reading. His expression behind thick-framed glasses was at first stoic and inscrutable as he beheld the man before him. Eventually, dry lips parted and brow furrowed. "Emet. How long has it been?"

Chastisement descended upon the sculptor as he let the door close behind him. "Probably too long."

The learned holy man sat up straight and set the paper aside. He offered a curious smile. "I am not sure whether to commend God or just chalk it up to serendipity. I was just wondering about you the other day."

Emet looked admonished. "Wondering why I haven't been back to temple, I'm sure."

Rausch shrugged. "Not so much," he said. His expression and demeanor became more grave. "Are you all right? I had heard you moved into the Devil's Block."

The sculptor nodded. "It's been a rough go of it lately," he admitted. He managed a smile. "But things are looking up."

The rabbi smiled. "Well, then, I suppose I am both sad and glad to hear of it."

"Thank you, Rabbi." He shifted on his feet, looking furtive.

The older man was quick to read Emet's anxiety. He smiled reassuringly. "Why don't we take a walk?"

* * * *

It was difficult to begin his narrative, but once he did, Emet prattled on with all the bubbly effluence of a teenager in describing—without too much detail—the circumstances of Galatea's animation and her subsequent amorousness. Rabbi Rausch listened carefully all the while as the two men strolled through a city park near the synagogue. Finally, he directed the younger man toward a park bench and sat.

"...I know this all sounds crazy, Rabbi, but I am speaking the truth," Emet insisted as he, too, took a seat. "I carved a

Emet snapped his fingers. "Done!" he declared before whistling his way out the door.

And so it went through the remainder of the morning and into the afternoon. At another store he was greeted with news that one of his pieces had sold just that morning, which resulted in much-needed money in the sculptor's pocket. After a quick lunch from the counter at a deli, Emet made the purchase of twenty more pounds of clay, in anticipation of a productive night.

In more than one way, he chuckled mutely to himself, his thoughts and libido turning to the beautiful Galatea. But he forced clarity into his mind. *There is still one last stop to make.*

If he had not pushed away thoughts of carnal pleasure before, they would certainly have faded upon approaching the steps of the synagogue. It had been quite some time since last he had stepped through the heavy doors, since last he had worn the yarmulke. Even with his minimal possessions, it had taken some digging through his dresser to uncover it. Somberness fell upon him like a giant hand as he settled the little knitted cap atop his head.

A faint hint of incense greeted him at the door. Through the heavy walls, he heard faint prayers from the sanctuary. No coherent words, just the haunting mumbles of devoted men. Though guilt gave him pause for a moment, he decided not to offer his own prayers to God; *after so many years, what would one prayer do now?*

The hallway to the offices were less austere. Emet found what he was looking for at the third door. After setting his heavy bag on the bench seat in the hall, he faced the door. His hand hesitated before knuckles rapped against the polished wood.

"Come in," a ragged but vaguely familiar voice called.

A lump settling in his throat, Emet pushed the door open, tentatively following it in. The office beyond was simple, nearly spartan. Merely shelves lined with books and a large black desk in one corner. Seated alongside the desk so that he

For the first time in more years than he cared to think about, Emet Lowe was smiling as he rode the train the following morning. He had patently ignored the shuffling homeless and shiftless dealers on the way to the station—the prostitutes would not be about for hours yet—as if they were little more than minor obstacles in his path. Nearly all of his thoughts were directed toward his lovely Galatea, who had awakened him that morning with her mouth and hands, bringing him swiftly to erection before impaling herself.

She had ridden him with enthusiasm, and though she made no noise, she became flushed with a wanton look which served to heighten her lover's enjoyment. Emet had briefly wondered how a construct composed of three hundred pounds of clay could be so light atop him before deciding he was happy that it was so.

The owners of the various shops and stores in the Deco District were surprised and even wary to see a smile upon Emet's face and buoyancy in his step. All they had ever known of the skinny, sunken-eyed man was dourness and angst, the hallmarks of the tortured artist. The man they now met had a brightness in his formerly pale, beady eyes and a smile upon thin lips.

"What happened with you, old man?" quipped one of the collectibles dealers he met, who then jabbed Emet in the shoulder. "Don't tell me you finally got some."

The sculptor—who often bristled when the dealer called him "old man" since, by definition, he was still only middle-aged—frowned. "A gentleman does not discuss the details of such things, Michael."

Michael shook his head with a grin. "Well, whoever she is, thank her for all of us."

"You can thank *me* by making an advance purchase of my statues," Emet responded readily. "I have a feeling I will be turning out some rather inspired pieces soon."

Michael mulled the idea over. "Tell you what. Bring me something in a few days, and if I like it, I'll take as many as you got."

street above could match my Galatea's skill at giving pleasure.

Such thoughts faded away, destroyed and cast upon the winds of lust as the pleasure continued. Emet grunted and moaned, settling his hands to either side of Galatea's head and entangling his fingers in her hair. He jabbed and pushed, feeding his lover the full length of his staff again and again, and never did she balk, or gag, or protest in any way. She merely continued sucking, pulling, massaging, coaxing out from within him the gift he had rarely shared with a woman throughout his life.

"Oh, Galatea! My angel! My goddess! My--" further appraisals became gibberish as Emet groaned and bucked against his lover, feeling the rush of supreme pleasure as it sped up from the ends of his limbs, gathered in his groin, then burst through the tip of his spasming penis deep within Galatea's mouth. He cried out in ecstasy such as he had never known before, clutching her head close to his tumultuous groin.

Stop! Stop, my love, he thought, as her oral ministrations became too much. *Suck it gently...bring me down slowly from the heights...*

As if in accordance with his thoughts, Galatea did as Emet wished, massaging his cock with slow, soothing caresses of her tongue, allowing him to soften in her mouth. Only when the sculptor sighed in gratefulness did he pull back, drawing his spent manhood from between the living statue's lips. He cupped her face in his hands, gazing euphorically upon her angelic, perfect face. A single thick bauble of milky cream decorated her lower lip.

She gazed upon his face, once again seeking direction. The dollop of fluid upon her lip dripped to the floor below.

Emet smiled beneath glazed eyes. "Come to bed with me," he whispered.

Wordlessly, Galatea rose and followed her master to the bed in the corner.

* * * *

statue and...she's alive!" He hung his head, smiling wistfully, leaning forward with elbows on his knees. "She's the perfect woman."

Rabbi Rausch pursed his aged lips, the wrinkles around his eyes darkening. "Perfect, you say."

"Yes. Perfect."

"Because she does as you command?"

"Because...because she knows what I want, before I even know what I want!"

"On the contrary," informed the rabbi. "She is merely feeding off your desires. The more base, the easier it is for your construct to respond. You must take care, for she will act in accordance with the simplest of your urges."

Emet grinned rakishly. "I don't mind it so far."

"Then you have not thought about it," chided the rabbi. "Consider the possibilities: lust is one of the most powerful basic instincts a man possesses. But so is pride. And anger." He spoke the last two words while looking the younger man directly in the eye.

Emet swallowed thickly, agreeing slowly with the learned man. "I need to be careful, then, how I express myself around her."

"More than that. You must guard against feelings such as hate."

A dark look of realization crossed Emet's face. "Truthfully, I expected you to tell me I'm crazy," he said with a nervous laugh. "But you talk like this is nothing new."

"It isn't," the rabbi answered simply. "Do you know the legend of the Golem?"

A deep furrow between Emet's eyes was his only response.

Rabbi Rausch rolled his eyes with a huff. "You never did follow up on your studies," he lamented, then cleared his throat. "When your mother first presented you to me, I wondered as to why she chose the name she gave you. It seemed, at the time, an appropriate name, especially considering the particular spelling. The circumstances of your conception, after all--"

Emet ground his teeth. "I know all about that," he said quickly. "Mother told me just before she died."

Rausch nodded. "I cannot imagine it would be an easy thing to accept that you were the product of a violent rape. I offer my sympathies for that. I only bring up the subject to offer context."

"What kind of context?"

Rausch met Emet's eyes directly. "Do you know what your name means?"

The sculptor frowned in confusion. "Well...no."

"You see, the name 'Emmet,' with two Ms, means 'universal.' But your name is spelled E-M-E-T." He glanced to the younger man to insure his attention. "The word 'Emet' means truth, or life, in Hebrew. I always assumed your mother wanted that name for you, with that spelling, in order to erase the horror of how you came to be."

Emet's face darkened. "You certainly know how to brighten a man's day," he remarked with sarcasm. "But what does my name have to do with this Golem?"

"In light of what you have told me, everything," the rabbi said. "You see, in the seventeenth century, a rabbi in Prague constructed a massive statue of clay in order to protect the Jews in that city from the mayor's soldiers. That statue was a golem. It could not be stopped or killed, and followed the wishes of its creator. In the end, the mayor of Prague gave in to the rabbi's demands and spared the Jews. The golem was sealed inside an attic, where it supposedly remains to this day."

Emet blinked, waiting.

Rabbi Rausch continued. "In order to animate the golem, the rabbi needed to inscribe a particular word onto his creation. The word was 'Emet.'"

The sculptor suddenly nodded in understanding, his memory flashing back in less than a heartbeat to his act of carving his full first name upon the foot of the statue. "And I did the same with Galatea. Every artist signs his work."

"I suspected as much. The moment you did, somehow, your statue became animated. But do not think that is the same as coming to life."

Emet looked uncomfortable. The strange coincidences of his life had led to the creation of a potential monster. He did not want to admit that.

"Emet?"

The slender sculptor nodded his head only once. "I'm listening."

Rabbi Rausch inhaled deeply, then let it out as a long, contemplative sigh. "I would like to see this creation of yours."

Again, Emet nodded, then rose wordlessly from the park bench. He did not look to see if the rabbi followed him; he knew the older man would.

* * * *

Apprehensive hands fidgeted with the lock to Emet's home. With the presence of the rabbi behind him, he felt to be under scrutiny. He was not entirely sure what awaited beyond the door. A small part of him wondered if the bliss he had shared with Galatea had all been a dream.

Finally, he slipped the correct key into the slot beneath the weathered brass doorknob and disengaged the lock. Carefully, he peered within before Rabbi Rausch could see anything.

Galatea sat like the statue she was upon the cinder-block pedestal in the middle of the room. Her skin glowed with ghostly pale radiance. Her eyes remained blank, and her hair matched the color of her milky skin. She was apparently immobile and unaware of her surroundings, until Emet stepped into the room, the rabbi following.

Pale clay turned a slightly more fleshy tone and the eyes came alive with color. Her hair splayed away from the round, angelic face as Galatea turned to look upon her master. She smiled warmly, glittering eyes catching the pale light of day flooding into the room. Only briefly did she glance to the aged man behind Emet, whose presence, apparently, bothered her not a whit. There was no modesty within her as she rose in her unabashed nudity.

"There," said Emet proudly. "My Galatea."

Rabbi Rausch cleared his throat. "You, eh, certainly took a lot of care in your, eh, rendering of her," he commented, looking over the woman's exquisite form.

"She is, without a doubt, my best work."

Galatea smiled demurely, eyes boring into Emet's while she awaited his commands.

The rabbi stepped around, gingerly approaching the animated statue. "Would you mind?" he asked carefully with a glance to the sculptor.

"Of course, rabbi," Emet said. "She is perfectly docile."

Indeed, as the Rabbi approached, Galatea stood straight, arms at her sides and breasts thrust out as if encouraging the elderly man's advance. The rabbi blushed, having trouble believing that this delectable woman before him was nothing more than a clay statue animated by a combination of ancient Hebrew mysticism and distorted luck.

His hands settled to her shoulders; they felt firm and warm, like any real woman's. His touch traveled down her arms, gently pulling them out so he could see the palms of the woman's hands. As he deduced, they were as smooth as the rest of her skin. Nor did she possess fingerprints.

He glanced back to Emet with a meaningful look. "You must trust me, Emet. What I am about to do may seem painful at first glance. But, if Galatea is what you say she is, it will not affect her."

Hesitantly, Emet nodded, then watched as the Rabbi reached for a long metal awl on the sculptor's stand. Holding the fingers of Galatea's right hand, he settled the point of the awl in the middle of her palm and pushed.

Emet winced at first, but a quick look to Galatea told him she was completely unperturbed by the rabbi's actions. Rausch pushed with as much strength as he could muster, causing a spike of clay-like skin to form on the back of Galatea's hand. There was no blood, no seepage of any kind other than a few drops of clear moisture around both the point of insertion and when the awl finally broke through the other side.

Rausch let go of the awl and turned Galatea's hand over. The skin retracted slowly back along the length of the slim metal tool. He shook his head in amused disbelief. "Truly amazing," he muttered.

"It is as I said," Emet gushed, smiling broadly. "Why, this can only be a miracle sent by God himself!"

The rabbi raised a cautionary finger. "Be careful of your words, Emet," he warned. "There are miracles, and then there are things unexplained."

"But, rabbi--"

Rausch silenced the sculptor's protest with a short hissing sound. "You must keep her hidden. Do not tell anyone about her. In fact, if you are adamant about keeping her, I would suggest you locate a more secluded place to live. This neighborhood has many wandering ears and eyes."

Emet frowned. "I am a poor artist," he bemoaned. "It's good that Galatea doesn't eat, because I could not even afford to buy more food! And you want me to move?"

The rabbi's look was direct and honest. "I said nothing of feasibility," he said, then softened. "But this place is not the best for keeping such a creature. You must be very careful about not allowing her existence to be known to the world."

Begrudgingly, Emet nodded, then smiled rakishly. "So I have to keep her locked up, and all to myself, then. At least until I can afford better accommodations."

Rausch rolled his eyes, but he nodded with a chuckle. "Just be careful, Emet."

The sculptor offered his hand. "I will, rabbi. Thank you."

* * * *

As soon as the door closed, Emet heard Galatea moving behind him. There came the clattering of metal as the awl fell to the floor, and the sculptor turned, watching as Galatea approached the bed. Obviously responding to the sudden spike in her creator's libido, she crawled onto the dirty mattress, settling on her knees with her thighs spread widely apart. She bent over, stretching her arms toward the pillows at the head of the bed.

Trembling desire overcame the sculptor. He hastily removed his coat, then shirt, shuffling toward the deliciously—and lewdly—displayed backside of his mystical lover. His pants fell around his ankles, revealing a stiff and ready cock. Hands caressed the firm round rump of his personal goddess. His eyes settled on the forbidden treasure of her anus, which was as pale as the rest of her skin with just the slightest hint of pink at the wrinkled aperture. Emet was certain the fact that Galatea had positioned herself at just the right height was no coincidence.

He trembled in bliss at just the barest contact of the tip of his erection against the puckered, pursed opening. "Is this what you want, my dearest?" he asked her. "Do you want me...in there?"

Golden hair bobbed about her head as Galatea nodded.

Emet found his throat dry, head light. The devilish kink of anal sex had always intrigued him, had always been an unsatisfied fantasy. Now, on the verge of making that fantasy real, he was nearly at the point of ejaculation already. With effort, he managed to control himself, taking his cock in hand and pushing the head against Galatea's nether orifice. He was surprised to find her damp there. His creation, it seemed, had the ability to make any part of her moist and accommodating.

He watched the pale opening spread slowly around his cock, revealing deeper and deeper shades of pink as the head popped inside. Emet groaned, gripping his lover's hips. Galatea pushed up on her hands and arched her back more deeply than even the most willing whore. The snug, gripping tunnel of her anus pulled his length in, sucking like a mouth, burning like a furnace. Inch by inch, the whole of Emet's phallus was consumed.

For a long moment, he simply leaned against her, relishing the incomparable sensations. His cock throbbed almost painfully, but exquisitely so, massaged along the full length by muscular movements no mortal woman could possess. He caressed her taut cheeks, the furrow of her spine.

Galatea looked over her should at him. Her face was flushed, sweaty, eyes blazing with an expression of pure lust. Lips pouted and trembled. Full breasts heaved. To further eroticize the moment, she took one of her hands from the bed and cupped a perfectly round, firm teat, pinching the engorged nipple.

Emet moaned, reaching for a handful of his lover's luxurious hair. It felt like silk as he gathered a fistful and jerked back. Galatea reacted as if grunting in painful pleasure, but of course, no sound issued forth. That little fact did not matter to Emet. The expression was enough. It showed her submission to him, his dominance over her. Pulling back until just the head of his heated cock was nestled within her ass, he shoved home to the hilt. Galatea bucked and writhed, shaking as he pounded into her again and again.

The cool, quiet air was filled the sounds of wet skin slapping together, Emet's groans and grunts, the protests of mattress springs. Emet alternately watched his creation's sweaty face—at one point, a tear trickled from her right eye—and the bacchanalian sight of his penis sliding in and out of that most taboo of a woman's openings. He was not sure which excited him the most.

He nearly screamed the arrival of his orgasm, pleasurably sending liquid fire into the body of his lover, creation, and conquest. He shuddered against Galatea, slapping both hands to her quivering buttocks to keep from falling atop her body. He felt every trickle of seed leave his cock as Galatea milked him of every drop.

Drained, dulled, and satisfied, Emet swayed on his feet, eyes closed and sweat dripping from his nose. "That was incredible, Galatea," he muttered. "You truly are...my perfect woman."

Galatea eased forward on the bed, letting her master collapse atop her. As always, she said nothing. The flush drained from her face and the "sweat" dried. As Emet slid off her to the mattress on his side, she stared blankly at the wall for only a few seconds before closing her eyes.

* * * *

The following several days saw a rejuvenated Emet obsessively at work, crafting figure after figure. His imagination sparked by the carnal experiences provided via his lover, he indulged in the motifs of Greek and Roman myth. Lustful satyrs, coy nymphs, and erection-sporting conquerors became his new theme. He found his hands and tools flying effortlessly about the mounds of clay, creating artful and intricate renditions born from his own base and lustful mind.

And whenever he was ready and randy, Galatea was available to him without him having to speak a word. Whatever his debauched desire, she acted out her part without hesitation or judgment. Emet allowed himself the fantasy of reading into the golem's sweaty and impassioned face a true desire for whatever it was she did for him. Ultimately, he knew none of it mattered; she was simply a creation, after all, with no more feeling than the tools he had used to create her. Still, a part of him wanted to ascribe to her at least some humanity, even if only to lend satisfaction to his acts of dominance.

Five days after Rabbi Rausch's visit, Emet oversaw the loading of three boxes of hardened clay figurines onto the back of a truck. Michael the art dealer had consented to accept twenty-three statues—the number surprised the younger man—in good faith, with the agreement that, if he did not like them, he would have his driver return them without charge to Emet's apartment.

Oh, he will take them, Emet thought assuredly as the hefty driver carefully arranged the boxes in the back of his truck. Emet had not allowed the man to enter his rooms; he had set the boxes just outside the door, which remained shut so as not to afford any accidental glimpses of Galatea.

Taking a moment, Emet opened the door to his basement apartment, peering inside. Galatea turned to look at him from her usual perch upon the cinder column. He smiled fondly. "I will return later, my lovely," he said as if to reassure her.

She nodded.

"And, do not go near the windows," he continued. "No one can know you are here. Do you understand?"

Again, she nodded.

Satisfied, Emet closed the door and locked it, then ascended the steps to join the driver in his idling truck.

He did not notice the curtain in Mrs. Rudolf's front window, the one which oversaw the stairwell down to his rooms, as it settled back into place.

* * * *

Who was he talking to? Mrs. Rudolf wondered as she stepped back from the window. Suspicion burned through her mind. *That little weasel of a man better not have anyone staying with him.*

She sipped her coffee in contemplation, maneuvering the bulk of her body around the cluttered living room.

He's been acting strange lately. When he came to pay his rent, he was actually smiling. Only two things make a man smile. Money and pussy.

She soured. *He clearly is not making money, otherwise he wouldn't be here. Which means...*

A distasteful look crossed her face. *He must be keeping one of those trashy, disease-ridden whores from down the street*, she decided. *And I can't have that. Not in* my *house!*

"Carl! Jeffrey!" she shouted in her shrill tone.

Within moments, a pair of large, dim-witted men assembled in the living room, one from the kitchen, the other from one of the rooms upstairs. She gave them a sneering look while taking a ring of keys from within her voluminous house dress.

"Go down to Mr. Lowe's apartment in the basement," she ordered. "See if there is someone staying with him."

"Yes ma'am!" answered Carl, the larger of the two.

"What we 'sposed to do if there is?" asked Jeffrey.

Mrs. Rudolf grinned evilly. "Send her back to the street and deposit all of Mr. Lowe's things onto the sidewalk. He has breached his rental agreement."

The two men nodded and grinned. Carl took the key Mrs. Rudolf held out.

"I have some errands to run," she announced. "I should be back in a few hours. I trust this matter will be cleared up by then."

"You bet, Mrs. Rudolf."

* * * *

Michael regarded the boxes of small sculptures with impressed eyes. He had always known Emet for creating rather typical depictions of woodland animals and other such fare. Well-rendered and with acute attention to detail, but not exactly eye-catching. What he saw now, however, went against the grain the middle-aged sculptor normally offered.

"Emet, old man," he finally said, reaching into a box to take up a detailed statuette of a nubile, naked woman astride a unicorn with an obvious erection. "I am impressed."

The sculptor grinned with pride. "As I said, I have been inspired."

Michael chuckled, replacing the diminutive statue and picking up another. "She must be one hell of a woman," he remarked, brow furrowed as he looked the detailed carving over. It showed a muscular satyr, standing with goat legs splayed wide. Two massive, detailed erections jutted out from the creature's groin, pointed toward a pair of crouching, naked fairies with their mouths open and tongues outstretched, as if about to catch the streams of the satyr's orgasm.

"She is unique," Emet responded. "So...?"

"Well, I'll be honest," Michael said. "I get a lot of customers looking for erotic pieces like this. Seems to be all the rage now."

Emet grinned. "These boxes constitute only a small sample," he said. "In fact, given the proper advance, I could purchase enough clay to make three times as many pieces as this."

Michael arched an eyebrow in interest. "Oh, really?"

The sculptor met the art dealer's eye. "Yes. Really."

The younger man contemplated the implied offer for a moment, then nodded. "I'll tell you what," he finally said. "Five hundred as an advance against sales. I'll put them right in the front window and price them from fifty to seventy bucks to start. If they sell quickly, I'll raise the price and settle at fifty percent."

Emet was quick to counter. "Twenty-five percent," he said. "The rest to me."

Michael narrowed his eyes. "Thirty-three," he counter-offered. "The rest to you."

Emet smiled and held out his hand. "My advance, if you please. Oh, and I will need the services of your driver for all the clay I'll need to take back to my apartment."

* * * *

As with the morning, Emet did not allow Michael's driver to enter his apartment. He had the burly man deposit four hundred dollars' worth of malleable clay in several boxes upon his basement doorstep, then sent the man on his way. As the truck rumbled away, the old, dented Cadillac belonging to his landlady sidled up along the curb. Emet gave her a disparaging look.

"Afternoon, Mrs. Rudolf," he said without disguising his contempt.

Her eyes searched the sidewalk, as if looking for something. She seemed displeased that she did not see what she had expected. "Mr. Lowe," she responded after emitting a small belch. Paper bags and fast food wrappers littered the front passenger seat. She wiped her slovenly mouth. "Is everything in order with your rooms? I like to make sure my tenants are well cared for."

"Oh, I'm sure everything is fine," he said. "I only just now returned home, but I am sure my apartment is unmolested."

She smiled mirthlessly. "Then all is well, Mr. Lowe. Good day."

"Good day." He watched as Mrs. Rudolf put the aging Cadillac in gear and pulled away from the curb, then as she drove around the corner to the rear parking lot. His dislike for the woman had grown with that simple exchange. Feeling a spike of anxiety stab through his heart, he turned to the steps and descended to his door.

* * * *

The sight which greeted him made Emet stumble in the doorway, gripping the handle of the door for support. His mouth gaped; eyes bulged. Even with the pale light which seemed to transform every color into lifeless shades of grey, the streaks, spatters, and puddles of congealed blood all but glowed with unnatural radiance.

Two large, muscular young men lay upon the floor, their bodies crushed and twisted at obscene angles. The closest one lay with his chest to the floor but his head turned all the way around. One arm was canted upward, broken in several places, the limp hand hanging down toward the middle of the back. The other corpse stared upward with an expression of perpetual pain. Both had apparently been bludgeoned to death.

"Oh, no," bemoaned Emet, looking upon the surreal scene of carnage. "What happened? Galatea? Galatea! Where are you?"

She emerged from the darkest corner of the room, beautiful sublime body decorated with blood. Both of her arms were streaked with drying crimson ichor, with more spots and lines upon firm, naked breasts. Her face remained innocent, unperturbed, as if heedless to the violence that had been committed.

"G-Galatea?"

She nodded slowly, and smiled, raising her blood-stained hands in welcome.

Quickly, Emet shut the door behind him. The spike of anxiety from moments before became a pounding wave against his chest. "Wh-what did you do?"

His creation lowered her arms and glanced to the bodies upon the floor. Her brow furrowed as she returned her gaze to Emet. It was as if she could not understand why he was acting the way he was.

I only told her to remain inside, he thought, remembering. *Not to go near the windows. I told her...*

His face paled as he recalled his words, and the chilling directive he had inadvertently given Galatea.

No one can know you are here.

He sighed deeply, heavily. *By telling her that, I opened the door to this carnage. If she was discovered by someone, how better to insure no one knew of her existence than by killing those who discovered her?*

And now I have a mess to clean up. He pinched the bridge of his brow, trying to stem off a headache. *Where did they come from? Thugs from the street, seeking to rob me?* A dark chuckle escaped his throat and he squatted beside the second corpse. "Did you find what you were looking for?" he asked with morbid glee. But his eyes narrowed in suspicion as he looked past the dried blood on the body's face. "Wait. I know you."

Hurriedly, he dug beneath the corpse's backside, seeking the wallet. Finding it, he flipped it open—forty dollars went into Emet's own pocket—and extracted the driver license. "Well, hello, Carl Wilson," he said with a sneer. Upon reading the address, Emet craned his head, looking upward as if through his ceiling to the rooms above.

A cold, malicious smile pulled at the corners of his mouth.

* * * *

Emet found the fat woman as she sat before the aged television in the living room of the house. She looked up from a box of cheese crisps with an annoyed frown. "Mr. Lowe," she grumbled. "You don't often crawl out of your hole, and today I've seen you twice."

He glared back briefly, then dropped a pair of well-worn wallets onto the coffee table. "I found these outside in the garbage," he said simply. "They belong to a couple of the other tenants, I believe. You might want to be sure they get them back."

A cold hand squeezed Mrs. Rudolf's heart, but only briefly. She gave Emet a dismissive look. "Thank you, Mr. Lowe. They'll be glad to have them back."

"I only hope I don't find any others," he said as he turned back toward the door. "No one wants to be caught *dead* without their identification around here."

* * * *

Mrs. Rudolf finally turned off the lights just before eleven o'clock. The world news was over, and she was no fan of late-night *Seinfeld* reruns. Still bristling over Emet Lowe's earlier smugness, she pushed away thoughts of how such an ineffectual little man could have fended off two hulking men as Carl and Jeffrey, as well as the location of her erstwhile tenants. She simply assumed the buffoons were avoiding her due to their failure.

This isn't the end of it, she told herself firmly as she ambled up the stairs. *I'll see that little weasel gets put on the street, along with whatever little tramp he's got stashed away.*

The muffled—but still loud—bass emanating from one of the apartments just past the landing made her scowl. She went to the door and hammered a fleshy fist against it. "Hey! No loud music after ten o'clock!" she yelled. "Or whatever you call that shit you're playing!"

Fucking losers, she thought to herself, smirking as the noise behind her abated. Most of her tenants, she knew, could not afford a late-night visit from the police for a noise disturbance.

Past the four rented rooms on the third floor, Mrs. Rudolf arrived at her own door. The exertion from climbing two flights of stairs was telling; her face was swollen and red, and sweat trickled down her neck from her temples. She recalled the days before the late Mr. Rudolf passed, when she rarely had need to leave the "penthouse" on the top floor. *Curse the old bastard for dying on me,* she mused darkly.

The room beyond was cluttered with stacks of newspapers, magazines, and other recyclables Mrs. Rudolf had long planned to have taken away. The odor of mildew and rotting food filled the room. The capacious woman wrinkled her nose briefly, but she was used to the smell. Ignoring the clutter, she headed for the kitchenette, looking for a last snack before bed. A half-full jar of pickles would do the trick, she decided.

Turning back toward the living area, she gave a startled gasp, inadvertently letting the jar slip from her grasp.

"Good evening, Mrs. Rudolf."

She glared, eyes blazing wildly. "Mr. Lowe! How dare you! I'll call the police!"

The gaunt man shook his head with a dark chuckle. "Oh, you know how long it takes them to respond around here, Mrs. Rudolf. Better to call the Salvation Army."

"These are my rooms," she hissed, spittle dripping from her lower lip. "You have no business here."

"Oh, I think I do," he responded casually. "Galatea, my darling, give the old hen back her pickles."

Mrs. Rudolf frowned, then looked to her left, where stood an unabashedly naked young woman with the most unearthly golden hair and glittering eyes she had ever witnessed. A disgusted expression twisted the fat landlady's face as she snatched the jar from pale, offering hands. "Have you no shame? Is this what the world has come to? Naked whores running around carelessly?"

Emet shook his head with a wan smile. "Oh, my dear creation is nothing like those pathetic whores who part their thighs for the chemistry gods. She is so much more than that."

"Well, I really don't care, Mr. Lowe," she bristled, even as she remembered their earlier meeting, and the implication that this slight, frail-looking man had somehow chased off her buffoons. She made an effort to be amiable, despite the context. "I would ask you to leave."

"In due time," Emet said, then gave a short nod to the silent Galatea. Without the slightest flicker of emotion, the alabaster-skinned woman raised a large butcher knife, taken from Mrs. Rudolf's own cupboard, and advanced.

The corpulent woman blanched visibly, eyes widening in fear at the sight of the knife. "Wh-what are you doing?"

"Have you ever heard of the term 'just deserts,' by any chance?"

Mrs. Rudolf backpedaled into the kitchen, raking a fleshy hip against the counter. She fell against the refrigerator, fear blatant in her eyes as the naked inhuman woman approached. "I'll give you whatever you want! Please! Tell her to stop!"

"But why would I want to do that? I can't stop now; you know too much."

"I won't say anything! I swear!" Even as she screeched out those words, Mrs. Rudolf raised her arms to protect herself, palms turned outward so the hands would shield her face. This, of course, left the insides of her forearms fully exposed.

She heard more than felt the quick slashes of the blade, metal singing wetly in the air. She cried out once, anticipating a death stroke, but it did not come.

With slow trepidation, Mrs. Rudolf lowered her arms, focusing past her own curled fingers to a sight which both sickened and unnerved her. Emet stood behind his voluptuous companion, chin upon her shoulder beside the ghostly, blank face. His hands had come up from behind to grope and knead heavy, fleshy breasts. His face grinned maniacally.

"Isn't she wonderful? So beautiful, so obedient, so...deadly."

Brow wrinkling with confusion, Mrs. Rudolf became aware of the sensation of liquid warmth running down the inside of her arms. Dreading what she might find, the loathsome woman turned her arms and looked upon the long, leaking gouges which ran from wrists nearly to her elbows.

Bloody flaps of flesh lay wide open, allowing the torrent of blood to spill freely to the floor.

"Oh, sweet Jesus in Heaven," she muttered, feeling her vision blur as light-headedness set in. She could barely focus upon the two figures before her as Emet Lowe bent the naked woman over before him, thrusting his hips firmly against her backside.

The degenerate, perverse vision of two lovers fucking while she died was the last thing Mrs. Rudolf would ever see.

* * * *

"Emet!" exclaimed Michael as the lanky sculptor stepped through his doors. "How's my favorite artist?"

Emet smirked arrogantly, meeting the younger man with outstretched hand. "Oh, I'm your favorite, now?"

Michael chuckled. "Well, sure! I've sold all your pieces. Even had people coming back all week asking when I'm going to have more."

The sculptor grinned. "Then you will be glad to accept the thirty new pieces I've completed."

"Thirty?"

Emet nodded. "Your driver should be bringing them in shortly."

Michael shook his head with a grateful smile and clasped Emet's bony shoulder. "I don't know how you did it, but you did. Just the other day, I showed some of your pieces to a couple of appraisers. They really liked what they saw, Emet."

"This is only the beginning. I have even more impressive works in the making."

"Can't wait to see them," Michael said honestly. His eyes softened. "Sorry to hear about that mess last week with your landlady."

Emet shrugged. "She was obviously not well."

The shop owner shook his head ruefully. "Dangerous place you live in, old man. Your landlady goes crazy, beats a couple of her tenants to death before slitting her wrists...you ever think she might have killed you, too?"

The sculptor smiled. "Not really, no."

* * * *

While the sun, as always, did not shine upon the Devil's Block, Emet could almost feel its warming glow as he left the train station and stepped lively along the street toward his home. The majority of his day had been spent glad-handing with the various shop and gallery owners who sold his wares. They had all agreed to the same deal he enjoyed with Michael, resulting in a flattering return for the struggling artist.

In a mere week, he had earned more than enough money to pay his rent, all other bills, and put some aside. It had been years since Emet had enjoyed a financial surplus. He looked forward to finding a better place to live, a better life, one which he would happily spend with his perfect woman, Galatea.

Head held high as he strutted through the filthy streets, Emet had no other thought in his mind than to return to his humble apartment and spend the evening indulging in all manner of carnal delights with his compliant lover. He flatly ignored the looks from dealers, pimps and prostitutes, until a lone voice called out to him.

"Well, if it ain't Emet Lowe!"

He stopped, eyes searching, finding the busty redhead as she strolled from her usual corner. Crimson lips glowed against pale skin as she smacked her gum. The bemused gleam upon her face sent uncomfortable chills down the sculptor's spine.

"Oh. You again. I thought perhaps you had died," Emet said snidely.

"Now ain't that a terrible thing to say," she chided him, stopping a few paces away with hands on her hips. "'Course, I was thinking the same about you. You ain't been coming and going like you always did. I was starting to miss my Emsie-Wemsie."

He scoffed derisively. "If you have to know, I've become quite popular for my sculptures. I dare say it won't be long before I crawl my way out of this disgusting pit." He smiled arrogantly. "But don't worry. When we leave this world behind, we'll be sure to give you a wave good-bye."

Dierdre's eyes narrowed. Her jaw stopped working. "'We?'"

He chuckled. "Did I say that? It must have slipped out."

The busty prostitute looked put out. "You shacking up with someone, Emet?"

He tilted his head to the sky as he laughed, then snapped it back down again before addressing the streetwalker. "In a way, yes," he admitted. "But she is nothing like you, rest assured. I would not waste my time with anything so cheap and tawdry."

Color rose in Dierdre's cheeks. "You always talking down about us, Emet," she snipped. "Like you think you're better. Well, you ain't, okay? Not much difference between you and me, you know, 'cept I got something other people want."

He glared. "As do I," he growled, then sneered. "And I don't have to get on my back to be paid."

"Oh, yeah?" she challenged, cocking her head haughtily. "What you got that's so damn good it pays better than me?"

The sculptor's bravado faltered. He looked away. "For you to understand art would be like a pig understanding the rich flavor of Beef Wellington."

The self-assured prostitute did not skip a beat. "So show me the beef, Emet. Unless you're afraid."

Heat rose to the lanky man's cheeks. He glared once more upon the prostitute. "Do you really wish to know?"

She smacked her gum and winked. "Show me."

* * * *

In the several days since Mrs. Rudolf's "suicide," the apartment building had been placed in a sort of escrow limbo. The tenants were allowed to remain, rent-free, until a new property owner took the place over. Everyone, it seemed, had accepted the idea that somehow, Mrs. Rudolf had bludgeoned to death two of her tenants—the popular rumor was that the burly men had raped her, and she had taken revenge upon them—then, feeling remorse for her actions, slit her wrists.

The police were doing little to actively investigate such a happening in an area of town well-known for crimes of passion and depression, many of which remained unsolved.

"Is this all some trick to get me to drop my skirts, Emet?" Dierdre asked suspiciously while the sculptor unlocked the door. "'Cause, if that's all it is, and you really wanna just bed me, why not come out and say it? Ain't nobody around now."

He pushed the door open into the shadowed environs of his home and cast a sneering look over his shoulder. "If I haven't made my contempt for you clear before, let me just say this: in a matter of moments, you will see why I despise such pathetic vermin as yourself. And once you have seen, you will be sent on your way with skirts fully intact, I assure you."

The prostitute's eyes clouded. "Fine. Let's get it over with, Emet. I've half a mind to charge you for the time. I could be getting paid right now."

His lip curled in disdain. "You are right about one thing. You do have half a mind."

He stepped in and flipped the switch, sending pale yellow light across the room from the standing lamp by the door. The inert statue of Galatea sat as always upon her simple cinder throne, eyes as pale and blank as the rest of her body. A veritable army of smaller figurines stood alongside the wall near the doorway, awaiting their march to the outside world.

Dierdre's eyes fell upon the lifelike, life-sized statue. An expression of wonder and awe decorated her pale features. "You did this?"

Emet frowned at his guest's reaction. He had expected the same sort of revulsion Mrs. Rudolf had shown, or at least a laughing condemnation. But the simple streetwalker appeared fully impressed with the results of Emet's skill. The redhead went so far as to approach, even touch the statue upon one sublimely-rendered thigh.

"Why...yes, I did. She took me weeks to complete."

Dierdre smiled. "She's beautiful," she remarked, then turned a smiling face toward the sculptor. "What do you call her?"

He blinked, somewhat perturbed that this pitiful prostitute could show any interest in art whatsoever. "Eh, G-Galatea," he stammered.

Dierdre's smile broadened. "Like the story," she remarked. "Pygmalion created the most beautiful woman in the world, and he named her Galatea. His love for her was so powerful that the Goddess of Love gave her life."

Emet stared upon the woman before him, dumbfounded that she would know anything about art, history, or culture. "You...you have *studied*?" he asked, incredulous.

She smacked her gum and winked. "I ain't always been like I am now," she explained. "Used to go to school, you know. But, life gets hard sometimes. Not like anyone's immune to stepping in shit, right? Not even you."

A feeling of admonishment coursed through Emet. He found himself unable to meet the prostitute's eyes. "Apparently not."

"So, this is the big secret, huh? What, you gonna sell it off and make a fortune, is that it?"

He frowned. "I could never sell my Galatea."

She looked haughtily upon him. "Women are sold all the time," she declared.

"It's not...she is more than a mere statue. She--"

Dierdre tittered. "Oh, I can see that," she said, sidling up beside the stony facade of Emet's creation. "Don't think I ain't noticed certain similarities."

He frowned in confusion. "What?"

She cocked her head with a chastising look. "Oh, don't play that game, Emet," she chided. "Look at her, look at me. We got the same white skin, the same lips, the same cheeks...hell, ten years ago, I had pretty much the exact same tits! What color is her hair, Emet? Red, like mine? Are her eyes blue, too?"

Emet stared, suddenly seeing the similarities. He ground his teeth. "No, she's not the same as you," he growled. "She is not cheap! She is devoted! To me!"

Dierdre looked amused as she licked her lush lips. She stood between Emet and Galatea, not noticing as a faint touch of color rose to the surface of the statue. "Like you wish I'd be? Huh?"

Emet shot to his feet. "No!" he cried. "Not like you, with the stain of the sweat of a thousand men upon you! My Galatea is pure! She has known only me, and will know no other!"

The redhead stiffened before the sculptor's vocal barrage. It was only then, after the echoes of his words had faded, that she detected the movement behind her. Spinning about, she stared with both wonder and fear upon the emotionless nude woman who now stood over her.

"Dear God," Dierdre whispered, before being caught up in the swiftly-sweeping arms of the impossibly animated statue. She was lifted off her feet, held aloft by a creation which should not have been given any kind of life, yet it was. Hysterically, she called out: "Emet!"

"Galatea!" he cried.

But his creation seemed to ignore him. Pale, strong hands spread across Dierdre's back, then pressed.

And pushed.

Crack.

Snap.

Crack.

Snap.

With each jolting crush of her spine, Dierdre convulsed, limbs kicking and flailing impotently. She made little noise beyond gasps and grunts, her face showing the paralytic effect of shock.

Finally, Galatea released her victim. Dierdre fell upon her back on the floor, body limp and twisted. She convulsed only slightly, blood bubbling to her lips. Her head turned toward

Emet as he crouched beside the dying prostitute. Wide, shocked eyes conveyed pain in a way words never could.

The sculptor found his own eyes dripping with tears. His heart pained as if squeezed by the hand of Death. He glared up at his creation. "How could you do this?" he shrieked. "I did not want to kill her!"

Galatea's only response was a blank stare. And a step.

Ssssmack.

Emet stiffened. "Keep your distance," he warned. He reached to the table near him, taking up the awl. "I command you."

Ssssmack. Galatea's eyes were like lifeless gemstones as she moved closer, weight balanced upon her right foot.

Fear blossomed in Emet's eyes. "You do as I wish! You are my creation!"

Still the golem advanced, lifting the left foot, then settling it upon the ground inches from where Emet crouched. The stark, emotionless expression upon Galatea's face became suddenly threatening.

"Do not make me do this!"

The right foot raised. She loomed over him, now, reaching.

"No!" he yelled, then stabbed down into Galatea's left foot, destroying the first 'E' in the inscription beneath her ankle.

Galatea froze instantly, the nearly flesh-like tinge of her skin vanishing as quickly as did the color of her eyes. Golden hair became as the clay from which it had been rendered, settling against her lifeless face. Still, the statue moved forward, bidden by the basic force of gravity. No longer alive, it nevertheless fell upon the form of its creator.

Emet fell back against the hard floor, pinned beneath the enormous weight of his creation. He felt the piercing of shattered bones within his body, puncturing lungs and other organs. Blood bubbled up through his throat and spilled from pale, thin lips.

His last act was to reach up and caress the cold, stony cheek of his lover.

* * * *

Rabbi Rausch stepped away from the "meat wagon" ambulance after offering a final prayer to the corpse beneath the glossy black bag. As the van ambled away, the aged cleric approached a disturbed man clad in an overcoat who stared down the dank stairwell toward the basement apartment.

"Detective Marks," Rausch said as he settled a hand to the younger man's shoulder. "Are you all right?"

The detective shook his head slowly. "Nothing's right about any of this," he said philosophically. "Last week, the landlady beats a couple of men to death, then kills herself. Then, tonight, a man kills a hooker before his own statue falls on top of him. It's all so...strange."

The rabbi nodded. "Strange things happen."

Marks scoffed. "Yeah, easy for you to say. But I don't have the luxury of answering to faith. I have to provide evidence. Only thing is –" He sighed in frustration. "– there's not a whole lot of that here, either."

"Man cannot find every answer," Rausch said.

"Well, we gotta look, rabbi," Marks answered, then grunted in resignation. "This is nuts. I don't even know how to file this case. What am I supposed to say?"

"The truth?" Rausch offered.

"Yeah? What the hell is that?"

Rabbi Rausch stared into the darkened stairwell which lead to Emet's apartment. It was like staring down into the deepest bowels of the earth, where only darkness and madness lie. "It's simple," he said at last.

"Well, then enlighten me."

The rabbi turned back from the stairwell and leveled his eyes upon the detective. "Emet Lowe created the perfect woman," he said. His eyes darkened as he finished. "And she killed him."

About Gabriel Daemon

Gabriel Daemon has been self-published online since 2006. He lives in San Antonio, Texas, where he cheers on his World Champion Spurs and sips dark German beer at his favorite pub. His first book, <u>Pretty Baby</u>, is available at eXcessica.

RED SMOKE
By Elise Hepner

He would be waiting for me in the forest.

Adrenaline chased through my body making me shake out my long limbs. He was ready for the hunt. As I dressed I could feel his eyes on me. A tingling on the small of my back. My pulse like the thundering of wolves in the woods at night. The door was locked and bolted. Candles lit on my night stand. Now all that was left was the ritual.

Smoothing up along my arms was the sweetest lotion that twinkled—like when the moon hit the water running in a stream outside my window. Vaseline coated my naked flesh like a bed of dancing reptilian scales that formed rainbow spots in the moonlight. My pussy shined with it and my excited juices. He liked me to be basted in shimmering liquid like a candy covered coating—good enough to eat.

The red silk teddy I picked skimmed my stomach, making me catch my breath from the cherry red reflection in the mirror. It's cloth licked around the tips of my thighs as it fell, creating a tickle that thrummed up my body. Heat along my sex.

He had picked out everything in the antique chest hidden under the mattress. This is where I had chosen my current selection.

Apple. Cinnamon. Cherry. I looked like food for the tasting. A hood traced the brown froth of hair secured in place by a tortoise shell clip which ripped into my scalp. It created a lovely frame for my small features and excited, upturned mouth. It was time to go. Not time to be late.

* * * *

As I run through the mass of trees lit by darkness and my hunger, brambles thwack at my tender calves encased in slick red thigh-highs. The pungent sweetness of my labia without panties crushes the rest of my senses as I run. Stones puddle under the red leather boots that stop just above my ankles. They twist them to awkward angles.

At night is when the whiskers create black shadow crevices in his jaw line. Where beautiful muscles twitch when he comes inside me. The dark hairs along his body probe my hips and belly, building the pressure that forces my pussy to bursting with liquid need.

I am shifted out of my thoughts because the clearing is ahead, fire burning, life-altering. My safe haven.

A tug along my scalp lifts me onto my toes, turning like a mechanical ballerina in a wind-up box. He is not subtle in letting me know he is here.

"You are a sight to behold. You ache with desire and freshness. I will beat that out of you tonight. Claim you raw and redder than the hood that you use to hide. I know what you really want little Red, and I will spare nothing in giving it to you."

My tongue swells, mouth clogging with dryness while his brown flecked pupils rake the silk along my breasts and lower still. His eyes are mental claws tearing me apart. A vulnerable part of me breaks into fragments when he gives me that look. It is special, just for me. His lips tremble with pleasure, teeth aching in a torpid smile, a baritone chuckle hitting me in the face.

His lean, muscled body is well lit against the fire he has made previously within the clearing. He likes to watch me writhe against a backdrop of chaos and heat. As his nails grip into my scalp I know these little jaunts into the woods are getting more dangerous.

A fine tremor along my bones makes my teeth chatter despite the warmth, licking up my sides from the rising flames. The tautness in my scalp makes a stinging moan escape my lips and I bite them quickly to suppress it. Any little noise of my submission will break his resolve for my flesh completely. Inside he is a powerful wolf on the prowl. Outside he is my calm, collected everything.

I am the prey.

The heat from the flames pricks at my legs as he moves me ever closer to its sparks. Each silken tie from my hood drops away as he plucks the fabric with his course fingers. I feel it give across my shoulders and swallow a gasp. That particular gift has been with me for a long time. It is a trademark—an everyday collar from a man who doesn't believe in them.

It slides down my back into the awaiting fire. I hear the hiss as it is eaten by the molten twists of red and I know this is going to be different from any other night. My nerves begin screaming to bolt. His eyes are locked away from mine on the crisp burning of our favorite garment. I can see the perverse glee dancing in the reflections of his pupils. My toes pinch from a lack of circulation. It is hard to breathe.

At best, my breaths are ragged. Taken from me by the realization that we had no established vocabulary for safe words. Yet it excites me. A fresh start. A chance to be free. We can explore everything now. I grow wet and palpable at the thought.

This could be my big finish, I think, as his jaws nibble at my neck. The tenderest piece of meat. A pinch from his canines make my nipples stand at attention within my now exposed, silken red night shift.

"Little Red, you might have come to me for the last time. What will grandma do when you're gone? Surely you should scurry back home?"

His hot breath in my face reeks of alcohol as his grip loosens on my hair. He is swift to catch my wrists at my lower back as I stumble across the ground which is slippery with fallen leaves. I watch as my heels pin the leaves to the ground.

My arms are locked into the back panel of my dress. A discomfort presses from my shoulders wrenched at awkward angles. A furious blush lights up my cheekbones. Tears of joy pulse down my face. His voice has the sweetest commandments. My grandmother worries about him finding me.

I worry one day I won't be able to find him.

"You trust me, don't you?"

I look into his eyes, which hold compassion, love, and a harshness I know from years under his hands.

A simple nod in his direction. A declaration to my affection, which is seeping down my thighs. My eager pussy betrays me as his fingers skim my pulsing clitoris underneath the dress. He dips into my slick slit. He is abrupt and skillful in his torment. I try not to smile. I know I give him all the power as his body presses against mine.

I squirm against his insistent stare as he pumps into me with his thick digits. I widen for him. Everything inside me expands to bursting. The pressure feels so good. Smooth chaos of my pulse in my wrists against the back of the dress. The fabric may burst against my trembling hands. I am trembling with joy. My legs may buckle.

"I know, you like it when I take it from you, careless of whether you want it or not. I know everything you love, I know everything you are. No one can come close to me." He whispers in my ear close to my hair. I know his secrets are true.

I try to be good against his insistent drumming across my g-spot. Everything inside me is building to tear me apart with pleasure. Heat from the fire beats up my back. His thick hand slips from me before a flutter of orgasm can break me into pieces.

The tiny straps of my little red dress fall to the forest floor. His jaws snap in my face as the fabric falls to my feet. I am wearing nothing now. I watch as he sucks the juices, my own, from his fingers. The ones he has used to bring me bliss. He offers a gentlemanly hand around my waist and another around my wrists so I can step over the offending material.

"We will be careful. Or will we?" He mocks in sing-song, a hand pressing against my throat.

Then we are reeling in a dance I know very well. The rope hisses out of his course pant loops and across my exposed belly from one hand to the next. Then I'm leaning back into his arms. He holds me with one arm in a graceful dip as my demise slicks around my midsection to a chorus of sparking flames at his back.

As I reel to my feet from the push up from his arms, the rope lashes against my back. Rough marks of a makeshift whip. Rope burn seeps up my sore back muscles to sit heavy in my pussy. Soft laughter plays in the back of my hair. Kisses at my neck, floating down my abused spine, a lick along the crease of my ass that makes me gasp from the cooling line embedded in so much fever. Then a clench of knots at my ankles that squeeze until I can't breathe. As if a matching pair was strapped over my lungs constricting my heart.

He binds my ankles from running.

There is no physical or mental escape.

He picks me up effortlessly against his broad chest. I have one second to nestle there in peace within the familiar outcroppings of his chest hair. The smell of him keeps me still within the cage of his corded biceps. His scent speaks to me, within the recesses of my brain that tell me to twitch and bolt.

I am trussed for the flames. A buzzing in my head builds over everything else as he shifts me more firmly against him. He throws me lightly against him, hair obscuring the vision of my surroundings. I am over his back where I can see nothing but a firm, tight ass. My nipples brush electric against his shoulders as his nails dig into the flesh at my thighs. The sharp indents bring back my breath, smoke filling my lungs as he tosses me across the plastic folding table facing the fire.

This is new.

"Open your mouth."

An order where there is no room for question regardless of what he is holding.

I accept the rubber ball gag on my tongue, holding me still like a lamb whose throat is about to be torn out. The sound of clanging surgical steel over to my left keeps my mind off my pounding pussy. My body is thrumming with life, knowing I could be devoured at any moment by the whims of the man I trust.

I see the spreader bars glow in the fire. He walks around me, drawing them over my body. I sigh as the rope releases from my ankles, leaving a trail of sting along my veins which makes me moan against the gag. The slip of cold, relaxing handcuffs in place of the rope, only serves to amp up my beating heart. He does the same to my arms, spreading me in an open, vulnerable arch of body parts.

Warm, rough hands caress down my needled back, tracing the outlines of his handiwork. It makes me blush more than the rough, splayed angles of my legs. He tickles, smoothes and massages down my back, working my meat until I am tender and practically purring against the cold night air, which has nothing to do with my heavy, erect nipples. Sweat pools across my chest as the first slap lands across the globe of my ass cheek.

He's just warming up. A few swats in my direction laid across me to show what he's capable of doing. They don't make me scream, but I cannot jerk away from their branding bruises. I wouldn't want to as the delicious, musky sweat smell of his palm coats my skin. I can smell his exertion and my pleasure as my excitable pussy fills with blood.

I am trussed to the spit of his burning fingertips as they catch me on my thighs, ass, lower back. My lover, my wolf, runs the gauntlet of possible places to hit me as the sting bites up my back—warm needling that will hurt for days whenever I walk, sit, stand still.

This knowledgeable tidbit removes all the desperate thoughts inside my head. Though we will not always be here, we will not always meet like this when the moon has grown pregnant with our secret, I will always bear his marks. This time will not be erased from my body.

I bear cane imprints from months ago, biting bitterly into my back. The way each stroke hit my flesh was decadent dessert on top of the intricate rope art he'd done all over my body. He knows how to bring me out, make me beg. He knows how to do things for me I cannot do for myself.

When he is gone, my skin will read like a map to our pleasure spots—living artwork to our relationship—the ups and downs in purple, black, red, and white traceable scar tissue.

I will be beautiful without my hood.

He notices my mind has gone somewhere else. The eager blows have stopped and I am deeply, immediately repentant for my selfishness. I would apologize, bow, but for the angle I am spread and the silencer hindering my mouth. There is no way to make up my indiscretion. The wickedness of my actions makes my pussy walls tight, clenching in a shaky rhythm.

I turn to try and read his face, eyes, the stance of his legs, But he's moved so I cannot see him. My head will not reach a comfortable angle so I bend it down low in shame.

A growl trickles from his lips.

He rips up my head, his fingers tearing into my scalp. The insistence rips a moan from my throat which comes out as whimper against the ball gag. I swallow down the urge to beg for more knowing that he would ignore me. I have earned nothing but strictness from him. I deserve penance. My spine is bowed in discomfort which makes my arms and legs tingle. He's forced my nipples to graze against the molded plastic of the table as he shakes my head to answer his questions.

"Do you like it when I punish you? Is that why you're so naughty?"

"Can you not obey for one second without being selfish, you little pain slut?"

They are not really questions he needs to speak or answers he doesn't know yet. But he asks them anyway, furthering the heat that's building between my legs.

Nothing is touching me now and the lower half of my body is singing with cozy warmth and tingle. I want the endorphin's sailing through my limbs to wait their turn as he flogs me with his fingers again. I'm not ready for release as he tears away the ball gag barring my mouth. I know I'm in for something good.

A small smile quirks my lips only for a second. He must know how much the lack of contact is killing me, the tension in my neck from his rough grip in my hair making me lose patience. He always said I was quick to lose my submissive state. It's why he trained me with extra love and care.

I can see that emotion behind his amber eyes along with the crackling heat that always makes me want to scurry away. An unpredictability that makes me shrink back in horror. He is stern with his hand threaded through my hair arching my neck, his palm forcing my jaw open. I am stiff and hard to work with but I lose all apprehension as he dips into his pants and pulls out his dick. My mouth opens wide from the joy of just seeing it glisten at the tip against the flaring backdrop of the night.

He gives me a moment to choke on my luck before I am choking him down my throat. The warmth of the fire has made him burn in the back of my throat. I am opening for him, blinking back the need to close my mouth and move my tongue around his length. I will not control this, he says, with a thrust of his hips which makes me gag helplessly, holding him with my mouth, eyes smiling with relief.

"Are you ready?" A ferocious smile lights up his face barely touching his eyes. He knows I know he isn't expecting an answer. There is only one answer to give: submission.

He pushes slowly into me, like he's testing a virgin. Each inch he gives me is wet silk against my tongue. I can hear his grunts as he takes me gently, going against his beastly nature. I am both grateful and apprehensive, the sweet pungent smell of him engulfing my nose as he moves as far as he can go in my mouth. I run my tongue along the underside of his shaft. He moans above me, which sings electric through my raw nerve endings. I can still feel my fluttering pulse against the red of my marked ass.

His fingers tighten and give in my hair with an unpredictability that sends shivers and spikes down my flesh. Goosebumps prickle my tied limbs while my breasts bounce with the sudden force of his thrusts. I can feel him down to my toes as the head of his cock plays along my sensitive bruised lips. The softness speaks to my hungry sex as I rattle against my bondage. The ache in my thighs feeds my desire to feel him in other places than my mouth. I close my eyes against the need, concentrating on the slip of his skin against the back of my throat, swallowing him in a tight rhythm.

"There you go, just like that, you love it like that. Such a gorgeous girl as you taking me in your mouth, so sweet and gentle for my pleasure." He sings my praises and it makes my heart warm with pride.

My clanging demonstration has made him rougher as he drops my head and keeps pounding into my mouth. I accept him as best I can without the aid of an angle for my head while my thoughts spin into my happy submissive space.

He is a primordial beast opening me up for sacrifice. The moans and groans of pleasure above me make my thighs and belly tight with need. The need for release pulses across my clitoris as I whimper against his cock. He slips out quickly, holding himself to his stomach as he offers me his balls to lick and suck. The slick, tender feeling of him on my tongue brings me close to the edge—I know he can tell, as he softly pets my head. He is gentle and loving, taking my mouth in his hands as he massages away the kinks from face-fucking me. I can't help but grin under his ministrations even as his cock juts out in my line of sight, taunting my needy vagina.

He moves the ball gag back into place. For a second I am buzzing with unused energy. I have no more sight of him. Sounds of crunching sticks and leaves let me know he is moving behind me as my pulse pounds for punishment.

I am as open as I've ever been, knowing our time together is coming to a close. I cannot keep hiding. Burning wood smoke puffs into my face as the wind changes direction. It chokes me even as I breathe it in with pleasure, one of my favorite smells. He always has a fire waiting to warm my body after my long trek through the woods to meet him.

My wrists work against my bonds, the smooth metal pricking my flesh with its pinch. I feel him hovering at my back. A fingertip traces the crack of my ass, swirling deliciously against my pert opening. A crack of his fingers against my slippery slit sends an electric current through my body and, with several more quick taps to my severally neglected pussy, I am writhing with lust against my bonds. Only several more short swats and I am seconds away from an orgasm. My head silently pleads for more as my body shifts awkwardly into positions I cannot reach or maintain for very long restrained.

He is unwavering in his determination to lead me by the hand to an orgasm which he'll snatch quickly away before it can be felt. As he pats my overly aroused pussy he sticks a finger just inside my sex tracing the inner lining of my opening. It tickles, spreading an agitating warmth up my chest which makes my ass clench. My muscles are still worn out from the spanking so each stroke of his finger brings a new firm spot of tension to my ass cheeks.

As quickly as he has entered me, he is gone, leaving a abrupt ache.

"You're being very good, little Red, the color of your ass almost mimics your hood burning in the flames. I won't make this any easier for you though—you haven't earned it." His voice was rasping, low.

He resumes his handiwork along my ass this time with a flare that brings lengthy screams strangled against the ball gag. A raw, smarting spread of lines up my torso makes me flinch. The throbbing marks renew themselves along every available source of skin, making me arch my back in desperation. The sensation relaxes the tension in my legs as he thwacks into them. My calves unwind like a screwed up massage. One need is fed as my other sexual yearnings draw up into the back of my mind with his steady hand.

I wiggle with my hips against the spreader bar which has taken away all chance of protection. As his blows grow in snap, flinging through the air with a solid crush of sound, I give up the pointless fight and move my ass to meet them. I embrace my kink as silent, gagged tears criss-cross my cheeks. I bite down on the rubber planted in my mouth. Its acrid smoothness against my tongue is soothing, reminding me of what I've lost. As each blow rains down on my tender skin, I bite into it for comfort, my mind falling to the pure sensation.

I count them in my head when I can, when I can't I'm satisfied simply listening to the sound cracking through the din of the night.

His breath is panting, urgent, hard as his love is never ending. Each strike washes over me like his pride. My ankles are stiff, arms tired as his stinging relentlessness eases across my bare skin. The tool drops to the ground as he spreads his fingers over the marks dotting my flesh. A hiss slips out through the rubber in my mouth at his tenderness. He smoothes away the ache into something more delicate. Soothing motions of his palm spread the fire while tickling my overheated sex. I nuzzle the plastic coating under my head in blissful delight.

With his soothing motions come my liquid placation. Then the swift pulling and positioning of my trussed body at the end of the table. An amazing bolt of sensation makes me thrash with delight as his cock sheathes itself inside my tight pussy. He wrangles a tight gasp from my throat, his cock fighting past my clinging, eager walls. His fingertips bruise my hips, making his first thrust hit that magical sweet spot buried deep within my body. Each roll of his hips brings a new sensation that arches my back as my tender knees thrust against the rough table molding.

The metal holding the table together shakes with our gyrations, making my blood buzz with adrenaline. Everything could break down. We could collapse, leaving me a broken rag doll on the forest floor at the mercy of a predator. Each stoke brings me closer to the full mercy of his pleasure.

Every struggle shifts me over the edge, forcing me over the orgasmic precipice, into an infinite world of exploding fireworks and trust. My head hangs low, panting as my hands claw at the table, crawling from the inside out with a building pressure that liquefies all my senses. He keeps on pounding into me with a relentless lust my pussy finds both painful and satisfying. Any harder and he could push through my stomach as his cock head finds my cervix in a sensitive line of pain and pleasure.

I cross it without looking back, grinding myself back into him until he touches my ass still speckled with brands. My throbbing heat flares as his skeletal, cut hip bones beat against my ass. He strikes a new shade of blue across me, slapping his palm against my parted cheeks to the rhythm of his strokes. The renewed vigor with which he touches me brings a chain of small orgasms stroking up my body until I am limp and hoarse against the gag.

When I can't take it anymore, his thrusts become more insistent, shorter, faster, concentrated for his pleasure alone. Still I writhe for him, knowing he delights in using me, turning me inside out and then back again. I can feel it's almost over as his grunts grow heavy, long and low. He ends it with a howl, forcing his way through me with one last tilt of his hips. I swear the world collapses at his pleasure, my own spurred on by his teeth gnawing into my hip. A jagged ring of clasping teeth will be my body jewelry until we do this again.

He pulls out of my dazed body, spent and shaking. Taking stock of my shape and glancing over towards the long-dead fire, my lover glances at the approaching dawn. Reality has come to take him from me. We are cresting across a cold morning high as he casually undoes my bonds. They are nothing to him now.

As I ease up, flinching and sated, he rubs my hands and feet, gently working back the circulation. I am grateful that he takes care of me even as I wince from the lack of care he has shown my back. But I know it will be beautiful when I glance in the mirror in passing—beautiful as I trace, pinch and irritate every last marking while I fuck myself.

While I hide it from my family and friends, inside I will be gloating over the secret sting—the tell-tale hiss, a nervousness to sit down with my back straight against a chair.

It's nothing my grandmother hasn't seen before. But it is also nothing she would notice. She may be wise in the way of herbs, but our playground is blocked off to strangers.

When he holds my chin in his hands, kissing me against the insistent urges of his body growing against my stomach, I want to stay. He dots my upper body with tiny touches of his lips, running his hands through my hair like the most precious pet that I am. He curls me in his arms. Knowing we must part, I close my eyes to the encroaching dawn, too bright for my midnight world. None of my fantasies can live here.

* * * *

When I wake up, there is nothing. I am on the ground soft with dew. I ache more from my heart than my body. I do not know if he will be back again the next moon. I know he watches me. He is my constant shadow. Whether or not he shows himself to me is up to him. Everything has always been his decision. I would rather settle for my wayward beast than the most handsome prince my grandmother shows me in the pages of the paper. They are goodness and light, shining through to cast the demons away from my chest.

I could not settle for someone so politically and emotionally cold. I'm sure there would be passion in our relationship. Maybe even a vine of love that could grow with time. But he would treat me as a delicate princess—then move onto the town whore. He would never understand my soft pleas to be used like the strumpet he sees once a month. He would beat me and feel bad about it later. He wouldn't understand my glow of pride as he came to me, wheedling for forgiveness. He would make me sick.

I would look to the woods at night with longing. Long after my husband had fallen asleep content with his sweet taking of me and my fake cries of pleasure, I would mourn a loss of myself. It would be a different kind of cage than the one I make now—a choking, clawing cage of docile compliance. My heart could not be in such a wicked lifestyle. I would rather be beaten than held back, loved after abuse than coldly ignored inside and out of the bedroom. This is my way to matter to myself.

My wolf prince is gone. Tonight I know I'll be promising the moon a lifetime of my happiness for one more shared night with her watching us writhe. Today I'll go to work in the gardens with my grandmother. Tonight I'll go the ball as planned. I'll stand and do my family proud with fake gentile breeding. I'll dance with men who'll wrap their arms around my marred waist and look in concern as I flinch from their touch. They will release their tight hold, not knowing I want them to grip me closer, forcing me through my pain.

I will be a princess of darkness or not at all.

About Elise Hepner

Elise Hepner has been previously published in The Erotic Woman for "Joy Button" as well as Clean Sheets for "My Little Pony." She got her erotica wings from writing short pieces for Alison Tyler's blog contests every Saturday and found her calling. This is her first foray into erotic literature though she has multiple non-fiction publications from travel magazines to medical magazines on her resume. She hopes to make erotica her main focus in the upcoming years. She enjoys getting down and dirty while exploring sexuality in a variety of ways which is why writing smut makes her heart sing. Look for anything new as well as tips and tricks of the erotica trade at <u>celise91writer.blogspot.com</u>.

GOOSE GIRL
By Giselle Renarde

Once upon a time, two old queens raised a beautiful daughter with the assistance of the community and a positive relationship with her birth mother. As mistress of her castle, Princess Svana grew into a happy and well-adjusted individual. Her ideology was based around freedom and justice for all, a philosophy not particularly common in the feudal era, but Svana always was ahead of her time.

Princess Svana was betrothed to a fabulous prince whose father was a friend of the queens' from way back in the disco epoch. Even the tabloid reports confirmed prince Everitt was honorable, open-minded and handsome as a fairy's own child. On the occasion of her eighteenth birthday, it was time for Svana to take her leave of the caring queens and marry the good royal. Unfortunately, prince Everitt lived at a great distance. In preparation, the aged queens packed for their daughter many costly trinkets, jewels and cups of gold and silver. In short, they sent with Svana everything which appertained to a royal dowry, for they loved their baby girl with all their hearts.

As you might expect, Svana was not particularly happy to leave behind her many friends, the beloved queens, her birth mom, her pets, and that green grocer who never forgot to import a few mangos from faraway lands. So, to appease their darling daughter, the queens sent along a maid-in-waiting, Rosamunda. The strong-as-an-ox servant was to ride with the princess and hand her over to the bridegroom, making very certain nobody messed with their baby girl along the way. And messing with Svana was a distinct temptation for all who beheld her, such was her incredible beauty. But, apart from that one time, which didn't really count since it was underwater, she'd managed to keep herself relatively un-messed-with.

Each woman, princess and maid, had a horse for the journey. There was something quite unique about the mare the queens' daughter rode. She was called Falada, and possessed the uncanny ability to speak. When the hour of parting came, the aged queens and b-mom stood around their girl, weeping into a communal handkerchief. *How sad they were to see Svana go!* That's when b-mom took out a small knife and cut her own finger until it bled. She held the tear-stained hanky to it, allowing three drops of crimson peasant blood to absorb into the white fabric. Feeling rather out in the cold, the queens tried to pierce their own fingers, but could not coax a single drop of blue blood from their bodies.

With a knowing smile, b-mom gave the hanky to her only daughter and said, "Dear child, preserve this carefully. It will be of service to you on your way."

Taking sorrowful leave of her mom and the queens, the princess stuck the bloodstained piece of cloth in her tight bosom, mounted her horse, and went away to her bridegroom.

* * * *

Having ridden Falada the Speaking Mare for some distance, Svana began to feel a delicious sensation between her legs. The metronomic bouncing pressure against her lower lips was her favorite part of riding bareback. Bringing Falada to a halt in the very centre of a vast field, Svana surprised her waiting-maid with a request.

"Oh, my dearest Rosamunda," she began. "Riding this way has my precious cavern flowing with love nectar. I feel I would die without immediate gratification. I beg you, dismount and take a drink from my cup."

"You have got to be kidding me," Rosamunda replied. "First of all, *precious cavern? Love nectar?* Who the hell talks like that, Miss Priss? If you're horny, you can bloody well get yourself off. I don't choose to be your servant."

So in her great thirst the princess alighted, bent down to grasp her skirt tails and pulled them up and well over her waist. Laying her head down against Falada's great rump, she tapped at her engorged lower lips. So sensitive were they from the riding that even the slightest pressure sent waves of happiness through her body. Rubbing her fingers against the juicy folds of her craving cunt, Svana panted and moaned. Her ample breasts jumped as she fingered herself, stiff nipples popping out from under her red and gold corset. Stroking through the waters of her swollen pussy, the princess rubbed faster and faster, big breasts bouncing, until the pleasure was so vast she had to squeeze her eyes shut just to stay sane. Gritting her teeth, Svana yelped like a pup as every fiber of her being jumped for joy. Oh, her thirst was slaked but how her hand ached! Perhaps she was developing carpel tunnel syndrome. Or repetitive stress disorder.

When the princess regained her composure, sitting upright on Falada's back, she realized how sopping wet her underskirts had become. A pleasant reminder of the day's pleasure. As she arranged her freed breasts back into her corset, Svana was suddenly overcome with panic. What had become of the bloodstained handkerchief from birth mom?

"Ah, heaven," the princess cried, hopping from her horse.

Nuzzling the distraught girl, it was Falada who indicated where the hanky had fallen, answering,

"If this your mother knew,

Her heart would break in two."

"What does that mean? If *what* my mother knew?" Svana inquired, picking up the square of fabric and shoving it safely between her breasts.

But the speaking mare only whinnied, saying nothing more. Svana mounted her horse again. But where had her maid-in-waiting gone? Her horse remained, but Rosamunda was nowhere to be seen.

"Rosamunda? Rosamunda!" Svana cried until the servant appeared on the scene with a jewel-encrusted cup of water in hand.

"You've slaked your thirst, now I am slaking mine," Rosamunda shrugged.

"But you drink from my golden cup! The queens packed that for me, as part of my dowry. It isn't yours to use."

Again, Rosamunda shrugged. "I would have asked, but I could see you were busy."

* * * *

Some miles further on, the women found themselves galloping over hill and dale, full speed ahead. Again, the princess ached with delight each time she fell hard against Falada's broad back. *Oh, the pleasure was too much to bear!* Bringing the horse to a halt on a grassy plateau, she turned again to rugged Rosamunda. Having occasional problems with short-term memory, Svana had already forgotten the girl's ill words of earlier that day.

"Oh, my dearest Rosamunda," the princess repeated. "Riding this way has my precious cavern flowing with love nectar. I feel I would die without immediate gratification. I beg you, dismount and take a drink from my cup."

Taking her mistress' reiteration for insistence rather than forgetfulness, Rosamunda's resistance wore away a touch. Rather than an outright *no* she asked, "If I do dismount and drink from your cup, what will you do for me? After all, I don't choose to be your maid."

The day was warm, the sun scorching the hilltop, and Svana knew her maid must be thirsty once more. "I will let you drink from my golden cup afterwards," the princess offered. "You may fill it with spring water again and again, as many times as you wish, if only you will do me this one kind favor."

"It's not a great offer," Rosamunda considered, "but what the hell? Not much else to do up here."

And so, dismounting from their horses, the women tumbled onto the green grass. Laughing with delight, Svana rolled onto her back while Rosamunda's powerful hands pushed up her many skirts. Between the blonde's snow white thighs, the maid-in-waiting found something she did not expect.

"Why, the bush down here is dark as night! How is that, when your hair is light as gold?" Rosamunda asked.

"I bleach my locks, okay?" Svana growled, wrapping her legs around Rosamunda's shoulders. "You try being a princess with mousy brown hair! It just doesn't work. If you're going to be loved and adored by your subjects, you have to be blonde."

"All right! Don't have a stroke," Rosamunda replied. She hadn't anticipated the ambush.

No stranger to cuntry ways, the maid-in-waiting nuzzled the wispy thing's tumescent clit with her wide nose, pressing against it as she licked the base of Svana's hole. The princess giggled with delight, tossing and turning in the grass. With her tongue flat and firm, Rosamunda licked the juicy folds of princess' pink and perfect cunt. What refreshment needed she, beyond these tangy waters? *Ah, did they ever get her blood flowing!* And that sweet and heavy smell of a sopping pussy...Was there anything better?

When Rosamunda stuck two fingers into her mistress' cunt, Svana dug into her corset of red and gold in search of hard nipples to squeeze. The maid flicked her tongue relentlessly at princess' clit, standing steady and strong as a soldier at arms. Purring like a kitten, Svana held Rosamunda's head down, pressing her lean white thighs against her ears until the strong servant could hardly hear. That's when the maid, petting the spongy spot inside Svana's hot pussy, began sucking vigorously at her erect pink bud. Kicking her feet in the air above, the batty girl cried out incomprehensible encouragements. With that sort of a reaction, Rosamunda just kept doing what she was doing. Slippery clit between her lips, she bit down gently upon it every so often until her mistress exploded. Pulling at the fiery woman's black locks, Svana shrieked like a banshee, soaking her maid's square chin.

Rosamunda pulled away, wiping her mouth on the sleeve of her simple green gown. In the grass, eyes closed and absorbing the fresh sunlight, Svana lounged like her bones had fallen out. That's when Rosamunda spotted something she could surely use. The precious hanky stained with b-mom's blood had fallen upon the ground when Svana was playing with her big tits. Scooping it up as the princess slumbered, the servant woman grabbed the golden cup and set off on foot to fetch some water from the nearby spring. While she was there, the waiting-maid launched the bloodied cloth into the waters and watched as it swirled and whirled and disappeared down the stream.

* * * *

When Svana finally awoke, flesh hot and bothered by the sun's mighty rays, Rosamunda stood against her mare holding the jewel-encrusted cup.

"Ah," Svana yawned. "You may go to fetch your drink now, Rosamunda."

But the waiting-maid laughed haughtily. "I have been and returned from my drink, and now I shall leave on your mare and marry your prince."

"You'll do what?" Svana asked, rubbing her eyes. *Was this a joke?* But Rosamunda was not one for foolishness...

"Check your bosom for that filthy hanky," the waiting-maid instructed.

It wasn't there. Neither was it in the grass nearby. What had become of that precious blood?

"I've disposed of it and now it's gone and you are weak and powerless," Rosamunda continued.

"I am?" Svana asked, very much surprised.

"You are," the waiting-maid responded. "And so I shall be princess and you shall be servant."

"Ah, heaven," Svana sighed. She felt no reason to question Rosamunda's divine knowledge.

The princess had to be content with this arrangement. Had she not sworn by the clear sky above not to reveal one word of this to anyone at the royal court, Rosamunda would have killed her on the spot. And, coming from Rosamunda, that was no idle threat.

Then the waiting-maid, with many hard words, bade the princess exchange royal apparel for her own shabby clothes. The maid undressed first, revealing a large body, firm with muscle. Her cunt was cloaked by a black bush, a dark trail leading the way to solid breasts culminating in purplish nipples surrounded by sharp hairs. However grotesque, there was something about Rosamunda's naked body that rendered Svana even less resistive.

Untying the princess' corset, the monster of a woman let the girl's gown fall to the grass. Rosamunda's hot breath harassed the back of her neck as she took firm hold of Svana's breasts. Her knees nearly gave out at the sensation. Spinning on her heels, the princess pressed her perfect tits against the waiting-maid's and kissed her spring-water mouth. Straddling the servant's leg, hairy as the green grocer's, Svana rubbed her ever-ready pussy lips against her hard thigh. Rosamunda grabbed her ass with both hands, rocking her like a swing. Svana grasped the maid's shoulder and her feet lifted right off the ground. Back and forth, back and forth her moist pussy lips tribbed against Rosamunda's thigh. The pressure on princess' mound increased until Svana screamed so loudly she couldn't see straight.

Rosamunda dropped the girl in a writhing heap upon the green dress, squeezing herself into the red and gold gown. She commanded Svana to get up and dressed.

"Whatever you say," the smitten Svana gushed.

With the dressing all finished, Rosamunda mounted her mare, cackling, "Falada is more suitable for me, and my nag will do for you."

But Falada saw all this, and observed it well, whinnying to Svana,

"If this your mother knew,
Her heart would break in two."

"Oh, mind your own business, you old nag," Svana scolded.

* * * *

The waiting-maid now riding Falada, and the true bride the bad horse, they traveled onwards until at length they reached the royal palace. There were great rejoicings over their arrival, and the prince sprang forward to meet the woman in red and gold, lifting the waiting-maid from her horse. *How strange!* The tabloids reported that his princess was a knock-out, and yet his consort looked quite gargantuan in person. *Just goes to show you can't believe everything you read.*

With Rosamunda conducted upstairs, the real princess was left standing below. Knowing not what to do or where to go, she stood in that spot for a day and a half. Fortunately, the old king derived a certain gratification from peeping on the blacksmith as he handled his red-hot poker. Thus, king Dolphus was every so often looking out of the window with binoculars. That's how he noticed Svana standing in the courtyard. Remarking how dainty and delicate she was, he instantly went to the royal apartment and asked the bride about the girl.

"What, that little prossie? I picked her up along the way for companionship," Rosamunda lied. "Give the girl something to work at, that she may not stand idle."

But old king Dolphus had no work for her, and knew of none, so he said, "I have a boy called Conrad who tends the geese, but I fear he's becoming a tad too friendly with the flock, if you catch my drift. A little prossie may help rid him of this queer affliction."

"Yes, you don't hear of many poultrysexuals, my liege," snickered Rosamunda. She couldn't have plotted this better herself.

And so it was decided the true bride had to help Conrad keep his hands and other body parts off the geese. But even this task was not torture enough, in cruel Rosamunda's mind. Soon afterwards the false bride said to the lanky prince, "Dearest husband, I beg you to do me a favor."

He answered, "I will do anything most willingly if you'll only agree not to molest me this evening. I fear I shall never recover from our wedding night."

"Agreed," said Rosamunda, tickling her scrawny husband. "I really ought to have stopped after the nineteenth round, but I couldn't resist your little cock-a-doodle-doo! Here's what I'll have you do: send for the knacker, and have him cut off the head of the horse on which I rode here."

And so, the faithful Falada was to die because Rosamunda was afraid the horse might reveal her true identity. When this came to the ears of the real princess, Svana despaired. Secretly, she promised to give the knacker a rim job, for his wife did not read to Cosmo and could not believe anybody would do such a thing. In return, the knacker would perform one small service. There was a gateway in the town, through which she had to pass with the geese, morning and evening. Would he be so good as to nail up Falada's head on it, that she might see him again, and more than once? For the knacker, it was a small price to pay to get his asshole tongue-tickled by a beautiful girl.

Early in the morning, when Svana and Conrad drove out their flock beneath this gateway, she said in passing,

"Alas, Falada, hanging there."
Then the head answered,
"Alas, young queen, how ill you fare.
If this your mother knew
Her heart would break in two."

When they'd driven their geese into a great floral meadow, Svana sat down and unbound her hair, which was like pure gold except for the slightest trace of dark roots. Conrad saw this and delighted in its brightness. Her hair reminded him of his first love, the golden goose, who had an unfortunate accident and was subsequently consumed. So heart-wrenchingly badly did Conrad miss his golden goose that his cock sprang to life in reminiscence. Having been scolded by the king for his fowl temperament, the boy thought perhaps the lovely Svana would alleviate the tension in his groin. Untying his humble rope of a belt, he brought the golden-haired girl face to face with his humble joke of a cock.

Alas, there was no way Svana was coming anywhere near that mother-clucker, and she told him so in no uncertain terms. But, grasping his drooling rod by the base, Conrad begged and pleaded with the righteous bride. Even as he shook his erection this way and that, Svana's answer remained no. When he approached her, stroking firmly on his humble shaft, there remained no choice but to summon the summer breeze, who owed her one. Turning her face to the heavens, Svana cried,

"Blow, blow, thou gentle wind, I say,
Blow Conrad's tiny cock away,
And make him chase it here and there,
Until I have braided all my hair,
And bound it up again."

And there came such a violent wind that it blew Conrad's penis far across the country. Of course, he was forced to chase after it because it was by far the most precious thing he owned. There was nothing else from which he derived such use and enjoyment. When he finally caught up with his dick, it was muddied, bruised and limp with exhaustion. Yes, that summer wind had blown Conrad's cock more skillfully than any, man, woman or goose ever could. He came back to the meadow with a smile on his face just as Svana finished putting her hair back up.

Though his body was blissful, Conrad still missed his golden goose. Could he not have one measly strand of hair to remember her by? But Svana guarded her locks jealously, and would not give the goose boy even one strand. Then Conrad was angry, then pouty, then surly, then a little itchy, then angry again. At any rate, he would not speak to her. Thus they watched the geese until the evening, when it was time to return home.

* * * *

Another day of bird-chasing was upon Conrad and Svana. Again, as they drove the geese out through the dark gateway adorned with the head of her beloved horse, the maiden said,

"Alas, Falada, hanging there."
And Falada answered,
"Alas, young queen, how ill you fare.
If this your mother knew

Her heart would break in two."

Heavy-hearted, the false maid sat down in the field, picking dandelions with her toes, and began to comb out her hair. The endearing but pervy Conrad ran and tried to clutch it. Offering her every pleasure in the world for just one strand of hair, the boy whipped out his rigid rod. In haste, Svana pronounced the words,

"Blow, blow, thou gentle wind, I say,
Blow Conrad's tiny cock away,
And make him chase it here and there,
Until I have braided all my hair,
And bound it up again."

Sure enough, the lecherous wind blew and blew Conrad's little dick, blew it so hard it flew off his body, and the goose-boy was forced to run after it. When he came back, Svana's hair had been put up a long time and he could get none of it. But after all that running and all that blowing, Conrad was too sleepy to argue. He took a nap while the goose-girl looked after their flock till evening came.

But in the evening after they had got home, Conrad went to the old king. Dolphus was busy watching the blacksmith with his red-hot poker in hand, but the boy took no notice and said, "I won't tend the geese with that girl any longer."

"Why not?" inquired the aged king, stowing his binoculars away.

"Oh, because she vexes me the whole day long," Conrad replied.

The aged king commanded he relate what it was about the girl that irked him so. Conrad said, "In the morning when we pass beneath the dark gateway, there is a horse's head on the wall, and she says to it,

"'Alas, Falada, hanging there.'
"And the head answers,
"'Alas, young queen, how ill you fare.
If this your mother knew
Her heart would break in two.'"

Conrad went on to relate what happened on the goose pasture, and how he was forced to chase his dick all across the countryside. Well, this was a revelation for the aged king, who commanded Conrad to drive his flock out again next day. As soon as morning came, king Dolphus placed himself behind the dark gateway, and heard how the maiden spoke to the head of Falada. And then he too went into the country, and hid himself in the thicket in the meadow.

There the king soon saw with his own eyes the goose-girl and the goose-boy bringing their flock. The moment Svana sat down and unplaited her hair, which shone with the radiance of a thousand hot oil treatments, that pesky Conrad was on her like a nose-print on a blacksmith's window. The boy offered her a deal: for a single strand of her golden hair, he would give her every awesome pleasure his penis could provide.

Allowing his trousers to fall to the ground, Conrad revealed his erection once more to the girl. As he traced his fingers around the rim of his glistening cockhead, thumbing the precum into his sensitive skin, he warned that this very well could be her last chance. Svana knew better and soon repeated the words,

"Blow, blow, thou gentle wind, I say,
Blow Conrad's tiny cock away,
And make him chase it here and there,
Until I have braided all my hair,
And bound it up again."

When a blast of wind arose to blow Conrad's erection across the countryside, a cry resounded from the nearby thicket. "No!" shouted king Dolphus, chasing the penis at break-neck speed. After all, it had been a while for the king, and even a small penis was better than no penis at all.

"What an odd occurrence," Conrad puzzled, watching the elderly king make chase.

"Well? You'd better get after him," Svana replied, combing her golden locks. "If the king catches your penis, I hate to think what he might do with it."

So Conrad ran far away, chasing the king who was chasing his penis, which was being blown by the summer wind, all while the maiden quietly went on combing and plaiting her hair. Well, both the king and Conrad were absent for quite a long time, and when they returned they looked utterly contented, so God only knows what they were up to.

Collapsing in the grass at Svana's side, the peeping cock-chaser asked her why she did all these curious things. She replied, "I dare not lament my sorrows to any human being. I have sworn not to do so by the heavens above me. If I had not sworn that oath, I would have lost my life."

The king urged her and left her no peace, but he could draw nothing from the goose-girl. "All right then," said he. "If you will not tell me anything, tell your sorrows to the iron-stove there."

By this time, Svana desperately desired to speak to somebody, anybody, about her troubles. Since she had no gold to pay the county therapist, the dear girl figured an inanimate object was her next best option. Creeping inside the iron-stove, the true bride began to weep and lament. She emptied her whole heart, crying, "Here am I deserted by the whole world, and yet I am the daughter of not one, but two queens! Yet, a false waiting-maid has by force compelled me to put off my royal apparel, and she has taken my place with my bridegroom. Now I am doomed forever to perform menial service as a goose-girl alongside that wretched poultysexual. If this my mother knew, her heart would break in two."

The aged king, that clever bugger, was standing outside by the pipe of the stove, listening to what she said. When the beautiful girl emerged, royal garments were placed on her, and Svana shone with the radiance of the stars. The aged king summoned his son, and revealed he had got the false bride who was only a waiting-maid. The true one was standing there, as the former goose-girl.

The young prince rejoiced with all his heart when he saw her beauty and youth. She didn't look half as threatening as his current wife, who had read about some kind of kinky strangulation thing and wanted to try it. He really wasn't into asphyxiation. Heavens above, Rosamunda's hands were so huge, he would be dead by midnight! This new girl was manna from heaven, as far as prince Everitt was concerned. Svana didn't think he was half bad, either. Together, the three royals hatched a plan so half-baked, it just might work.

* * * *

That evening, a great meal was made ready for prince Everitt, princess Rosamunda, and the minor celebrities with whom they were acquainted. While the guests feasted on mole-rat, the specialty of their kingdom, the prince suggested it might be kind of kinky if he went down on his wife under the dinner table. Rosamunda's two greatest pleasures were mole-rat and public sex, so she agreed whole-heartedly.

So down went the prince, under the tablecloth and beneath her many skirts until an anxious tongue fought through the false bride's jungle of pubic hair. When that tongue struck flesh, Rosamunda's folds released a veritable waterfall of love juices. Heavens above, the prince must have taken lessons since they'd done this at the breakfast table! Instead of flitting about like a lost fly, his tongue licked her lower lips full and hard. His teeth bit at her thighs before he stuck his ample tongue straight up her hole. Swirling every which way, he flailed it against the pleading walls of her cunt.

When the aged king had eaten and drunk and was merry, he turned to the enraptured waiting-maid to pose a riddle. Of course, with a wild tongue wrestling her spasmodic pussy, Rosamunda could hardly concentrate on Dolphus' question. "What punishment deserves a person who steals the identity of a rightful royal, marries her prince, kills her horse, and leaves her no option but to tend geese for a living?"

Just as Rosamunda started to process the riddle, the head between her thighs took her erect clit into its mouth and sucked like it was drawing poison from a snakebite. Oh, the waiting-maid nearly lost her head! Struggling desperately to retain her composure before the king, Rosamunda fought to transform her moans into words.

With an expert mouth sucking relentlessly at her cunt, words came tumbling out. "She deserves no better fate than to be stripped entirely naked and put in a barrel which is studded inside with pointed nails." Unable to keep quiet under the harangue of one tongue that felt like many, Rosamunda continued, "Two white horses should be harnessed to this barrel, which ought to drag her along through one street after another…" The maid, dizzy with cunnilingual delight, had one wild scream left in her before she could be still. "…till she is dead!"

And then the tongue ceased its thrusting and the mouth ceased its sucking, and Rosamunda lay back in her chair in blissful relaxation.

"Ha! It is you," said the aged king, "You have pronounced your own sentence, and that's exactly what shall be done unto you."

"What?" Rosamunda stammered. "But, but, but…"

And then a great cry rang out from under Rosamunda's skirt, and who should come climbing out but the rightful princess!

"No!" Svana cried. "No, I beg you not to harm my darling Rosamunda!"

"Don't harm her?" asked the king. "But this was your plan!"

"What can I say? I'm complicated," the goose-girl replied. "And I realize now the full extent of my infatuation with this hairy maid. She's large and rough, and she really screwed me over by stealing my identity, but now all has been put right. I should like to keep her as my lover, my liege."

"Your lover?" cried prince Everitt. "But you're supposed to marry me!"

"Have you never heard of a sham marriage, you great twit?" Rosamunda cackled as Svana pet her dark head.

"A what what-age?" puzzled the lanky prince.

"Well, I certainly have," guffawed old king Dolphus. "I lived in one for forty-seven miserable years! The only things that made it bearable were the blacksmith and my unfathomable wealth. Do you really think I am that scrawny boy's father? I should think not. No, Everitt, your mother chased after anything in pantaloons. As for me, well, once you go blacksmith you never go backsmith."

"How disturbing," said the prince. "And I suppose it could work, but is it really fair to me to have no lover of my own?"

Svana observed the prince's golden hair and shot the king a quick glance. "I should like to introduce you to the goose-boy."

About Giselle Renarde

Eroticist, environmentalist and pastry enthusiast Giselle Renarde is a proud Canadian and a great lover of the vast forests of the Great White North. For Giselle, a perfect day involves watching a snowstorm rage outside with a cup of tea in one hand and a chocolate truffle in the other. Ms Renarde lives across from a park with two bilingual cats who sleep on her head.

Giselle Renarde has contributed short stories to numerous anthologies, including Tasting Her: Oral Sex Stories (Cleis Press), Love Bites (Torquere Press), Coming Together: With Pride, and Coming Together: Out Loud (Phaze). Online, Giselle has contributed erotic content to such websites as For The Girls and Hips and Curves, and editorial content to Lucrezia Magazine.

For desirous commentary and hyper-analysis of every facet of social existence, visit Giselle's blog, <u>Donuts and Desires</u> or visit her site <u>here</u>!

BLACK AND GOLD
By Tessa Buxton

Once, a long time ago, before men started measuring these things, there were two worlds—the world above inhabited by men and the world below inhabited by fairy. These two worlds were as much as one as the other and the men and the fairy walked side by side under the sun of the world above and through the waters and mist of the world below.

Over time, the two worlds split apart—the bright and shining retreated to the world below and the men, brutish and strong, turned to the world above where the living was harder. When the fairy needed to, they walked among the men to drink their breath and their life and become stronger, and as such, the millennia passed.

Just as the world above formed into kingdoms and clans, gathering under charismatic leaders and their children, then so the world below. And just as the people of the world above changed, so each clan was distinct unto each self, then so too did the fairy, and each had a task.

The Cancanagh were golden and shining, drinking the lust and life of the men above. They wove stories and, when the men above told tales of the fairy, it was the golden Cancanagh they spoke of.

Hidden deep in the lands below was the Demon Door, the door joining the world above and the world below. It was guarded by a clan of fairies who named themselves for birds, who kept to themselves. Their lord had wings of darkest night and eyes which could open a dimension. Of their clan, it was said, a girl would be born with wings the color of the sun of the world above and the two would marry and protect the gate from all and everyone, married at birth and destined to love each other.

But as the fairy separated more and more into clans, they formed into two people—the Daoine Sidhe and the Unseelie

Court—and each formed into kingdoms with monarchy, and the crowns became cruel and demanding.

One king of the Unseelie took his warriors and took slaves from each of the people, and took a boy with wings of solid black and placed a powerful seal over his eyes so he could not open a dimension to harm them. To win the favor of his queen, he gave her the boy with the black wings along with a golden boy of the Cancanagh whom she called Findbhair.

* * * *

Now it happened that Findbhair was favored of the queen—he had golden hair and shining golden eyes, and when he laughed, it sounded like light upon rippling water. She dressed him in the richest cloth of finest streith—the way they wove light into clothes. She would sit and brush out his golden hair, and rub oils onto his golden skin and cradle him to her breast and sing sweet nothings into his ear.

So the boy, Findbhair, became spoiled, and as he grew older, he grew lovelier and the queen doted on him more. She offered gold and diamonds for his hair and rose petals for his bath. She gave him small mischievous fairies to make him laugh and slaves to wait upon his every whim.

The boy, Findbhair, saw the dark boy with the seal over his eyes, who was of an age with him, and found his greatest pleasure in tormenting him. He would pour cold water over his skin whilst he worked. He would order him whipped. He would sit beside the boy and laugh and laugh and his laughter was like the light falling upon the rippling waters of the lake.

It amused the queen to see her favorite so happy as she fed him sweet meats and sweet breads, candied rose petals and the drops of water that caught in the folds of orchids. She would sit beside him, stroking his hair and watching as he tormented the nameless boy with the black wings and the seal over his eyes.

The boy never responded.

When Findbhair knocked the food from his hands—coarse bread—with cruel laughter, the boy said nothing.

When Findbhair poured icy water over his head, the boy said nothing.

When Findbhair struck him, the boy said nothing and continued with what he had been doing.

Findbhair was fascinated by him. He wanted him to react, and when the queen cuddled him in the night in her palace, it was the boy with the black wings he dreamt of.

Findbhair, old enough to please the queen the way she wished, asked of her a single boon. He asked that the boy with the black wings be given to him as his own slave and the queen, lying there with his golden head on her bosom as she stroked his hair, she gave him his whim.

Findbhair found new and varied ways to torment the boy, who answered him calmly and never lost his temper. He washed his master. He fed his master. But no matter what his master did, he never lost his temper.

Even when Findbhair threw the all of the petals from the queen's rose garden across the courtyard and commanded he went to lift each one as he was told.

Even when Findbhair took an entire jug of wine and poured it over his slave's head, the boy just slicked back his hair and continued to lift the petals.

* * * *

But things must change, the way time means that they must. Slaves saw the way the queen favored the Cancanagh and whispers started about the boy and the queen, which were unfortunately true.

Time took the whispers to the king, who saw his queen, beautiful as she was, stroking the hair of her Cancanagh slave, and became enraged with jealousy.

He threw the boy aside and asked the court if his queen was unfaithful and jealous courtiers lounging upon their thrones told him it was true, that the boy was Cancanagh and beautiful and how could she resist such beauty.

The Cancanagh seduced her, the court said—he used his golden hair and laughter like the light upon rippling water, and took her to his bed so she would favor him above all others. When they said the Cancanagh had taken the boy with the wings of solid black to his queen's bed as well, the king was driven mad with jealousy and rage, so he asked the boys one last time if they were true to his service or if they would be condemned.

Findbhair told how the queen touched him in the quiet hours between midnight and dawn, and that he had no choice, for he was her slave, and surely that, too, was service. The boy with the wings as black as pitch said the same.

The queen denied this—she told her husband how the Cancanagh seduced her, how she loved only him, and that the Cancanagh were seducers and not to be trusted. She said she had been wooed by his golden hair and winning smile and laughter that was like light upon rippling water. The king believed her.

So the boys, for they were in truth barely older than children, were sent to the wild lands between the Daoine Sidhe and the Unseelie where the monsters lived to die of either hunger and thirst or be torn to pieces.

* * * *

The two boys walked for days through the vast empty plain, as the saliva dried on their tongues, making them thick and like leather. Their limbs were heavy and their hair, both golden and black, slicked back with quickly drying sweat in the harsh sun of the world below. Their clothes tore, thick with salt, ragged with grit and heavy with dust. They limped over stones, each driving the other one with their silence and their reticence to show weakness. The plain was ice cold when night fell and they found shadows under larger rocks to huddle together against the cold. The Cancanagh was pressed against the ice of the basalt against his back and the boy with the wings of blackest night against the chill of the sky. They would shudder, drawn up against each other, as warm as they could be whilst the night growled and expanded around them.

Sometimes, in the shelter of their small rocks, they would hear the steps of the great beasts to whom they would be a snack, or even a morsel caught between their teeth. They would hear the slither of their great tails on the dust and packed dirt, and their roars into the chill of the night. And Findbhair, hearing them, would involuntarily flinch into the chest of the boy with the black wings, and the boy would curl around him just a touch to soothe him back into sleep. They never spoke, but sometimes Findbhair would reach up his golden Cancanagh fingers and touch the seal that the king of the Unseelie had placed over his eyes. The boy with the black wings would soften to the touch, and something silent, and painful, would pass between them.

Days passed like that, through the austere heat and the icy cold, hiding from the great beasts and stumbling on, with the only hope in sight the eventual death that waited for them amongst the upturned rocks. Sometimes they froze, hearing the rustle of rough fur through wind or the sibilant hiss of scales upon scales. Sometimes they looked at the grey sky and prayed for rain, but never a word passed between them.

* * * *

When the beast found them, hidden in the hollow of a large black rock where some small shadow pooled, Findbhair found himself ready for death. The monster was large with black mats in its ragged fur, its golden eyes rheumy with madness and hunger as its roar shook the mountains. Claws as black as basalt unsheathed with a wet slick noise and the monster brought down its muck brown arm and Findbhair stood there and waited for death.

The pain was bright and brilliant along his face, hot and wet like tears along his right cheek and mouth, the air thick with the fetid stink of the beast and the brilliant smell of copper pennies. Then he felt a second, duller ache and he fell—the boy with the black wings pushing him to the side— his sword-like basalt claws ripping the seal from the left side of his face.

There was a sound like thunder and then the two of them were soaked in the thick and briny blood of the monster, a terrible spray as the boy with the wings of pitchest black, his eyes, blacker even than the shadows of his wings, opened the door between dimensions and ripped the monster in twain. Findbhair looked at him, his hand to the terrible wound on his face, over where his eye had been, ripped out by the beast, and wondered why, even now, thick with blood and fetid gore, drinking the blood because there was nothing else to drink, consuming its meat because there was nothing else to eat, that there were no words between them, and why the boy with the black wings had saved him.

* * * *

With silence as a companion between them, they travelled across the plain, keeping blood and meat as sustenance, to the end of the world below, where there was a small village whose fairies had wings like those of birds. When they saw the boy with the black wings, they rushed forward with exultant cries and lifted him, and for the first time in Findbhair's memory of him, from when they were infants before the queen tore them apart, he smiled.

This, Findbhair discovered, as they tended to the wound on his face where his eye had been, medicating it so to prevent scarring, was the family of the boy with black wings. He had a name, and he was called Raven.

Last among those to welcome home their prodigal child was a girl with hair as golden as Findbhair's own, but eyes as black as Raven's—she was like a cross between the two, with the beauty of the Cancanagh but the silence and stillness of the boy with the black wings who was called Raven. She wore a soft pale blue gown the color of a misty morning and her wings were sun-bright golden. Raven, when he spoke to her, called her Canary, and called her his beloved wife, and something inside Findbhair died that day.

* * * *

Years passed there in the village in the shadow of the demon door, where the fairy with the bird wings lived and Findbhair was welcome among them, treated as one of their own. He ate with their men, as their ladies smiled at him, he ran with their boys as the women choralled their voices but stood apart from him, as Raven watched him with strange eyes, with Canary, tiny and sunflower brilliant beside him.

And Findbhair hated her.

The more the people spoke to him, the women with their heavy eyes and men with their soft fingers which lingered upon his skin, the more Findbhair pulled apart from them, his eyes turning to the black wings of Raven and the warm yellow of Canary where they stood apart from them, and his eyes were full of hate.

He found a way to the human world, the world above, and lingered in the misty woods of the emerald lands where women walked, and of those with black hair and black eyes he drank down their breath until there was nothing left.

Findbhair locked his door, he stood at his window and he watched them, drunk on the breath of emerald maidens, and the liquor men made, and saw the satin black wings of Raven and turned away.

Just as when they walked through the lost plains, words never passed between them.

* * * *

Then Canary fell ill.

It started with a cough that would not fade, that came when she laughed in her soft brittle voice. It was a cough like the braying of a donkey.

Tinctures and lozenges did nothing to soothe it.

She took pale and fever, bright from hour to hour, her hair slick with sweat and harsh with salt.

Sleep abandoned her and the pain came long and hard and Raven was beside himself.

Raven turned to the house he had put aside for the Cancanagh. He opened the door with a violent flourish and looked at the golden man sitting on his bed, his missing eye covered with black lace and he was beautiful, made perfect by his flaws and the scar that was not quite covered by the lace. It looked like he might shatter into a million pieces and could never be brought back to one whole.

"You drank the breath of Canary," Raven said and his voice was like a whisper, "I have felt your eye upon us when we walk, I have felt your ears when we speak. I have given you nothing but kindness in exchange for your cruelty. When we were children, I saw what was done to you and I did what I could. When we walked through the desolate plain, I shared all I was to bring you home, to my home, for you had known none. Tell me why you do this? Why do you watch us and hear us? Why would you hurt her who has done nothing to you?" He stopped, his face red with rage. "Answer me, Cancanagh."

Findbhair said nothing.

"She has done no harm to none. Would you hurt me for what I have done, and if so, why hurt her and not me?"

Findbhair smiled, with his wondrous, glamorous smile, and lay back on the bed. "What would you do?" he asked Raven. "What would you give, to save her? If she died, what would you lose?" He stretched out supine on his bed, amongst the fine cloth and popped the bones of his spine with a delicious sigh. "Perhaps I am still the boy who was favored of the Queen of the Unseelie."

Raven looked at him, his eyes as black and hard as diamonds. "Such a child never existed," he said with his whispery voice. "You do this for a reason other than the cruelty you would espouse given chance. I know you, Findbhair, I have known you as the boy who was favored of the Queen of the Unseelie. I have known you as the boy who walked with me through the desolate plains, and I have known you as the man that you have become. There is something that you wish from me. Tell me what it is that you are ransoming for my bride, for my golden Canary."

"Give yourself unto me," Findbhair said spreading open his legs on the primrose patterned bed spread, kicking off his leather soled shoes to bare his slender toes to the lamp light of the room. "Give yourself unto me and I shall tell you what it is I wish, and I shall save your Canary for what you ransom unto me, and I shall leave here. I shall go to the lands of the

Cancanagh and throw myself upon their mercy. I have known you all my life, Raven of the Demon's Door, let me drink of your breath so that I will regret nothing when you give me what I request."

So Raven of the Demon's Door stepped forward to the small neat bed whereupon the Cancanagh lay. With eyes dull and black as coal, he undid the collar of his shirt and bent down to kiss the golden Findbhair.

He forced upon the Raven's mouth with his tongue, moving it strong and firm as he laid himself between the open legs, toeing off his shoes as his hands moved to either side of the golden shoulders, his heat bearing down on him.

Strong hands stretched over his back, a scent as sweet as lemons and peace roses washed through him as he forced his hips against those of the Cancanagh, rubbing and rippling.

It surprised him, the passion in the golden breath as Findbhair drank him in, feeling the heat of him like a burning volcano the over flowing bliss that ran through him. He had heard the Cancanagh fed off this, and had known Findbhair for almost all of his days, but he had restrained everything his entire life. He bucked into the kiss as Findbhair reached around and began to stroke his wings, fingers through the feathers as their crotches rubbed together. It felt better than anything Raven had ever known—it was fire and it was ice and it was air and it was metal at all of the time. He undid his flies and those of Findbhair so they were pressed skin to golden skin as the Cancanagh used his foot against the bedspread to raise his hips, even as he ran the fibers of the feathers between his fingers.

It was the heat of the sun of the world above and it was the cold of the waters of the seas below.

It was the dazzle of the court of the Unseelie and the machinations of the Daoine Sidhe.

It was fingers and tongues and heat and rubbing and balls tightening and bodies arching and it was all of these things and it was none of them.

It was the everything of creation and it was the nothing of chaos.

When they came against each other it was with the force of mountains colliding, it was with the heat of volcanoes, it was with guttural cries and a stuttered golden moan.

As Findbhair laid upon the primrose patterned bedspread, shirt ripped, feathers about him, and trousers open wide to the air, his breath hitching and catching in his golden throat, Raven asked, "Tell me what you want. Tell me what it is that will save my Canary?"

"I want your eye." Findbhair said as he touched the patterned lace that covered his own disfigurement, "I want the right eye stolen from me. I want all that was taken from me. I want the Emerald maiden whose blind eyes saw me. I want the Unseelie queen to suffer for what she did to me and I want you to see me. I will leave this place, as I did promise, but I want it that every time I see myself, you see me."

So the Raven flexed his mighty wings of feathered black and brought his fingers to his eye and plucked it out, throwing it upon the ebbing chest of the Cancanagh, with blood and gore still upon it.

So Findbhair laughed as he held the eye in his hand. "I shall leave you, my Raven. I shall leave the world below and feed only among the breath of the mortals, but know this, my love." He drew the words out slowly, tasting each of them on his tongue. "Your Canary is dead."

And as he left, Raven sat alone on the bed with his head in his hands and heard the La La La of the women mourning and knew it was true.

And so the Raven touched the blood upon his cheek and remembered the boy he had known in the Unseelie Court, the boy he had travelled with in the desolate plains and the golden man he had grown to be, and knew that some day they again would meet, and then and only then, would he know the truth of what it was that the Cancanagh had truly desired.

About Tessa Buxton

Tessa Buxton knew she was going to be a writer pretty much as soon as she discovered the comma. Inspired by the work of Jayne Fisher, she's been writing since she was a small child, finishing her first novel at eleven. Published for short stories and poetry by the age of fifteen Tessa then took a time out from publishing, but not from writing, whilst she garnered herself an advanced education in literature to better improve her work. She currently lives in Derbyshire with a small dog who owns her completely, an Internet connection and new publishing credits to her name.

She has a novel currently available with Eternal Press called **East of the Sun**, *as well as short comedy story called* **Fey**. *She is better known as the fan writer Seraphim_grace and her copious amounts of work can be read at http://seraphim-grace.livejournal.com*

THE LITTLE MERMAID
By Karenna Kolcroft

Once upon a time, in the palace of the Sea King, a party was in full swing. It was the eighteenth birthday of the king's youngest daughter, Ariana, and every had come to celebrate.

But Ariana didn't enjoy her party. She preferred peace and quiet to the loud celebrations that often occurred in the palace, and usually managed to slip away after an obligatory few minutes of attendance. Unfortunately, she didn't have the option of leaving her own birthday festivities. Too many people wanted to speak to her, to congratulate her on becoming an adult or to dance with her. If she left, everyone would look for her, and her father would be furious.

Instead, she stayed in the palace ballroom, chafing in the decorative shells and anemones her grandmother had adorned her with. How much longer would this torture go on?

In addition to her discomfort, Ariana had another reason for wanting the party to end. On this, her eighteenth birthday, she finally had the option of rising to the human world to see the wonders her sisters and friends had told her about. Granted, she would have to remain in the water, and would therefore be unable to see everything that made her so curious, but at least she could get a glimpse of the life humans lived. If she could ever get out of the ballroom.

Her father came over to her, followed by a merman Ariana hadn't seen before. "Daughter, I wish you to meet Lord Havian," the Sea King said. "He has traveled quite a distance to attend your birthday ball."

"It's a pleasure," Ariana lied. She didn't want to meet yet another potential dance partner.

"The pleasure is mine, Lady Ariana." Havian took her hand and brought it to his lips. "I have heard of the beauty of the king's youngest daughter, and wanted to view it for myself."

Ariana rolled her eyes. She'd heard many compliments and propositions that night, but none as corny as this. "I hope

I meet your expectations."

"You surpass them," Havian replied.

"Daughter, Lord Havian has requested the pleasure of your company tomorrow," the king said. "He wishes to court you, and I have agreed. Your maid will accompany you tomorrow, and you and Havian may spend the day becoming acquainted."

Court her? She had just turned eighteen! True, three of her sisters had married at her age, but she had no intention of marrying so young. There were too many things she wished to do, too much to see. "Father, Lord Havian, I appreciate the attention and the compliment, but I do not wish to be courted," she said firmly.

"Daughter, you will follow my wishes," the king replied, glowering. "Lord Havian has made a respectful request, and you will grant it with your company tomorrow. And if all goes well, a wedding will be planned."

Over her dead body. She didn't even like the looks of Havian. She could hardly imagine spending her life with him, let alone sharing her body as she knew a wife would be expected to do. She didn't intend to marry at all, and certainly wouldn't marry someone her father had chosen. He might have her best interests at heart, but he, like the rest of her family, did not understand her in the least. "Father, I don't feel that one day's acquaintance would be sufficient basis for a marriage," she said.

"And as your father, I overrule that decision," he countered. "This is a discussion best held in private, daughter. You do not wish to argue in front of Lord Havian, surely."

Ariana didn't actually care who they argued in front of, but she knew that to her father, appearances were everything. "My apologies," she said through gritted teeth. "Father, I wish to take advantage of my option to visit the surface. When might I do so?"

Havian chuckled. "I have heard that you are quite fascinated by the tailless beasts who live outside the sea, my dear. Perhaps we could visit the surface together tomorrow."

"Perhaps. But for my first visit, I would prefer to go alone." Ariana turned back to her father. "Father, when, please? When might I go on my own?"

The Sea King paused. Ariana was his favorite child, the last his wife had given him before her death, and she greatly resembled her mother. Ariana knew that he might not wish her to go to the surface unaccompanied, but she was certain he would allow it, if for no other reason than he might see its importance to her. Finally he said, "Remain here for a short time longer, and then you may go."

Ariana flung her arms around him. "Thank you, Father! I promise, I'll be careful not to be seen by the humans."

"I trust that will be the case," he said adamantly.

"I would be pleased to accompany you tonight," Havian offered.

"That would be unwise," the Sea King said before Ariana could protest. "Ariana's maid has been dismissed for the evening, and there would be no one to chaperone. I am not willing to permit you to be alone with my daughter until the engagement is definite. It would not seem right."

Havian inclined his head. "As you wish, Sire. Ariana, perhaps I could trouble you for a dance before you go?"

Now that she had gotten her way, Ariana felt more courteous toward the lord. "Of course. It would be my pleasure."

"Again, lady, the pleasure is mine."

He took her hand and they swam into the center of the dancing crowd. Ariana loved to dance, and was generally very graceful. But Havian was clumsy and clunky, and Ariana found herself unable to move the way she wished. Havian seemed to notice no problem; he smiled and chattered as though they were the most graceful couple in the room. Ariana was thankful when the music stopped. "Thank you for the dance," she said politely.

"Thank you," Havian replied with a bow. "You're a wonderful dancer."

Ariana couldn't bring herself to return the compliment;

that would be too untruthful. "Thank you," she said instead.

"Havian!" A large merman swam to them. "You old dogfish! It's marvelous to see you." He realized who Havian was with, and his face went red. "Princess Ariana. I apologize for my rudeness, lady."

"It's fine," Ariana said graciously. "I can see you know Lord Havian. I'll leave the two of you to talk."

"I'll find you afterward," Havian promised.

Not if Ariana could help it. Havian's friend had given her the opportunity to escape for her visit to the surface. "Until later," she said.

As she swam away, she heard Havian say, "I can't wait until her father approves our engagement. She's a gorgeous little piece of tail, isn't she?" His friend rapidly hushed him; one didn't say such things about a princess. Havian's comment made Ariana more determined than before to avoid spending any time with him.

Without bothering to tell anyone where she was going, she left the ballroom. After overhearing Havian, she had no desire at all to remain. Her father would figure out where she had gone, and she would make her apologies to him and to any remaining guests when she returned. But now she needed to be away from the noise and the crowd. She needed to see the surface world.

Once out of the palace, Ariana swam swiftly upward. Her older sisters, who had already made this journey, had pointed her in the direction that would bring her to what they claimed was one of the most interesting parts of the surface world. "Buildings higher than the palace!" they'd claimed. "And so many humans! You'd never believe it if we told you."

Maybe not, but Ariana had always wished they would tell her more. Now, at last, she would have the chance to find out for herself.

She broke the surface of the water and looked around. Above her hung a large, white globe, surrounded by many points of light. "Moon and stars," she reminded herself from what she had learned about the human world. "They're beautiful!"

Ahead of her, she saw the city her sisters had told her about. She swam closer, drinking in the sight of the glowing lights and huge structures. How had humans built such enormous things?

A roar sounded from above her. Frightened, she looked up and saw blinking lights passing over her. What was it? It appeared not to notice her, so she relaxed and continued her swim.

As she neared the city, she saw some familiar things. Boats. She'd only seen them from below, of course, but they were immediately recognizable. Humans walked about on the decks of the boats, and in the still night air she could hear their voices, though she couldn't make out the words they said. They were fascinating creatures, even more than she'd imagined they would be: the way they moved about on what she knew were called legs, the strange items that covered their bodies. Perhaps they needed those items in the air; it seemed colder than the ocean to her.

Cautious not to allow herself to be seen, she swam still closer. Nearer the land, the boats became smaller, each occupied by only a few humans. Music played from some of them, some soft and beautiful, some loud and painful to her ears. But all of it fascinated her. Despite the stories from her sisters, she'd never expected anything like this.

Suddenly she heard a scream from one of the boats. She turned in time to see a human body hit the water. Rapidly, she dove beneath the waves and swam to the site. She knew humans couldn't live below the ocean; this one might need her help.

When she reached the place, she saw a beautiful young man. His eyes were closed, and bubbles came from his nose. His long legs dangled beneath him. He seemed unable to swim to the surface. Ariana knew she wasn't supposed to interact with humans, but she couldn't allow this one to die. She grasped him beneath his arms and pulled him toward the land.

As she got closer to the land, the water became shallower. Long posts sank from above down into the sand below her, holding up flat structures to which some boats were tied. Looking up through the water, Ariana saw humans on the flat structures. Perhaps they would be able to help the young man. She pushed him ahead of her to the surface and held him, hoping that none of the humans would see her.

She heard a shout. "Someone's in the water!"

A splash sounded beside her. Quickly she let go of the man and swam away. She didn't want to; she wanted to remain with the young man and make sure he was all right. She wanted to stay with him in his world. She had never seen anything like him; she wanted to see more.

But she couldn't stay. She wasn't human, and it made no sense to her that she would want to stay with such a strangely-shaped creature. Nor would it be safe to do so; her entire life, she had been taught not to let humans see her. She waited until she saw the young man pulled from the water, then returned to her home.

The party had ended; her father awaited her to confront her about leaving without notice. Ariana pretended to listen, but all the while, her mind was on the young man she had rescued. When she finally retired to her room for the night, he filled her dreams.

* * * *

The next day, Lord Havian arrived at the palace before Ariana had fully awakened. Reluctantly, she allowed her maid to assist her with the shells a princess was required to wear in her hair and on her tail. Of course, she left her breasts bare; mermaids had no reason to cover themselves. Ariana knew that mermen considered breasts alluring, but they were as much a part of the body as a tail or hair. It would never occur to her, or any other mermaid, to hide them.

Havian awaited her in her father's throne room. Her father stood beside him, indicating without words his approval of the man. Ariana's maid followed her and waited deferentially at the doorway to the throne room. "Daughter,

Havian has arrived to spend the day with you," her father said. "Your maid, of course, will accompany you as chaperone. I trust that you will allow Havian to take you where he will, and that you will make an honest attempt to become acquainted with him so that you might make a wise decision as to his proposal."

Ariana had already decided. She wouldn't marry Havian under any circumstances. But it would only anger her father to hear that. He wanted what was best for her; she just didn't agree with his assessment of what was best. "Of course, Father," she replied, eyes downcast.

"Enjoy yourselves." The Sea King returned to his throne, dismissing them.

Havian took Ariana's hand. She cringed at his touch, but managed to hide it. "Where shall we go, lady?" he asked. "What have you always wished to see?"

The city above the waves, she thought but did not say. "I shall go wherever you wish to take me," she replied.

His mouth curved into an unpleasant smile. "Very well. I know of a beautiful area nearby, filled with rocks and anemones. I think you will enjoy it. It is nearly as lovely as you."

Ariana rolled her eyes at the compliment, and did not thank him for it. Something about his words rang insincere. This man thought nothing of her, save what he would gain by marrying a princess. He would play the part, she could see; he would act as though he loved her until he had what he wanted. But she hadn't forgotten the overheard comment at the ball. What he wanted was something far less innocent than her time.

At least with her maid along, he would be unable to make any attempt at anything inappropriate. The maid had served Ariana nearly all her life, and would allow no harm to come to her. Ariana trusted the woman with her life.

As he had said, Havian brought them to a small garden-like area not far from the palace. Ariana wondered that she had not discovered it herself on one of her exploratory trips.

"It is lovely," she said, a genuine note of awe in her tone. "Thank you for bringing me here."

"Its loveliness pales in comparison to yours."

Havian pulled her to him and pressed his lips to hers. Ariana struggled, but he was much stronger than she. His tongue insinuated itself between her lips; his hand came up to cover one small breast. Ariana slapped his arm, but he did not let go. And her maid did not speak up to stop him.

Finally, Ariana managed to break the kiss. But Havian did not release her breast. "I suggest you move your hand," Ariana said coldly.

"Do you not enjoy my touch, lady?" Havian asked lewdly. "All women like to have their bodies admired by men."

"I do not wish you to touch me at all." Ariana looked around for her maid, who waited at the edge of the garden. "Why don't you help me?"

"Lord Havian is doing nothing wrong." The maid smiled. "This is what womanhood is, my lady. This is what marriage will be. Enjoy what he offers."

"Indeed, enjoy it," Havian said, smiling. "Your maid already has."

Stunned, Ariana looked at her maid, who met her eyes with a lascivious smile. "You planned this," Ariana said, stunned. "You planned to bring me here and- and-"

"Of course, lady," Havian replied. "Surely you don't expect me to propose without sampling you." He caressed her lower back. "What shall I sample first?"

"Nothing!" Ariana jammed her elbow into Havian's ribs and rapidly swam away.

Once out of danger, Ariana burst into tears. How could her trusted maid have betrayed her this way? She had expected no better from Havian, but she had thought she would be able to depend on her maid to ensure her safety.

She swam toward the palace, but stopped before she reached it. What would she tell her father? He might not believe the truth. He had seemed pleased about the impending match with Havian. Perhaps he had known Havian's intentions. Even if he hadn't, he would be angry, and Ariana was uncertain at whom he would direct the anger. She had done nothing wrong, but her father might see it as rudeness on her part that she had fought Havian rather than simply turning him down.

She didn't want to return to the palace anyway. She knew where she wanted to go. Thoughts of the young man she had saved still filled her mind, and she felt undeniably drawn to him. In her current form, she would be unable to find him, but if she could become human...And being human, she would be able to live in the human world as she'd often dreamed, and would be away from Havian and others like him who sought to bed and wed a princess. In the human world, no one would know her as Princess Ariana.

Only one merperson could help her with that, and it was one Ariana feared to encounter. The Sea Witch, she who assisted the merfolk when she desired and made their lives more difficult when it pleased her to do so. Ariana knew the Sea Witch had the power to make her human, but she would have to offer something in return. She shuddered at the thought of what that might be; the Sea Witch coveted things most merfolk would loathe to give up.

As she swam to the Sea Witch's cave, Ariana searched her mind for something to offer. All the treasures she had were at the palace, and she had no way to retrieve them. The only item she had that the Sea Witch might find of value was a beautiful shell that had belonged to her mother. Ariana didn't want to give it up, but if it meant she could go to the human world and find the man who had taken over her thoughts, she would do it.

At the Sea Witch's cave, two large sharks met her, swimming back and forth in front of the entrance, preventing any but the bravest from going inside. Ariana swallowed her fear and swam directly toward them, singing as she went. To her surprise, they allowed her to pass.

The Sea Witch waited just inside. "Greetings, Princess,"

she said. "I have been expecting you."

Surprised, Ariana asked softly, "Then you know why I'm here?"

"Indeed," the old woman said, as though the question were frivolous. "You wish to be a human, one of those poor unfortunates who never know the joy of the sea, who are forced to walk about on two spindly sticks rather than gliding effortlessly through the water. Why do you wish this, Princess?"

"I visited the surface last night during my birthday ball," Ariana replied. "I encountered one of them, a man who had fallen from a boat. He was beautiful, and I wish to find him again, for I can't stop thinking about him."

"It is unlikely you would be able to find him," the Sea Witch warned. "The city which you saw contains thousands of humans. Most of them do not even know each other, and you know nothing of this man save what he looks like. How would you locate him?"

"If you can make me human, you can give me something that would enable me to find him," Ariana argued. "Please. I can't return to the palace; my father wishes to marry me off, and the man he has chosen is, in my mind, far from suitable. I want to marry for love, and I love the human I saved last night."

The Sea Witch regarded her as one might look at a foolish child. "Love does not develop as quickly as that. It is cultivated over time. However, you are clearly infatuated with the man, and therefore I will help you. I can transform you into a human woman, and I can aid you in finding this man. However, once you find him, you must attract him on your own. You must gain his love. Should you be unable to do so, you will die in human form, and will never see your home again. Are you willing to give this up for a man you have seen only once?"

Ariana didn't give herself a chance to hesitate. "I would give up anything for him. If I die, at least I'll have experienced humanity. And maybe I will gain his love."

The Sea Witch nodded. "Then first I must have your payment."

"I haven't much to offer. Only this shell." Ariana held up the shell that had been her mother's. "It is dear to me, but I will give it up for this opportunity."

"Keep your bauble," the Sea Witch replied scornfully. "I wish something that is more a part of you. I will take your voice."

Shocked, Ariana couldn't answer for a moment. She had known the price would be high, but she could barely conceive of this. "My voice?" she stammered finally. "But without that, how can I speak to the young man? How will I get him to love me if I cannot talk to him?"

"Women have many ways to attract men," the Sea Witch replied, her tone leaving no doubt as to her meaning. "Your form, your movements, the swing of your hair, all these things will draw the man to you if you use them properly. Your eyes speak volumes, Princess, without you uttering a sound. You will find a way. Your voice is the payment I require. Will you give it?"

What choice did she have? Return to her normal life and risk being married off to a man she despised, or give the Sea Witch what she demanded and chance finding true love. "I will," she said quietly.

Those were the last words Ariana ever uttered. The moment she gave her agreement, the Sea Witch forced her mouth against Ariana's, as Havian had done. The witch's slimy tongue pushed into Ariana's mouth, and Ariana felt something give way and flow into the witch. She wanted to vomit from the sensation of the alien tongue in her mouth, but mercifully, the witch released her before that occurred. "Open your mouth, Princess," the witch ordered. "Try to speak."

Ariana tried to say something, but no sound came out save her breath. She couldn't say a word.

"Wonderful!" the Sea Witch exclaimed. "You have paid your price, Princess, and now I will keep my end of the bargain." She took a vial of foul-looking, smoky stuff from a shelf and held it out to Ariana. "Swim to the surface, then drink this. Your tail will split in two and become those 'legs' of which humans are so proud. You must leave the water within moments of your transformation, or you will drown, for you may be able to swim as a mermaid but you will not have the skill as a human. There will be pain, Princess, make no mistake about that. With each step you take on those legs of yours, it will feel as though you are being stabbed in the soles of your feet. And there may come a time after you find your man when you will feel a sharper pain and will bleed. You have seven days to win his love or you will die, and will turn to sea foam as do all merfolk. Any questions?" She waited a moment, but of course Ariana said nothing. The witch laughed. "Of course, if you had questions you could not tell me. One more thing I will give you."

She took a strip of skin—Ariana tried not to think about what that skin might have come from—and on it wrote with a quill and ink. Handing this to Ariana along with the vial, she said, "You cannot tell your love your name, but you are being brave and deserve to be known by your true name. That is what that skin says. Ariana. Study it and perhaps you will learn to write the human language so that in time, if there is time, you might communicate with him."

Ariana bowed her head to show her thanks to the witch and left the cave. The sharks did not hinder her; they were there only to prevent people from entering, not from leaving. Ariana swam rapidly toward the surface, hoping she would not encounter any other merfolk. But her passage went unnoticed, and she arrived at the surface within minutes.

The Sea Witch had told her she would need to leave the water immediately after taking the potion, so Ariana swam as close to land as she could without being seen before she uncorked the vial. A foul smell emanated from it, and she almost lost her nerve. But this was her one chance to find her love, her one chance to escape the life her father had planned for her. Ariana took a deep breath, then swallowed the contents of the vial.

The effects were immediate. Her tail tore in two; she almost passed out from the excruciating pain, though mercifully it didn't last. Looking down through the water, Ariana saw her beautiful green-blue tail change into two legs the color of the flesh on her upper body. Between her legs was a patch of hair the color of that on her head. A strange place for it; Ariana was not quite certain of its purpose. And her mind was unable to focus enough to figure it out; although the pain had abated, she could not get used to the feeling of legs rather than tail.

Her time was running out, as well. The Sea Witch had told her she would drown if she did not get out of the water. Ariana tried to swim to the land, but could not coordinate her legs to get her there. With her arms alone, she dragged herself through the water, hoping she would be found before she sank below the waves. She couldn't drown before she found her love.

A shout came from above. "Someone's in the water!"

"What the hell?" another voice said. "It's the week for drownings, I guess."

A splash beside her and strong arms gripped her, pulling her from the sea. She turned to see the face of her rescuer and almost fainted when she recognized the young man she had saved. Clearly the Sea Witch had kept her word that she would enable Ariana to find him.

He pulled her to the edge of the water, and his friend assisted him in bringing her onto dry land. For the first time, Ariana felt something dry and solid beneath her. She almost laughed with joy at the feeling, but stopped herself. She would have been unable to laugh anyway, without a voice.

"She's naked," the man's friend said, looking stunned.

"Yeah, well, sometimes people try to drown themselves without clothes," the young man retorted. "Close your mouth and get your mind out of the gutter. She looks like she's in shock." Lowering his voice to a gentle tone, he said to Ariana, "Are you hurt? Where did you come from?"

Ariana shook her head in response to his first question,

but of course could not answer the second. Even had she been able to speak, she wouldn't have known what to say. Surely she couldn't tell him the truth of where she was from.

"Can you talk?" the man asked.

Again Ariana shook her head. Remembering the strip of skin she still clutched in her hand, she held it out to him. "Ariana," he read. "That's your name?"

Ariana smiled and nodded. She loved the way her name sounded in his mouth, as though his lips and tongue were caressing it. "My name is Finn," he said. "Are you from around here? Do you live nearby?" Ariana shook her head. "Do you have friends near here?" Finn asked.

Another head shake. "Good grief," Finn's friend muttered. "Apparently she just appeared out of thin air. What are you going to do with her, Finn?"

"The first thing is to get some clothes on her and get her warm." Finn took off his shirt, revealing a broad, muscular chest. He handed the shirt to Ariana. "Put that on. Garrett, go to the truck and get my spare swim trunks. Those will work as shorts for her. When we get back to my place, I'll call my sister and see if she has any clothes she can lend her."

"Your place?" Garrett repeated skeptically. "You're taking a strange girl to your place? You're nuts! She could be a psycho or something."

Finn looked into Ariana's eyes. "I don't think so. I think she's just lost, and I want to help her. Ariana, put the shirt on."

Ariana looked at the garment, clueless. She had seen how the shirt looked on Finn, and how he had removed it, but she didn't know how to put it on. After a moment, Finn took it from her. "Hold up your arms," he said. Ariana obeyed.

"Okay, either she has a head injury or she's really stupid," Garrett said.

"Shut up." Finn eased the shirt over Ariana's head, then manipulated her arms through the sleeves. He was taller than she, and the shirt hung nearly to mid-thigh on her. "That's better," Finn said. "Garrett, thought I asked you to get those swim trunks."

He grinned. "I wanted one last look at her body. She's hot, even if there is something wrong with her."

Finn smacked him. "You want to walk home? Stop saying shit like that. Come on, Ariana. You understand what's happening, right? You're going to come back to my place until we figure out where you belong."

Ariana nodded. As far as she was concerned, she belonged at Finn's place, but she couldn't tell him that. Perhaps she would figure out how to write enough to tell him her feelings, someday. Someday before her seven days ended.

"All right, then let's go," Finn said. "And don't pay any attention to Garrett. He just doesn't know any better."

"I know better than to bring someone you just fished out of the harbor to my house," Garrett countered.

"That's because you still live with your mommy and daddy."

Finn led Ariana to a large piece of metal. As she walked, just as the Sea Witch had said, a stabbing sensation covered the soles of her feet. It hurt, but Ariana kept her mind on Finn and barely noticed the pain.

Round rubber objects sat at the bottom of the metal object, and it had glass through which Ariana could see inside it. She rested the palm of her hand against it, feeling the warmth that the metal had soaked up from the sun. "It's not much, but it's mine," Finn said. He opened one of the doors. "Get in."

"Where am I supposed to sit?" Garrett demanded.

"You're a pain in the ass," Finn said. "Ariana's small; she can sit in the middle."

Ariana climbed into the vehicle and slid to the middle of the seat. The seat was hot beneath her thighs, painfully so. "Sorry about the seat," Finn said. He fished a piece of cloth from behind the seat and gave it to her. "Sit on this towel. That will make it better."

Ariana lifted her buttocks from the seat and placed the towel beneath her, then sat back down. The towel covered the unpleasant heat, though she could still feel warmth through it. The men got into the vehicle on either side of her. "Fasten your seat belt, Ariana," Finn said.

Ariana had no idea what he was talking about. She watched as he and Garrett brought strips of fabric and metal across their chests and abdomens and fastened them beside Ariana. "Seat belt," Garrett repeated, enunciating each word. "Good lord, Finn, I don't think she get anything."

"It's like she's never seen a car or truck before." Finn reached between himself and Ariana and pulled out a similar strip of fabric and metal. "This one doesn't go across your chest," he said. He brought it over Ariana's abdomen and fastened it between Ariana and Garrett. As he did so, his hand brushed Ariana's belly, making her shiver.

Finn inserted a small piece of metal into a slot in front of him and turned it. The engine was much louder than that of any boat Ariana had ever heard, and she jumped. But she did recognize the sound. "Are you scared or something?" Garrett asked her.

She shook her head. The noise had startled her, but she knew that with Finn beside her, she was safe from anything. And after the initial sound of starting up, the engine was a pleasant, relaxing noise.

Finn moved a lever and pressed a pedal on the floor. The engine sounded louder, and then the vehicle began to move, Finn's hands on the wheel in front of him steering it onto a street where many other vehicles moved. Ariana was thankful for what she had learned of the surface world; although these objects were unfamiliar to her, she realized now what they were, and was fascinated. Just as boats moved through water, these vehicles moved on land, rolling along on the round rubber beneath them.

She watched intently through the glass as they passed other vehicles and buildings. She was so occupied with trying to see everything at the same time that she barely noticed Garrett's thigh pressing against hers. Then he placed his hand on her leg, and she started. "A little jumpy, huh?" he said softly. "What do you expect when you walk around naked."

Ariana slapped his hand. The movement caught Finn's attention, and he glanced over. "You want to get your ass out of my truck, Garrett?" he snapped.

Garrett played innocent. "What are you talking about?"

"Keep your hands off her, or I'll drop you off right here. Without stopping."

"Why? You want her for yourself?"

"I don't think she's like that," Finn said quietly. "She's too innocent. Just leave her alone. You have plenty of women to choose from; you don't need her."

"Whatever." Garrett shifted himself away from Ariana.

Ariana studied Finn gratefully. Garrett wanted the same from her that Havian had attempted to take, and Finn had stopped him. She began now to understand what the Sea Witch had meant, that her body would attract men's attention, that she had means other than her voice to earn Finn's love. He clearly cared for her already; he had treated her with so much kindness without even knowing who she was. She sent a silent thanks to the Sea Witch for her assistance in finding him, a task that might have been impossible otherwise.

After several minutes, he stopped the vehicle in front of a large brick structure. "This is my apartment building," he said. "You can come in. Garrett, go home."

"Yeah, whatever," Garrett snarled. "Thanks for nothing."

"Asshole," Finn muttered.

Garrett got out of the vehicle and slammed his door so hard the vehicle shook. Ariana shuddered. "Don't worry," Finn told her. "He'll get over it. He just thinks any female is fair game to drag into bed."

She looked at him curiously, not quite understanding what he meant. He smiled. "You don't have to worry about me. I'm not trying to get anything from you; I just want to help you. Garrett doesn't grasp the concept of helping someone without expecting something in return. Come on, let's get you inside and find something else you can wear. You look very nice in my T-shirt, but it isn't exactly acceptable to wear in public."

They got out, and he led her into the building. Several doors lined the hallway. Did he live in this entire structure? It was as large as her father's palace! But he unlocked one door and pushed it open to reveal a small room containing a pair of stuffed chairs and a small kitchen. "It isn't much, but it's big enough for one," he said. They went inside, and he closed the door and pointed to another door beside one chair. "That's the bedroom. You can sleep in there while you're here; I'll sleep in my recliner."

She shook her head. It wasn't fair for him to give up his own comfort for her. But then she realized it was another indication of how much he cared for her. Perhaps seven days would be enough to gain his love and make her transformation permanent.

"Yes, I will," he said firmly. "Don't worry; I don't mind it. I fall asleep in the recliner sometimes when I'm watching TV. I can manage to sleep there for a few days, till we find out where you're supposed to be."

She smiled thankfully at him. But in her heart, she wanted him to sleep beside her, not in another room. The touches she had experienced from Havian and Garrett filled her with revulsion, but from Finn, she would not only tolerate but enjoy such caresses. Even if he laid no finger on her, feeling the warmth of his body beside her would be wonderful.

He opened the bedroom door. The room was so small the bed took up nearly the entire space. "Sorry it's so small," he said. "You can take a nap if you want. I'm going to call my sister and see if she can bring over some clothes for you to borrow. You're about her size."

Ariana nodded her thanks and lay down on the bed. The T-shirt she wore rode up, revealing the tops of her thighs and what lay between them. Finn gulped and said. "You can get under the sheet if you want. Sleep well."

He backed out of the room and closed the door. She slipped under the sheet. Why had he seemed so flustered? He hadn't reacted that way when he'd seen her nude at the shore, but it seemed the sight of the place between her legs upset him.

She touched the hair down there. It was soft and curly. She slid her fingers lower and encountered a hard nub. Touching it made her shiver; she hadn't felt anything that pleasurable before. Experimentally, she pushed on it harder and caught her breath. What an amazing sensation!

What else was down there? She was reluctant to stop touching the nub, but was curious. She felt a small opening right behind the nub; when she touched it, she felt the need to urinate. How did humans do that? She got off the bed and opened the door. Finn was sitting on one of the chairs, talking into a small device. "I don't know where she's from," he said. "She doesn't talk." He noticed Ariana in the doorway. "Ariana, do you need something?"

She nodded, but was unable to think of a way to explain what she needed. "If you're thirsty, there's some bottled water in the fridge," Finn said. "And that door right there is the bathroom. You might need to go; sorry I didn't think of it."

The word "bathroom" was unfamiliar to her, but she decided to check it out. Inside were a low porcelain seat, with a large hole in it, a stall enclosed by a curtain, and a taller porcelain item. This last looked somewhat familiar to her; she had seen things like it in the piles of cast-off surface items she had found on the bottom of the sea. She turned one of the knobs and water gushed out. This must be how humans cleaned themselves.

The seat was a mystery to her. She sat on it and relaxed. To her astonishment, water gushed from her! The relief for her bladder was immediate. This was how humans urinated? How strange!

She stood and turned on the water again. She ran her hands through it, enjoying the moisture on her skin, then left the room. "Ariana, next time you go to the bathroom, please close the door," Finn said wearily. "And you need to flush the toilet, please."

Ariana looked at him, confused. The toilet? Which item was that, and what did "flush" mean? "You have no idea what

I'm talking about, do you?" Finn said. "Here, let me show you."

He led her back into the bathroom and pointed at the seat. "This is the toilet," he said. He pushed a metal lever, and with a loud noise, the water inside the toilet was sucked down. "And that's flushing. Do that every time you use the toilet, okay?"

Ariana nodded. "Where do you come from?" Finn mused. "Where is it that doesn't have cars and toilets?"

He seemed to be talking to himself more than to her, so she didn't worry about answering. She touched his shoulder in thanks and went back to the bedroom.

With the door closed, she lay on the bed again and resumed her exploration. Beyond the first hole between her legs was another, larger hole. She slipped a finger inside. The feeling was wonderful. She moved her finger in and out, longing for something, though she didn't know what. After a few moments, she returned to the nub, rubbing and pressing it until suddenly it felt as though every atom of her body was coming apart.

Frightened, she lay still until the feeling subsided. She wasn't sure what had happened, but although it scared her, it had also been the most incredible thing she'd ever felt. Was this what a man might make a woman feel? What would it be like if Finn's fingers instead of her own touched her there?

She turned onto her side and closed her eyes. Within moments, she was asleep.

She woke to the sound of voices in the other room. Cautiously she opened the door and saw two women sitting in the second chair in the room. Finn noticed Ariana and smiled. "Ariana, come meet my sister Jackie and her friend Petra," he said. "Jackie, this is Ariana, the mystery girl."

Jackie looked at Ariana suspiciously. "She's very pretty. Hello, Ariana. I'd like to know more about you. My brother's a little too trusting sometimes."

"Oh, Jackie, stop it." Petra smiled. "Hello, Ariana. Finn's been telling us about you. It's nice to meet you." She wriggled out of the chair and picked up a pile of fabric from the floor. "We brought you some clothes," she said. "I hope they'll fit. Finn's right, you can't walk around in that T-shirt."

"You guys astound me," Jackie said. "How could she not have clothes? How come she can't tell us anything? Ariana, you can write, can't you? You could write down stuff, if my brother hadn't been too clueless to think of it."

"I'm not clueless," Finn protested. He got up and took a thin stick and pad of paper from the top of a tall thing in the kitchen, and brought them to Ariana. "Here. You can write, right?"

She studied the stick. She'd never seen anything like it, and had no idea what it might have to do with writing. After a moment, Finn pulled part of it off and ran the other part over the paper. It left a mark behind. "This is writing," he said. He wrote the same letters the Sea Witch had scribed on the piece of skin. "And this is your name. Can you write anything about where you're from?"

She shook her head, but took the stick and clumsily copied the letters Finn had formed. "Good job," he said. He turned to his sister and her friend. "Guess writing is out. Petra, why don't you help her with those clothes? She had trouble with the T-shirt when I gave it to her to put on."

"This is ridiculous!" Jackie exploded. "No one is that ignorant!"

Petra took Ariana's hand and pulled her into the bedroom. She shut the door. "They'll argue for a while, but we don't have to listen to it," she said. "Now, let's see what you should try on first."

Ignoring the raised voices in the other room, Ariana and Petra passed the next while looking at the clothes. Petra patiently helped Ariana try things on, in the process teaching her how to put them on and take them off herself. When they finally emerged from the bedroom, Ariana was dressed in a pine green tank top and denim shorts. Finn's eyes widened when he saw her. "You look very pretty, Ariana," he said.

"Yeah. Really pretty." Jackie sounded completely

insincere. "It's a good color for her, I guess. So are we going shopping, Petra? I guess we need to replace the clothes she's borrowing."

"Jackie, give it a rest!" Finn snapped. "I don't know what your problem is, but Ariana isn't here to take advantage of anyone. She needs help, and I'm helping her."

"You're too nice. But whatever." Jackie stood. "See you later, little brother."

Petra gave Finn a peck on the lips. "Don't worry about it, Finn. She'll get over it." She followed Jackie out the door.

Finn looked at Ariana and forced a smile. "Don't worry. Jackie's always been a little overprotective of me. Did you have a good nap?"

Ariana nodded. "That's good," Finn said. "Maybe tomorrow we can go somewhere, get out of here. I mean, I'm sure you don't want to spend all your time in my apartment." He yawned. "But right now, I think I need to sleep. See you in the morning, okay?"

She nodded and gestured toward the bedroom. "No, you sleep there," he told her. "I meant what I said. You sleep in there and I'll sleep here. It'll be fine." He pulled a lever on the side of the chair and a footrest sprang up. He pushed back against the back of the chair until he was lying almost flat. "See? I'll be all right. Good night, Ariana."

She smiled and went back into the bedroom. She thought she wasn't tired anymore, but she fell asleep almost immediately.

* * * *

Over the next few days, Ariana and Finn grew more accustomed to each other. He worked, but taught her how to use the TV and the DVD player so she was entertained while he was gone, and took her out to see the city when he returned home at night. Although the walks they took were painful to her, she never minded. At least she was with him. A couple of times, Petra joined them. She seemed to like Ariana, and flirted constantly with Finn, though Ariana thought it was just a game between the two of them.

After they returned home on those nights, Ariana listened while Finn talked about himself, his past, his dreams. She sensed that he didn't often open up to others, and was honored that he felt he could talk to her. She only wished she could return the favor; she wanted him to know everything about her, but despite her best efforts, she still could write only her name, and of course couldn't speak.

She spent much of her time alone trying to decide how best to show her feelings for Finn. Her love for him deepened daily, and she was certain he felt the same, though she desperately wanted him to say so. She also continued her explorations of herself. She discovered the kind of touch that made her feel best, and experienced many more of the bursts of pleasure she'd given herself on the first evening. Among the DVDs Finn had, she found some that showed men and women together, touching each other and doing what the people in the films called "fucking". After watching those, Ariana always felt the desire to touch herself, or better yet, to try what was in the films with Finn.

But with only two days remaining of her seven, she was no closer than on the first day to winning his love. He cared for her, clearly, but she needed him to truly love her and to express that love. Finally, she made a decision. She understood from watching the DVDs what Havian and Garrett had wanted from her, and she determined that she would give that to him.

He came home from work exhausted and sat in his recliner. "Ariana, I'm sorry, but I'm not up to going out tonight," he said. "It was a really long day, and I just want to rest. Is that okay?"

She nodded and went to him. On one of the DVDs she'd watched, a man had come home tired and his woman had rubbed his neck and shoulders. The man had seemed to enjoy it, and it had led to more. Perhaps Finn would enjoy a shoulder rub. She stood behind the recliner and began to gently rub. "Mmm," Finn murmured. "That feels nice, Ariana. Keep going, please."

She massaged his neck and shoulders, pleased with his sounds of appreciation. After a few moments, she gave into an impulse and bent to kiss his lips. "Ariana?" he said hesitantly. "What are you doing?"

She replied by pressing her lips more forcefully against his. He pulled her around the chair and onto his lap. His tongue slid between her lips; unlike that of the Sea Witch, his tongue felt pleasant against her own. The kiss brought a feeling of tingling moisture to the spot between her legs, and the feeling grew stronger when his hand caressed one small breast.

Abruptly, he broke the kiss, though he didn't remove his hand from her breast. "What am I doing? Ariana, I'm sorry. I shouldn't..."

She covered his hand with her own and smiled reassuringly. "Do you want this?" he asked hoarsely. "Do you understand what's going to happen if we don't stop now?"

She didn't understand, not completely, but she knew it would be what the men and women in the DVDs did, and she knew she wanted him to do that to her. She nodded and moved his hand from her breast between her legs. "Ariana," he moaned. "All right. All right. I've wanted you since I found you. If you want me, then okay. But in bed. This chair isn't comfortable enough for fucking."

She gracefully slipped from his lap. More clumsily, he got up from the chair, almost falling over the footrest. Was he this flustered because of her? Now she knew why he'd seemed so nervous her first night there, when he'd seen her naked parts on his bed. She extended her hand to him and he took it and followed her into the bedroom.

Beside the bed, he pulled her close against him and renewed their kiss. As his tongue explored her mouth, his hands roamed her body. He didn't touch between her legs, not yet, but his touch on even the bare skin of her legs set her body on fire. She felt as though she would explode from the pleasure of it. Growing bolder, she moved her own hands over his body, feeling his chest beneath his T-shirt, caressing his buttocks.

Against her belly she felt something hard, and reached between herself and him to touch it. It was a large bulge in the front of his pants. Cautiously, not wanting to hurt him, she put some pressure on it. "Oh, god, Ariana, that feels good!" he exclaimed. "Here. Wait a minute."

He let go of her and peeled off his clothes, then helped her off with hers. For the first time in real life, she saw a naked human other than herself. Between his legs he had what the men in the DVDs had, a hard shaft with two small sacs hanging beneath them. In person, the shaft looked larger than the ones in the films. She reached for them, then looked at him questioningly. He nodded. "You can touch. You can touch me anywhere you want," he said hoarsely. "Have you done this before?"

She shook her head and cupped the sacs in her hand. He moaned. "Ariana, wait, please." She took her hand away, and he caught it in both his hands. "Ariana, have you ever had sex before? Ever done anything with a man?"

Again she shook her head. "Are you sure you want to do this now, with me?" he asked. "I want to. God, I want to. But if it's your first time, it will hurt, and I don't want to hurt you."

Hurt? How could it hurt? She stroked his shaft and a thought occurred to her. Her fingers felt good when she put them inside her opening. This part of him was much larger than her fingers. If it was meant to go inside her, it would hurt; his shaft looked too big to fit. But she knew she wanted him to try. Wanted to join with him that way, to be as close to him as possible. She looked into his eyes and smiled. "You want to make love to me?" he asked huskily.

She nodded. "Then lie down," he commanded. "If this is your first time, I want to make it incredible for you."

She lay on her back on the bed. Finn lay beside her and pressed his lips to hers. His hand moved over her breasts and down, down to the place between her legs. He pressed a finger against her nub and she caught her breath. "That feels good, doesn't it?" he whispered in her ear. "Ariana, you're so wet! I can't wait to be inside you, but I want to do something for you first."

He moved down the bed, leaving a trail of light kisses from her neck to the junction of her thighs. She waited to see what he would do, and was astonished when his tongue touched the nub. She jumped, then relaxed into the pleasure as he licked and sucked it lightly. She felt the now-familiar sensation building, and knew she was about to burst, but had no way to let him know until the strong pleasure hit her, stronger than she'd felt with her fingers. She bucked, and he looked up with a grin. "Did you like that?" he asked.

She nodded and smiled enthusiastically. He slipped one finger into her opening, then two. "God, Ariana, you're so tight," he said softly. "It's going to hurt when I fuck you, but I'll go slow, all right? You're still sure you want me to fuck you?"

His fingers felt amazing; Ariana was sure she was going to explode again. If his fingers brought her that much pleasure, she had to know what his shaft could do. She nodded and spread her legs wider apart, inviting him to lie between them. He accepted the invitation, covering her body with his own, and she felt the head of his shaft against her entrance. "Are you ready?" he asked softly.

She replied by kissing his lips. He pushed his shaft forward, and she felt her opening stretch to accept him. There was discomfort, but at the same time it felt so wonderful, as though she was connecting completely with him.

Slowly he pushed into her, then stopped. "The next bit is going to be the painful part," he said. "But it will only hurt for a minute, and then it will feel very, very good. Okay?"

She nodded, and with one fast thrust, he was fully inside her. Tears came to her eyes at the sharp, searing pain between her legs. He lay still. "I'm sorry, Ariana," he said softly. "I know that hurt, but just wait and it will stop, I promise."

As he'd said, after a moment, the pain subsided. She moved against him, and he took the hint, beginning a slow, steady motion in and out of her. "Is it okay?" he asked.

Better than okay. It was the most incredible thing she had ever felt! She meet each of his thrusts with one of her own, savoring the intense pleasure, until another burst came and she opened her mouth in a soundless cry. "You came again?" he asked, astonished. "Damn, Ariana, you're amazing! I can't believe how good you feel!"

He picked up his pace, thrusting harder and faster into her, until he shouted, "I'm coming!" She felt him push hard into her, then he rested on her. "That was so fucking good," he said. "Did you enjoy it, Ariana?"

He looked at her face to see her response. She couldn't speak, but it occurred to her that she could still move her lips in the shape of the words she needed to say. "I love you," she mouthed.

He stared at her, stunned. "Ariana, no," he said finally. "No. You can't love me. You don't know me. And I- I care for you, a lot. Having you here has been wonderful. But Petra and I...God, Petra's going to kill me. Ariana, Petra and I've been dating for a long time. We're planning to get married in a couple years. I care about you, but I love Petra."

She felt her heart shatter. Finn loved Petra? That explained the flirting and teasing between them, but why then had he introduced Petra as his sister's friend, not as his girlfriend? And why had he entered Ariana as he had if he loved someone else?

"Ariana, I'm so sorry," he said. He moved away from her and sat on the edge of the bed. "I never meant to hurt you. I just...I can't explain. I love Petra, but I wanted to make love to you. But it can't happen again, okay?" He stood up. "I'm going to go take a shower. We can talk about this after. I need to think."

He left the room, and after a second Ariana heard the bathroom door close behind him. She got off the bed; where she had lain was a bloodstain, which she realized must have been from when he had buried himself in her. Just as the Sea Witch had predicted: pain and blood.

She gathered her clothing from the floor and put it back on as best she could. Her hands shook, and she fought back tears. She couldn't stay here, not anymore. Finn loved someone else, and she could never gain his love for herself. There might be two days remaining of the seven the Sea Witch had given her, but as far as Ariana was concerned, her time was up. She would turn to foam, as the Sea Witch had predicted, and would never see her family again.

Once dressed, she slipped out of the apartment. It was best to leave while Finn was in the shower; he might try to stop her otherwise. But there was nothing left for her, no reason to stay with him. She had come here for love, but he had none for her. Her heart was broken, and she felt her body failing her. With Finn's denial of her love, her time had indeed ended.

Fortunately, in their evening walks, Finn had shown her how to get from his apartment to the harbor. She walked straight there, ignoring the looks from passers-by and the catcalls she heard from some of the men. At the edge of the water, she hesitated. This was the end for her, she knew. Mermaids had no souls; there was nothing beyond death.

She was about to dive into the water when she heard singing a distance away. She looked out into the harbor and saw her sisters, all missing their beautiful hair. Stunned, she waved to them, and they swam closer. "Dear sister," the eldest said, "we've been searching for you. Father was so saddened when you didn't return!"

"We went to the Sea Witch, and she told us what you'd done," the next said. "We made her tell us where you were."

"We gave her our hair to save you," the third told her. "She told us of a way that you can regain your true form and not crumble to sea foam if you do not win the love of the man."

"You've already failed to win his love, haven't you?" asked the fourth, who had always been close to Ariana and recognized the sadness on her face. Ariana nodded. "Then in two days' time, you will die if you do not do as we say," her sister said.

The fifth sister swam right up to the platform on which Ariana stood and held up a sharp knife. "The Sea Witch told us that your man has a true love," she said. "If you can find them together and run this knife through their hearts, you will be restored to your true self and will be able to return home."

"But you must do so tonight," the eldest said. "Go now. We'll wait for you here."

Ariana took the knife from her sister and turned it over in her hands. Stab Finn and Petra? How could she? They'd been so kind to her, Finn especially. But then he had taken the love she offered him without loving her in return. If she didn't take his life, she would lose her own.

She nodded to her sisters and set off back through the city. Would she find Finn and Petra together? If Finn had found her gone, he might have called Petra for help in finding her. They might be together now in his apartment, or in his bed. She set her heart against the man she loved; she had no other choice.

She turned the final corner and ahead of her saw Finn and Petra hugging on the sidewalk in front of Finn's building. It was a perfect opportunity; the way they were holding each other, it would be easy to run the knife through both their hearts. She moved slowly, carefully, toward them, thankful that neither was looking in her direction. She raised the knife, ready to strike-

And lowered her arm. No matter how hurt she felt, no matter what Finn had done to her, she couldn't bring herself to kill him and his true love.

Although they hadn't spotted her, Ariana had been seen. A police officer standing nearby shouted, "Drop the knife!"

Finn and Petra jumped apart. "Ariana?" Finn gasped. "What are you doing?"

"Looks like she was about to stab you," the officer said.

Ariana shook her head, but she couldn't bear the look of fear on Finn's face. Dropping the knife, she ran.

The officer ran after her. "Stop!" he shouted. "You're

under arrest!"

He was fast, but she was faster. She ran straight for the waterfront, knowing now that there was no hope for her. She had seen enough TV in her few days with Finn to know that if the officer caught her, she would be locked up in jail. There, she would die far away from the ocean. At least if she escaped, she would die near her home.

"Stop!" the officer shouted again.

For blocks he pursued her. A few people tried to grab her, but she dodged their hands and finally reached the water. She ran out onto one of the long platforms and, without hesitating, dove from it.

Death didn't hurt. She had expected pain, but there was none. She felt her body dissolving into foam, then heard a voice, one that sounded like music, and felt her form rising from the waves. "Child, you are one of us now."

She looked around. Surrounding her were dozens of transparent beings. She and they hovered above the water. She rose higher, and the beings rose with her. "Where am I?" she asked, and was astonished to hear her own voice. "What's happening?"

"You are with the children of the air now," said the voice which had first spoken. "We have chosen because of your love for your man and your choice not to harm him or his lover to bring you to us. You have no immortal soul, but if you stay with us for three hundred years and perform good for the humans over whom we watch, you may gain a soul and will live forever. Do you wish to remain with us?"

"Oh, yes!" Ariana breathed.

"Then so shall it be."

Ariana looked with new eyes at the city below her. At the water's edge, she saw Finn and Petra, heard them calling her name. Both had tears in their eyes. She went to them and pressed her lips to Petra's forehead, to Finn's cheek. "I wish you every happiness," she said, though of course they could not hear her. "And I wish you all love."

Then she rose with the children of the air.

About Karenna Kolcroft

Karenna Colcroft is the naughty alter-ego of a shy, sedate mom of two and teacher. She lives in the Northeastern United States with her children, assorted cats and fish, a couple ghosts, and half the time a boyfriend. Karenna began writing erotica about three years ago on a dare, and quickly became hooked. Her favorite thing to read is paranormal romance, and her favorite thing to write is whatever her characters tell her to. To learn more about Karenna, please visit her <u>website</u>.

JACK AND THE BEANSTALK
By Phineas Magnus

Jack fought against the strange lethargy and opened his eyes. It was a Herculean effort, for they each weighed as much as a bus. With that accomplished, he looked around the dimly lit room and tried desperately to make sense of the strangeness of it.

"Try to relax," a feminine voice said behind him. "I know it's difficult the first time, but please trust me; I'll try to do this as gently as possible."

"Urf?" Jack grunted, his mouth dry and throat sore. He felt like he'd been drinking heavily for about a week and was only now drying out.

"That's the transportation effects. They didn't design it for humans and we don't handle it well. The sickness will go away," she explained.

Her voice was pleasant enough, smooth and almost husky. She had an American accent. Not the southern one with the twangs and the y'alls—something more correct. He tried to turn his head to look at her but found he could not see her. Worse, he was confined in some type of chair or bed or…something.

Jack struggled, trying to push himself free of whatever it was that bound him. Within moments he realized he was truly immobilized. He was strapped down securely, but at least the device he was on was padded. Multiple straps held him, two on each arm and three across his back at different points. Even his neck was strapped, keeping his head snug to the table. What disturbed him were the straps that held his lower body. Each thigh was held by two of them, and two more held his calves.

None of those straps were nearly as disconcerting to him as the position his body was forced to mold itself into. His ass was up in the air, legs spread and enough feeling had returned that he knew without a doubt he was naked.

"Try to relax," she said again, a tremor in her voice. "I really hate doing this the first time...you're scared, confused...I know. I guess it's not any better any other time, but at least you'll know what's going to happen then."

"What the bloody hell are you doing to me?" Jack gasped, his voice raspy.

"An Englishman? Oh, we don't have many like you here. Somebody once told me the English are more into this sort of thing." She sounded surprised and a little excited, or at least happier. "Now hush and let me do this. The sooner it's over, the better."

Jack struggled again, to no effect, then stiffened in surprise when he felt something cool touch his bottom. Her fingers were rubbing something against him. His cheeks immediately flushed red with embarrassment, but he struggled anew as soon as he realized what she was doing.

"Relax," she murmured, putting pressure against him slowly.

Jack tried to resist. He clenched every muscle he had. He squeezed and tried to tear himself away, but ultimately it just made the pressure she was exerting that much more painful for him. Whatever substance she used to lubricate her fingers made resistance futile.

Teeth gritted against the humiliation, he felt one digit enter his rectum and press against him internally. She was an expert, he realized, as she found what she was after immediately and began to stroke her finger inside of him. The pressure felt horrible at first. Almost painful. It abated and soon began to cause him to stiffen involuntarily. Jack cried out, groaning in misery as he again tried to struggle in spite of her repeated suggestions for him to relax.

A warmth spread through, him though he struggled to deny it. He felt something happening, something disgusting and embarrassing. His body shuddered in spite of his intentions, causing him to wet himself slightly. It grew worse as she continued, until, at long last, something powerful swept through him. Jack gasped silently, unable to protest as his body betrayed him. It was the strangest feeling he had ever felt, and even though it felt good, he refused to accept it.

His body relaxed, all tension gone from his muscles. He struggled to catch his breath and fight, but he had not the strength.

"I'm sorry," the woman said, sounding truly miserable. "I...they make me do it. There's one milkmaid for every twenty men."

She wanted to say more, he could tell, but instead she turned and left the odd room. Jack struggled to look around again, but all he saw was the light brown wall and the edge of the strange couch he was trapped upon. He wondered at her term—milkmaid. What did that mean? Was that what she had done to him, milked him?

The straps released on their own, leaving him suddenly free. He picked himself up slowly and looked around. The room was featureless, every wall identical in color, all a pale tan. The light came from nowhere and everywhere, leaving no shadows. The only thing in the room was himself and the strange couch. He looked at it again, burning it into his memory with just a glance. A glance that, he was sure, would visit him in his nightmares.

When he turned again, he saw that the wall had opened. Not the entire thing, just a portion of it that was sized perfectly for him to walk through. Having no other options, he stepped through and found himself in a larger room filled with beds. Not beds like he was accustomed to, but beds nonetheless. They were thin pads on the floor with a single blanket on top. The pad was molded in such a shape that at one end it had a pillow.

"You must be Harry's replacement," a deeply tanned man said. He walked up to him and offered his hand.

Jack did a double take. *Harry? Replacement?*

"Yeah, sorry, that didn't make sense. Look, I'm Patrick, I'll introduce you to the guys," he said, turning to point to the rest of the men who were looking at Jack with a mixture of interest and apathy.

"Sorry, but why are you all naked?" Jack asked, noting the one thing they all had in common.

Patrick smiled sadly. "I been here twenty-two years I think, it's hard to know really, but they don't give us clothes to wear."

"They? Who?"

"The giants," he said, glancing up at the ceiling for effect. "They live up there, in their cloud city. The ground's too dirty or something; it's beneath them. Anyway, we do their dirty work and they live up there and do...well, whatever it is they do."

"What the bloody hell is going on here?" Jack asked, confused and wondering when he would wake up from the dream.

"Beans," another man said, shrugging. "We grown beans."

"Beans?" Jack asked, more at a loss than ever. "That's it then, I've gone mad."

Patrick chuckled and shook his head. "'Fraid not, but this place'll make you feel it," he said. "This is all passed down, mind you, but what we can figure is that these giant folk been using us for hundreds or thousands of years, maybe. There's something about the beans we grow on Earth, something they like. Maybe they need it, like we need water, or maybe they want it, like I miss a Camel and a Budweiser. Don't really matter I guess, except that they make us grow 'em. Three crops to about a year, best we can figure, and you don't never see them except when they come to harvest. Even then, it's just one of them pasty white skinned fellers in a weird looking plane."

Jack looked around, unable to comprehend what he was being told. "I was a banker," he muttered. "We were going through a merger...I just met a girl…"

Patrick nodded. "Yeah, I know, it don't make sense. Hang in there, you'll pick it up."

"Pick it up? Pick what up? I don't want to do this! I've got a life! I…"

"You got no choice," Patrick snapped. "You don't do the work, we're all in for it. It's easy enough right now, mid-season, but if you ain't helping come harvest or planting time, then we don't make the schedule. They don't like it when you miss a schedule. People have a way of dying, and trust me, I seen it, they don't make it quick or easy."

"I'm not a farmer," Jack managed to say. "I've never...I mean...how did...why…"

"It's a shock, you'd best have a seat. You can have that bunk over there, that was Harry's." Patrick pointed to a bed on the floor.

"What happened to Harry?"

"Harry figured he was closing in on his eighty-seventh birthday," another man said. "His heart gave out in the fields."

"That's Ben—he's a good man if you're in a bind," Patrick said, introducing the other man.

Jack nodded woodenly and sat down. His consternation about his own nudity was fading rapidly. Everyone else was naked and nobody seemed to pay it any mind, even if it was bizarre.

"Harry'd been here the longest in our group, fifty-two years, by counting seasons," Patrick continued. "He's the one that told us a lot of what we know."

"Harry had a sense of humor, that's what got him through," Ben added, then chuckled. "Might be he made up everything he told us and that was his private joke."

Patrick frowned. "Naw, that ain't it. It fits with what others have said. That and what little I get out of the maids."

Jack's head jerked up even as his cheeks flushed. "Maids?"

"Yeah, you met ours. Nobody's seen her, but she sounds like a pretty thing, don't she? She's new too, only been here a couple of years. The one before her, phew, she had a right cruel finger on her!" Patrick said, then he shrugged. "Anyhow, that's how they figure they keep us tame, like we're animals or something."

"What...what did she...I mean, I never...I didn't—"

Ben chuckled. "You ain't gay, if that's what you're worried about. Well, you ain't unless you are, I mean."

Patrick shook his head. "Ben means what they done, that happens to all of us every five days. Like it or not, it's just something our bodies do. Don't mean you have to like it and don't mean you want to snuggle up with any of us. Anyways, four men each day get to visit, your next one will be in five days."

The color drained from Jack's face at the thought of going through that ordeal again. "What...happened?"

"It's called prostate milking," Patrick said. "Right kind of pressure on it and it drains the juice out of a man without letting us enjoy it the way God intended us to, if you know what I mean."

"He means holding a woman in his arms," Ben said with a distant look in his eyes.

"What else would I mean?" Patrick asked with a scowl. "Anyways, there's no fraternizing with the milkmaids. We do our thing, they do theirs. The giants figure if we get to breeding, they can't control us, or at least that's what Harry said."

"I'm not going back!" Jack blurted out, remembering the situation. It reminded him of some memories of his past at prep school that he desperately wanted to keep buried.

"Ain't got no choice, son," Patrick said softly. "They know what goes on, the giants. You miss your time and bad things happen. You wouldn't be the first—some even fought so hard they got killed."

Jack stared at him, his eyes threatening to fill with tears of frustration and fear. He blinked and turned away, staring without seeing at the plain walls of his new and underserved prison.

"Get some rest, son, we'll take care of you and show you the ropes tomorrow." Patrick clapped him on the shoulder.

Ben followed suit, then moved off to his own bunk. The others dispersed as well to their own areas, leaving Jack to stare woodenly at the ceiling while the sourceless lights in the room faded softer. Eventually exhaustion overcame him and he drifted off.

* * * *

The week passed quickly for Jack. It was exhausting for the former banker, even though Patrick and Ben assured him repeatedly that it was easier mid-season than at harvest or planting times. All they had to do was water their crops. It had to be done manually, with buckets made of the same strange material that everything else was made of. There was a fountain with fresh clean water, but they still had to lug each bucket to the fields.

Jack learned what he could, even though he continued to doubt his sanity. The fields stretched for acres in all directions, each tended by different groups of men. He saw, in the middle of the fields, some strange device that was connected via a beam of some kind of light or energy to a great disc far above them. The bottom of the disc flooded the area with light for growing the beans. That same disc, Patrick told him, was the sky castle or cloud city that the giants lived on. Away from the city and the light it produced, the strange alien world was dark and filled with mist and haze. Harry had opined that they built their city so high up so they could get above the clouds and see the stars.

Jack's five days were up before he knew it. He turned a blind eye whenever someone was called away by the woman's voice to the door that opened in the wall. Now it was his turn, and when she said his name, he could only stare for a long moment at it. Sweat beaded on his forehead and fear and shame raced through his belly, making it flutter and tighten.

Finally, after her third call, he rose up and began to walk. The third time, it seemed, was too late. He was suddenly overwhelmed with agony. It felt as though his hands and feet were on fire, then his arms and legs. It dug deeper into his limbs, setting into the muscles and threatening to burst his bones open. Jack was writhing on the ground, crying out incoherently and struggling when it ceased as quickly as it had come.

"Jack," the voice called again, for the fourth time. His breath shuddering in his chest, he pulled himself to his hands and knees and started forward in a crawl. He managed to climb to his feet before he reached the door, and wondered as he did so, how it was possible that his body appeared untouched. He felt as though he had been burned alive.

He stood in the room, the aches in his body fading to memories. He was alone, aside from the couch. He glanced behind and saw the door had shut silently, sealing him off from his fellow prisoners.

"Please Jack, lay on the table for the procedure," said her disembodied voice.

Jack stared at it for a long moment, hesitating. He remembered the pain then, even as he was ready to refuse to do it. He could not forget that he had wished he had the strength left in him to smash his head against the floor until he felt no more. With a ragged sigh, he climbed onto the table and settled himself into position.

Immediately the straps shot out and secured themselves around him. A few seconds later, he felt her hand on his lower back, just resting there softly.

"Do as they say, Jack," she said compassionately. "I promise I'll give you what pleasure I can...it's all I can do."

"Who are you?" Jack managed to say.

"Hush Jack, just relax," she urged, spreading the lube against him gently.

"Why do you do this?" He insisted, struggling to turn his head back to her.

"They make me," she said so softly he could barely hear her. "We don't have a choice."

Her finger probed against him. She was soft and gentle, but firm and insistent. Jack groaned in discomfort at the full feeling that invaded him against his wishes.

"Bollocks! There's always a choice," Jack hissed. To prove his point, he tried valiantly to resist the procedure, bending all of his concentration to it.

"Jack, you're making this difficult," she said reproachfully. "I know you don't like it—neither do I! But we must, or they'll punish us both. The first time they hurt you is just a taste, just a warning of what they can do. The second time drives some men mad. Nobody's survived a third punishment."

Still Jack resisted, but the milkmaid was persistent and he was forced to feel disgusted by his body for its betrayal in the end. The hand departed, though not until he felt it pat him sympathetically on the hip. When she left the room, the straps retracted and he was able to dismount and return to the others, sore for his fight but otherwise physically relaxed even if he was in emotional turmoil.

The weeks came and went and before long, harvest was upon them. Jack quickly learned that the others were right—harvest was a brutal time. The beans were gathered by hand and taken, in buckets, to great bins stored in the transport craft the alien giant had flown down. Jack got his first glimpse of his captors and had to be reminded by Ben to stop staring and move on. They were a white skinned race, twice as tall as a man. They looked humanoid, although hairless and only possessing three large fingers on their hands, each opposable and multi-jointed.

Jack also found himself growing stronger. Gone was the baby fat a sedentary life behind a banker's desk had given him. Now, like the others, he was deeply tanned by days spent working under the alien lights and stronger than he thought possible. Their food was never satisfying—some paste with varying bland flavors made, largely, he was certain, from the beans they grew. It was available every morning and every night. What it lacked in variety, it seemed to make up for in nutrition.

Planting season was torturous as well, requiring farming tools the likes of which he imagined had not been used on

Earth for nearly a hundred years. His team of twenty men was responsible for fields five-thousand paces across. He had counted it off and it matched what the others had counted as well. Nearly five kilometers of fields, hand sewn by twenty men. Their fields were near the center, judging by the beam of energy that erupted from the ground nearby, but some of the other fields were dozens of kilometers away.

Still Jack fought against the milkmaid as well. It almost became a game, after more than a dozen weeks had passed. She would talk to him, soothingly and reassuringly, while he struggled to fight against what her skillful fingers coaxed from him. Occasionally she would let slip bits of information as well, things about her life before she had been taken or, less frequently, what she knew about their captors.

Jack began to realize, after a fashion, that when she had finished draining him, he missed their contact. He certainly did not miss the sodomy, but he did miss the chance to talk with her, even if she was the closest thing to an identifiable oppressor he could find.

It was nearing the time of Jack's second harvest when another of their crew, a quiet man named Andrew, threw down his water bucket and stared up at the giant city above. He opened his mouth and screamed a primal roar that shattered the silence of the fields and made everyone stop and look up in surprise.

"Andy! No!" Patrick called, but he was too far and too late to do anything.

Andrew was already running. He aimed for the base station of the beam that tethered the cloud city to the ground and made it well over halfway there before he stumbled and fell. Andy rose up, fighting against the agony that threatened to overwhelm him, and struggled on several more steps before he fell to the ground again. He continued writhing, rolling over and going into the tell-tale spasms of a seizure. Several minutes later, his jerking rapidly decreased. With a final twitch, he lay still.

A few seconds later, the man's body dissolved into nothingness. Nothing remained save the impression on the ground where he had been. The remaining nineteen went back to work, although some more slowly than others. Jack stared the longest, and finally fell in beside Patrick.

"That's why nobody ever runs, old son," Patrick told him before he could ask a question.

"So this is it?" Jack hissed. "We work until we die, no love, no family, no success? And if not, then we die early? That's bloody brilliant."

"You never know what can happen," Patrick told him, eyeing him warily. "But I'll do what I got to in order to keep breathing just in case, you know?"

"You're mad," Jack spat. He glanced at the others, tending to their own tasks. "You're all institutionalized, you know that?"

Patrick shrugged. "I got everything I need here," he said defiantly. "Andrew snapped, get it? They don't let nobody near that energy beam! No warnings, they kill anyone that goes near and he knew it."

Jack slowed to a stop and watched Patrick as he kept walking with his bucket of water. He shook his head after a moment and hurried to tend to his own assigned crops, wondering all the while what he had just seen and why the beam of light was so important.

* * * *

"We lost a man yesterday," Jack said when he felt the milkmaid gently stroke his left leg. Her touch was familiar now, intimate even. He wondered if she treated the other men this way.

He heard a catch in her breath before she responded. "Who was it?"

"Andy," he said. "He just...snapped. Screamed and ran towards the…"

"Andrew? What a shame. He was a good man. Quiet guy, but he had a tender side." She reflected sadly. "What was he

- 124 -

running towards?" she asked, moving slowly again to apply the warm lubricant.

"Whatever the thing on the ground is that connects to the city above," he said, not tightening up at all for the first time as she began to work her finger against him.

"You're not fighting me," she pointed out.

"Sorry," Jack said. "I was thinking. Distracted."

"That's better," she said, a bit of humor in her voice as she had to work more tenderly to fight her way past his clenched muscles.

"Humph," Jack said disapprovingly. "Better would be if you were on the table instead of me."

She laughed softly, but quickly silenced herself. "I'm sorry, that was inappropriate. I don't want to mislead you."

"Mislead me about what?" Jack groaned, fighting the beginning stages of the warmth threatening to spread through him.

"Into thinking I would enjoy you having me on this table or into thinking that I have come to care very deeply for you. That would be inappropriate, if I were to ever let you think anything like that," she said, her voice trailing off in a whisper.

Jack jerked a little, trying to lift his head, and failing. He nodded and smiled though, understanding her message. "I understand," he said, and gave her finger a squeeze the only way he could.

Jack relaxed then, allowing the milkmaid access without any resistance. It felt strange for him at first, but the sudden intake of breath he heard from her and the way in which her finger began to move inside of him reassured him of his decision. She even brushed up against his testicles and penis, pretending to do it accidentally, while she milked him.

When it was time, he groaned as the feelings overwhelmed him. It was a groan of relief and pleasure this time, not one of dismay. He felt his release issue forth and collect in the receptacle built into the table, then felt her continue to stroke him, coaxing out a second, weaker surge.

He could tell she was leaving reluctantly by the way her hand hesitated. He was left alone on the table at last, all the unspoken promises between them doing him no good.

He walked back into the room and headed for the open door that had breakfast waiting within. He stopped briefly as he passed Ben and Patrick. "Ever see a sunrise over the ocean?" he asked them, then moved on before they could respond.

Jack glanced back to see them staring, confused. He smiled and winked, then turned into the room.

"Maybe he is gay?" Ben mused, confused.

"Naw, he's just English—they're all like that." Patrick shrugged.

* * * *

"Fishing," Ben said. "That's what I miss. My dad and I could spend a lazy Sunday on the boat catching pan fish until we had no more room for them."

Jack glanced up at him. They were in line for their nightly showers and next to one another. Jack smiled and nodded approvingly. The showers themselves were not only communal, but really little more than a giant spray from above that was spread out enough to cover the room. It was quick and to the point, but given the lukewarm water, there was little encouragement to stay for more.

Back in the sleeping quarters, the door opened and a new recruit emerged. He was a young man, soft around the middle but with wide green eyes and close-cut dark hair. He looked around frantically, taking everyone in and gaping like a fish out of water.

"Welcome to paradise," Patrick quipped. "You must be Andy's replacement."

"R...re...replacement?" he asked, stunned.

"Bollocks, was I that bad?" Jack asked Ben.

"Worse maybe," Ben replied with a smirk.

"What's your name, son?"

"Mmm ...Mark," he replied. "Mark Wa—"

"Don't need no last name, Mark," Patrick said. "They never give us two guys with the same first name."

"They? Who...what's...where are your clothes?"

Jack snorted. "We got no clothes. They don't give us any," Patrick said. "And 'they' is the giants that live up there and make us do their dirty work."

"Dirty work? What is this place? What happened? Who is she, the girl in the room? What did she do to me?"

"That's our milkmaid," Patrick responded even as Jack's throat went dry. "They figure having her around keeps us docile. Every five days you get to visit her, and that's the only woman you'll ever be seeing again."

His eyes widened and the color drained from his cheeks. "Only…woman? Are you...I mean, do you…"

"We're not gay," Patrick assured him. "Nobody'll be poking your cornhole late at night or making your drop your soap in the shower."

"Don't worry, mate, the finger in the arse keeps us from being Nancies," Jack added somewhat mysteriously. He knew that when he showed up, if someone had said that, he'd be clueless.

Ben jumped in to change the subject. "I'm Ben, that's Jack. There's not much to see yet, but it's coming up on harvest time. We'll show you what to do tomorrow."

"You're Jack?" he asked, turning to look at Jack.

Jack nodded. "Why?"

"The girl...she said...she said to tell you she was sorry."

"Sorry? What for?" Jack asked, confused. His heartbeat had picked up at the thought of a message. What could it possibly mean?

"Something about her being forced to leave," he said. "I didn't understand...it was...she was...you know, doing things."

Jack rushed over to him, hovering inches from his suddenly white face. "Try real hard. What exactly did she say?"

He tried to shrink back but Jack grabbed him. Patrick and Ben were there a few moments later and pulled the two apart.

It was only when Jack relaxed and showed no signs of going after the man that they let him go.

"Old son," Patrick began. "You got a thing for the maid, don't you?"

Jack scowled at him.

"That kind of closeness, I ain't saying I blame you none. I seen it happen before though, and I 'spect we'll have a new milkmaid by tomorrow."

"What about her?" Jack growled.

"Killed maybe, or reassigned. Depends on what else she done I guess."

Jack swore violently and burst past both of the other men to head for the wall. He slammed into it where the door to the milking room was, to no effect. He punched and kicked it, and even ran his shoulder into it three more times until he finally gave up and walked sullenly away from it.

"Jack..." Ben said, searching for something to say. Jack just walked past him, not caring. He went to his bunk and crawled in, staring at the ceiling without seeing anything. Tears slipped down the sides of his face late into the night while sleep eluded him. The one thing he knew was—enough was enough.

* * * *

The next morning, four men went in one at a time, including Ben, and each reported they had a new milkmaid. Mark had avoided Ben all morning as well, but now that they were headed for the fields, the two found themselves side by side. They were gathering buckets for harvesting.

"Jack...I'm sorry," Mark stammered in a low voice. "I didn't know..."

Jack grunted.

"She said something else too," Mark whispered, glancing around nervously. "I was afraid, you know, to say anything? I didn't know who or what was going on. I mean...what is going on here?"

"What did she say?" Jack asked, stiffening and turning to look at him.

Mark jumped a little but nodded. "Yeah, okay...sure...just...just calm down, okay? She said don't ever forget her, and she meant everything she didn't say."

Jack stopped walking. He just stood there, digesting Mark's words.

"Jack, get your ass moving," Patrick called over to him, seeing the man standing there looking clueless.

Jack turned to look at him and then nodded. A smile split his face. He turned to Mark and grabbed his hand, then shook it. "If I don't get a chance later, thanks mate!"

Mark looked at him, confused, as Jack hurried away from him and headed to Ben and Patrick. "You're wrong Patrick," he said with a smile. "This is not living. We may be breathing, but bugger me if this is living."

"Jack, don't do nothing stupid," Patrick warned in a low voice.

"Come on, Patrick, what do you miss? It hasn't been that long, has it?" Jack pushed.

Patrick stared at him, swore, then nodded. "I had a little place in Northern Wisconsin. I'd sit on the porch with Dolly, my yellow lab, and drink a beer while the sun set."

Jack smiled and clapped him on the shoulder. "If this don't work, and I've got bugger all reason to expect it will, then it's been a pleasure knowing you mates."

"What are you gonna do?" Ben asked, looking around nervously.

"I think Andrew had the right idea. I'm going to see if I can take out that beam of light."

Patrick swore again and Ben just looked at him for a long moment. Finally he shrugged and smiled. "Tell me when," he said.

"Ben...no, I don't want—"

"Shut your mouth," Ben snapped. "I didn't say I was going with you. I just said you tell me when."

Jack looked at him, then nodded. "All right."

They broke apart and went about their duties, picking the beans by hand and taking them to the bins on the transport plane. The day stretched by, broken only by the fatigue carrying buckets of beans caused. Jack waited until he saw that Ben was nearby. He glanced around, seeing the activity from the other harvesting taking place in other fields, and nodded. Ben returned his nod ever so slightly.

Jack grew closer to the bin and saw Ben standing next in line to empty his beans. Ben cried out, as though in pain, and stumbled into another man, Tyler, who was also approaching. Both of them went down, spilling beans and distracting everyone.

Jack grinned and acted. He bolted, running so fast he nearly tripped over his own feet until he adjusted for a strength in his legs he didn't know he had. He felt free, for that heartbeat of time. Free from the giants, free from slavery, free to do anything.

The fire erupted in him, stealing his breath and sending him flying through the air a few short feet until he collapsed on the ground. He saw his bucket land nearby, spilling some of the dirt he had collected in it. He remembered the pain. He remembered well what it would do to him if he gave it a chance. He fought his way up against it, stamping down on it as it made the flesh on his heels sear in agony. He grabbed the bucket, forcing fingers that were cramped in agony to bend and contract. Then he was moving again. Ten feet away, then five.

The fire bit deeply into him, sending spasms of agony through his very bones and making him jerk about. He staggered closer, feeling it spread into his torso. This, he realized, was the final stage. When the fire reached his heart, he was done for.

His lungs refused to obey him. They were paralyzed with agony. He flared his nostrils, trying to pull in air, but found himself dropping to his knees instead. He was there, at the base of the power station. With the bucket in both hands, he twisted and flung his arms, letting go in time to see the dirt-filled bucket sail up into the air and bounce against the side of the structure. It tipped, spilling dirt as it did, and fell into the unknown beam.

The beam sputtered, not entirely, but in part. It was partially blocked by the debris and that weakened it. Far above, the lights on the giants' cloud city dimmed, then flickered. A moment later they went out and the world was plunged into shadow.

Jack lay on the ground, staring up and smiling, though his grin was twisted with agony. He sucked in a deep breath and coughed, then just lay there watching as the massive disc so far above them shifted faster and faster to the side. The beam of energy erupted skyward again, having burned away the offending bucket and dirt, but its receiving end was no longer in position.

It took several minutes for the giant's floating city to come down completely, but gravity would not be denied its prize. The flat bottom caused it to float with the strong winds of the upper atmosphere many kilometers away from the fields below. When at last it smashed into the ground, it did so with enough force to send tremors through the ground for hundreds of kilometers.

"Jack! Jack! Are you all right? Jack, you did it!" Patrick was shouting.

Jack saw his friend emerge from the shadows and stand over him. The man was grinning wildly as he leaned down and picked the abused Englishman up. "Jack, you did it! You killed the giants!"

Jack was not sure which hurt worse, the hug Patrick gave him or the giants' strange torture device. Patrick let him go at last, and the two of them walked back to the transport plane where the others, who had been watching, rushed to overpower the giant who had piloted it. Ben was standing as well, though he looked a little bit the worse for wear.

"They zapped me too—good thing you stopped them!" he said, clapping Jack on the shoulder and pulling him in for a hug.

"What about everyone else?" Jack asked, though he could hear the cheering going on all around him. "And the...where are the maids kept?"

Patrick laughed. "Never figured you English boys cared so much for the ladies."

Ben laughed and Jack could only shrug. "We're not all poofters," he said, prompting more laughter.

They ran off, heading towards their communal cells. Normally everyone went to their designated area—failure to comply meant punishment. Now, with no overseers to stop them, they explored and found other areas. One large building stood out from the others, and no one claimed it as their dormitory. Tools were improvised, from rocks to buckets to broken pieces secured from the shuttle. It took a lot of brute force, but eventually even the strange alien material succumbed to the violence and yielded an entry. Inside, dozens of terrified women were huddled, staring out at the men forcing their way through.

It took several minutes for the ensuing chaos to clear. The woman fought the men off, terrified, while many of the men fought their fellows to have a go at them. Finally Jack managed to get in front of them, along with Patrick and Ben, and they turned to face the huddled and equally nude women.

"The giants are dead," Jack announced loudly, which brought about a fresh wave of cheering from the gathered men both within and without.

When it finally died, an older woman stepped forward, her body slender and fit in spite of her years. "How is this possible?" she asked.

"We blocked the energy that powered their city. It crashed. You can go and see for yourself if you like," he added.

"Wasn't 'we' who did it," Patrick interrupted. "It was all Jack here."

"Hey, I helped," Ben said indignantly.

Ben's addition was ignored though, for another timid voice from the back spoke up, "Jack? Jack from unit twenty-seven?"

Jack peered through the women, trying to see the source of the voice. It sounded like the maid, but he couldn't be sure. "I don't know what my unit number is. I'm just Jack."

She forced her way through the crowd then and stared at him. Jack stared back, seeing a curly haired woman, slim and beautiful. Her eyes were a grayish green and filled with moisture, her face that of an angel who was not sure if she should laugh or cry.

"Turn around," she said softly.

Jack did so without question. He supposed he would have even crawled up on a table in front of everyone gathered had she asked him to do so.

He felt her hand a moment later, brushing against his hip and over his buttock, raising goose bumps in its passing. Then she put her hand to his shoulder and pulled him back around to face her.

"You have a birthmark," she said, tears running down her face.

Jack wrapped his arms around her and pulled her to him, crushing her in his embrace and feeling her sobs. She held on tightly, more tightly than he would have thought possible, but he didn't mind. He had no intention of putting her down anytime soon.

Patrick and Ben took up another cheer and soon it was echoed by everyone as they prepared to face their newfound freedom.

About Phineas Magnus

When a rather plain and average person steps into the shadows unobserved and reaches deep within to wrestle with their inner demons, a being such as Phineas Magnus emerges from those same shadows. Equally at home at a tennis club or speaking Swahili amongst African mercenaries, Phineas allows no boundaries to interfere with his exploration of the great wonders that perplex mankind. How else would such a man have been able to determine the proper width and depth necessary to build a pit in his basement—purely for educational purposes, of course? Likewise, many a flock of penguins in Antarctica may have never laid witness to a world record setting 6 meter naked dash across the frozen tundra. At the end of the day, the only thing that Phineas will truly be concerned with is whether he managed to provoke some sort of open, controversial, or disturbing reaction deep within the minds of those he was lucky enough to supply a fresh bit of prose to.

ANNIE AND THE YOUNG MASTER
By Bekki Lynn

Chapter One

Devastated, Lillian Basford stared at the whitewashed door. She tried the knob, but the door wouldn't open. She banged on it. "Father, let me in! Tell me how I wronged!" No one came to let her inside.

Saddened, she walked down the path and a ways from the house. Veering off, she went into the garden her mother had loved so much. Lillian sat on a bench for what seemed like hours, wondering why her words angered her father. Didn't he understand her love was the highest of all his daughters?

She looked around, but no one came for her. The sun was going down and the early summer evening air started to cool. Surely, she wouldn't be left out in the night. Gazing upward, stars appeared one-by-one in the darkening sky and tears streamed down her cheeks. "Mama, help me see my wrong," she prayed.

Uncontrolled sobs burst from her as she lie with her arms wrapped around her. Soon the night closed in around her and closed her eyes with hopes of hearing footsteps approach. Maybe one of her sisters would sneak from the house and bring her in.

"Miss Lillian, Miss Lillian," a lilting voice came to her.

Opening her eyes, she saw Celia, a servant, standing over her. She must have fallen asleep for she did not hear the woman approach. Lillian sat up asking, "My father wishes to see me?"

"No, miss. He wishes me to show you to the gate before it's bolted."

"But…Ceila, what have I done?"

"I don't know. Those were his orders."

Lillian nodded then followed the woman to the gate. With a glance back at the house, she asked, "What am I supposed to do? Where am I to go?"

"I do not know. Get on now."

She walked through the entrance to the house, fear welling up in her when she heard the bolt of the gate behind her. Daring one more question, she asked, "May I have a cloak, something to keep me warm?"

"I'm to give you nothing," she replied then headed back to the house.

Trudging along the dirt road, her eyes darted around with every rustling sound of the forest. The wild beat of her heart, the soft pad of her shoes on the dirt road, all seemed louder in the dark. She feared she'd drown out the sounds of danger approaching.

A growl pierced the silence nearby in the trees. She screamed and turned tail, running back to the bolted gate. Breathing hard, she rattled it and tried to reach through the slates to move the bolt. "Help! Help me, please!"

Lillian slunk down near the stone pillar holding the gate upright, distraught and frightened. She huddled against the stone, taking little comfort in the sun's warmth it held. Watching the space around her, she hoped nothing dared come near.

* * * *

At first light, Lillian awakened, surprised she'd slept. Letting her eyes focus as she took in her surroundings, she pulled herself up. The gate remained bolted and the property off limits due to the ferocious wire with barbed knots strung around it.

Hard reality set in. She'd been barred from her home–dead to them. Lillian turned away and walked along at a slow pace, trying to think. She could work, but who would hire the daughter of a prominent barrister to serve and clean for them. Some would think it a joke, others wouldn't dare go against her father. Her belly grumbled, coupling her worry about finding a place who'd take her on.

Weary and sure she'd walked miles, she found a stump to rest on. Wiping moisture from her brow, she studied the rushes off in the nearby ren. She wondered if they hid a stream. The land was somewhat barren and seemed safe enough. She walked with purpose and did find water.

Cupping her hands, Lillian tasted the water. It was good. She drank until thirst left hunger then stood and saw the hem of her dress muddied. This gave her an idea. Reaching down in the muck, she grabbed a handful and splattered the dress. When she finished, she worried the style of the dress, maybe the fabric would still give away her stand. Sighing, she set her mind to think how to get around it.

Lillian studied the rushes with her mind working fast. She could weave a covering, but she needed something with a sharp edge and looked along the water's edge. A ways along the water, she found a flat, sharp-edged stone to cut the stems of the tall weeds. She set to work until the pile seemed large enough.

Once she'd made herself a resemblance of a cloak with a hood to cover her light disheveled hair, she went along the road until it split. She took to her left, a route she'd never been as it went away from the town of Milltown where her father worked.

The sun came higher and warmed her through the cloak, but she daren't stop to remove it and risk no work. On she went, even when hunger pained her belly and her feet begged for rest.

Past a grouping of trees a field of black currents beckoned her. Unable to resist, she dared to do the punishable. She left the road, making her way through the brush grown up along the road.

With her stomach grumbling at the sight of the plump dark fruit, Lillian plucked one and tasted. "Mmmm." Sweetness filled her mouth. Taking the bunch, she walked back toward the road and sat among the tall grasses. She savored each morsel until the sound of horses hooves pounding the packed dirt road came near. She stilled, certain her cloak would keep her hidden if one should look her direction. The carriage passed her by.

"Whoa," a male voice said.

Closing her eyes, she feared he owned the field and would have her jailed. Careful not to move, she listened. From the single sound of boots slapping the hardened dirt, she he'd jumped down. She held her breath as he came closer.

"Pilfering fruit from the vine, are we?"

His voice startled her, but she didn't turn.

"Come up here," he said, grabbing her by the shoulders.

She rose, facing him as his hands insisted. Before her stood the man who spent a fortnight in her dreams. Lowering her head from his view, she remained silent.

"Why are you wearing such a garment?" His hands came up and moved the hood from her head, revealing what must look a tangled mass of haze.

Lillian swallowed the embarrassment of being less than presentable. "I've no other," she said with a meekness his presence caused.

She let her eyes meet his when silence seemed to linger from him. Samuel Wadkins studied her face with his deep gray eyes. Shivers swept through her as snippets of her dreams swam before her: his hands were gentle on her, making her feel warm, special—like a woman; his words were soft and loving as his face closed the distance between them. She always woke before the touch of his lips.

Samuel wiped his finger along her bottom lip then licked the juice from it, his tongue moving slow up to the tip. Tingles twirled in her belly.

"Mmm, I wonder…"

His young, smooth face became taut and strained…she wasn't sure why, because she sensed no fear for herself.

Fingers grazed her cheeks. "Your skin is soft like silkweed," he murmured.

"It is your touch that is smooth and tender." Lillian's heart drummed within her. How he could not hear, she did not know.

He reached for her hands and turned her palms up, caressing them with his. She wavered on her feet as fire seared through her veins.

"Tender flesh. I think you're not a homeless waif, nor a worker."

She yanked her hands back, wishing she'd considered her under-worked flesh. "Please, sir. You're being too familiar."

"Not yet, but I feel…"

Before he finished, his arms were about her and his mouth was on hers, moving, tasting her lips and left while shock held her still. Fingers kneaded through the cloak, relaxing her. She dared to rest her hands on his waist while her mouth succumbed to his, even opening to him when he attempted to slip his tongue between her lips.

He teased her into playing and she became the lover she wanted to be for him. Letting her hands move up and wind around his neck, she slipped her fingers into his dark hair, enjoying the flavor of coffee and cinnamon as she mirrored his movements, kissing him with equal need, hunger.

Her knees bent as he lowered her, coming down to lay over her as she opened to see him. He watched her with eyes darkened by his need, his face drawn with what she also wanted. Waiting for him to guide her into what was new to her, a niggling voice said she was behaving unladylike. It didn't override what the unfinished dreams left her wanting. She wanted to know him as her heart ached for him to know her. She felt her dress rise and her pantaloon pushed down. She searched his eyes, willing to give him what she'd been told was sacred to the man she'd marry.

"I feel as I know you and don't. Please, tell me your name," he requested, his voice more gravelly than before.

Lillian caught herself before she told him her given name. He might associate it with the name of the attorney. Rather, she told him her second name. "Ann."

Chapter Two

Samuel caressed her most intimate place and she arched into him, enjoying the feel of his fingers against sensitive flesh. "Touch me, Ann. Know my cock wants you," he whispered and placed her hand on the flap of his trousers.

Despite the crude reference, she found him harder than a cob of corn and her mother's words came back to her. *Men want with ease, but we must be the bearer of wit and hold them off.* Reaching up, she caressed the side of his face. "We should not be doing this. Someone could come along." His fingers plunged inside her. "Oh," she moaned. "Such wonder, pleasure."

"Your pussy wants me as I want…"

"Deeply."

He moved in and out of her…pussy…with a steady rhythm, controlling her body as it moved with him. Her eyes fluttered closed as she gripped his upper arms, somehow wanting it more for the hearing of the words she'd only heard from the men who worked for her father. "I should…shall not stop you."

Lips brushed her brow and his breath lingered over her mouth. "I've never felt such a burden of need. I cannot prolong."

He withdrew his fingers and she watched him undo his belt and lower his trousers. His length protruded, large and purple. Excitement beneath hesitation had her searching his eyes. She needed to see caring in his eyes. Samuel moved to kneel between her thighs, and it was there with intense passion. He grasped his shaft, moved it over her folds and pushed into her. "Oh, God! Stop!" she cried, as it seemed part of her ripped and his body set against her.

"I'm sorry," he croaked.

"Mama didn't tell me it'd hurt so," she said, feeling foolish.

He covered her face with kisses, wiping the tears with his lips. "I didn't mean to cause you pain, but it will go and pleasure will revive."

She nodded, trusting him without question. He groped beneath her cloak, finding her breast. His warm hand was as adept at drawing her thoughts from the hurt as his lips were pulling her deep within the heat of his mouth.

Lillian's thighs began to relax and her hips tilted into him. Slow and easy, he began to move, swallowing her moans as renewed fire flamed between their loins. She found her body matching his as he hovered on his hands. Her heart melted and fell the rest of the way in love with the man she felt connected to from that first look a fortnight ago.

"Oh," she panted when a current, much like the rolling creek after a hard rain, snaked through her midsection.

"Hold onto me, Annie," he mumbled.

She grabbed his shoulders, feeling him tremble while he rocked into her with quickness and force.

"Mmm, oh, mmm," he moaned.

The energy, his pleasure, carried her into uncontrollable convulsions of spiraling euphoria she'd never dreamed possible. He followed her with his own shudders, jerking before collapsing on her, their bodies quaking with tremors. There were no words known to her to describe the happiness her body yielded. Holding him to her, she breathed deep to catch her wind and kissed his head.

"I've never known a woman to lose herself so," he spoke into her neck. "Never have I...so fast. I want more of you." His lips trailed along her neck.

"Samuel," she moaned.

"You know who I am?" He rose, looking down into her face.

"I do."

"Where do I find you on my return from town?"

Panic filled her. For the moment, she'd forgotten. She had no place. He could not look for her. With her hands, she pushed at him. "You must be on your way."

"I am late," he admitted as he pushed himself up. "Where do I find you?"

"You mustn't think of me. It would not do for you."

"I beg to differ. I want to see you again."

Flattered, she watched him pull his britches up and realized she needed to put herself back together. Scrambling to put her clothing right, she sucked in her breath at the soreness she felt.

"The Hammond's are over the hill. Go beg to work for the stolen fruit."

"Yes, sir," she whispered, feeling as if she'd been put in her place beneath him. Will he now boast to his friends how he bedded a servant on the side of the road? She didn't want to think that of him, but she'd heard how men would talk—even of untruths to be truths.

He returned to his carriage and settled in with the reins in hand. Before he flicked to move the horse along, he looked back at her. "If they don't have work, or have you jailed, I'll pay and you can work it off for me." His face lit up with a smile aimed at herm much like the one he'd beamed at her sisters on that heart-felled day.

She stared after him, long after he'd gone from her sight, then sighed. "Not exactly how I wanted us to be, Samuel Wadkins." She wiped her face, put her hood back in place and turned away, determined not to let her heart turn at what truth she didn't know. There were other matters to be concerned with. Turning away, she walked on, hating the moisture dampening her undergarment. She much wanted fresh clothing as well as to bathe.

Once over the hill, Lillian saw a grand white house with shutters of polished coal. Walking up the lane, she prayed those tending the grounds wouldn't turn her about. She rounded the house and knocked on the kitchen door. An elderly woman answered.

"Are you in need of a maid?"

"No!"

The woman started to shut the door. "Please, I need to repay for fruit I staved my hunger with."

Old, bluish eyes looked her over. "Your age?"

"Barely eighteen, ma'am."

"You can stay the morning and scrub pots."

Without a word, Lillian followed her into the small, darkened room. Only lanterns gave off light for the tasks tended. Near the sink, pots and other dishes were stacked high. She filled the washbasin from the pump and, for the duration of the meal, preparation and serving of, she scraped, scrubbed and washed until there were none left.

She looked around and found herself alone. Not daring to be so forward to wander the house to gain permission, she slipped out the door with no destination on the horizon.

Trudging along the road, her head lowered, she fought the desperate need to return to her home to plead her father's forgiveness.

"Hey! Wait! Girl! Cap 'o Rushes, wait!"

Lillian turned around when she realized the girl called for. "Yes?"

"The misses want to see you."

"Why?"

"No question the misses, just do as asked."

"All right." She returned with the girl and followed her to the parlor.

A red-haired woman set her embroidery aside, casting her eyes on her. "What is your name? Where did you come from?"

"I've been wandering with no place to go." It was not a lie, but she could not reveal where she hailed out of respect for her father. "Lil is my name."

The woman nodded. "I've been informed of your honesty and you work hard. Our staff is full, but you have work until I place you elsewhere."

"Thank you, ma'am."

"Remove that horrid cover-up and let me see you."

"I mustn't. My dress is not presentable."

"Have Mable find you something."

"Thank you, ma'am."

Lillian retraced her steps back to the kitchen where she'd been given the task of readying beans for the pot. It wasn't unknown to her, since her father's cook had allowed her time and taught her to keep her busy.

The young girl came into the room, giggling. Mable quickly shushed her and pointed to the basket of potatoes waiting for peeling.

"Yes, grandmother," she said as she sat. "Master Wadkins came by asking for Ann. Misses told him no one by that name here. He wanted to see all staff and she wouldn't disrupt her household for she knows all the names."

Lillian squelched the pleasure of Samuel remembering her. Although, it'd do him no good to take up with the servant she'd now become. Again, since she'd seen the woman called Callie rubbing her protruding belly, she prayed his seed didn't do its intended.

"Would you be the Ann, he's looking for?" asked the granddaughter.

"I'm called Lil," she answered. Concentrating on the task, she forced Samuel from her mind.

"I'm Emma. I'm learning to fill Callie's place for when she has her baby."

Lillian nodded, realizing how, in the short hours she'd been there, she felt at home. No one talked over her as her sisters had done. No one sent her from the room because she was deemed too young or in the way.

Weeks, two months worth, passed, and Lillian heard no further word of Samuel's search for his Ann. She figured he moved on to another girl—maybe three or more by now. It saddened her to think him such a womanizer. She worked hard and slept soundly, except when dreams of Samuel woke her with fire of longing and wetness between her thighs. The creek cooled her on these nights, but it hadn't removed the ache of knowing her prayers hadn't been answered. Samuel need not be troubled with knowing, nor would she tell who fathered her child.

Lillian sighed as she dried and dressed to start her day. In the kitchen, she set to work amongst the excited chatter of the kitchen. The annual harvest celebration the Wadkins held seemed to be all they could talk of. This would have been her first year to attend the three-day event.

Now, if she went, she'd stand as a servant and watch the festivities. It didn't sit well, knowing her sisters would be in attendance and vying for Samuel's attention. Worse, would Samuel take them as he had her? Lillian shook the horrid thought aside. It wasn't right to put bad traits on him without cause. Nor did it help lessen what her heart knew. She set to cooking the pork for the morning meal.

Another worry felled her when she realized the servants of her father's house might recognize her. The talk of her place away from her father might not fare well. It could further anger him. Mrs. Hammond could put her out. She shuddered at the thought of wandering until she found another house to take her on.

"This is the first year for the Master Wadkins to be in attendance. He's looking fine, too. Think he'll choose a wife, grandmother?" she heard Emma go on.

"You remember your place," Mable told her.

Feeling her heart swell with sadness at missing out, she buried herself in more work. Her life had gone a half-turn and she had to focus on how to go from here and leave all she knew behind.

"Daydreaming, are we?" Callie asked her.

"Fancy a dance with the handsome young man?" Emma asked, teasing her.

Lillian felt her face warm at the mere joke of her once-cherished fancy. "Don't talk nonsense."

Emma's excitement carried her on. "You will go, right? We all go every year. And this year, it's a masquerade."

"I'm sure I'll be too tired." Even if she wanted to go, a dance such as this required a decent dress. She had but the one she came in, and the loaned servant dress she wore. She could not attend in her own with raising questions.

"Emma, go fetch the milk." Mable told her.

The chore would give them a reprieve from her incessant chatter, Lillian imagined. Still, there were days to go before the date of the event and she imagined the excited and curious chatter of the girl would grow.

The day came upon them and Lillian could handle the elevated talk no longer. She went about gathering the eggs, bringing in the milk, even doing the laundry to avoid being amongst it. However, it didn't take near enough time. She set her mind to steel off her heartache and help with the noon meal.

"Cappa, you have to go with us," Emma told her.

"The day is young. There is much to do. I'll be too tired, I should think." She dumped scraps into a bucket for the hogs and busied her hands with scrubbing pots.

As the hours passed, she found the desire to attend the dance growing. Her mind toyed with ways to hide herself from others and since a face cover was expected, she held a bit of hope of pulling it off.

Chapter Three

Once the evening meal ended, Lillian hung back as the other servants left, excited talk fading away with them. She pulled her laundered clothing from beneath her cot and took it from the cloth she'd found to wrap it in.

Determined to pull this off, she let her hair down from the bun twist she'd begun to wear. Looking through the box of spare items she'd been given by others, she managed to brush a bit of a shine into the blond strands, coil and pin it up into a fashion of sorts, much as she used to do with the trusses of her sisters.

Lillian's mind spun with ideas and rushed from the servants' quarters to pick a handful of wildflowers. Sitting on her bed, she braided them around bits of wire she'd found inside the barn. She mirrored a flowered hair barrette she knew lay on her dressing table in her old room.

From under her pillow, she pulled the mask she'd weaved with practiced ease from various plants outside the barn, while she'd taken a rest. It was the one thing she'd learned from her mother and continued to do, hoping one day to sell wares as she'd done. She looked at the mask piece and thought the sprigs of flowers would do well with the hair ornament so she ran out for more flowers.

Satisfied it looked as well as any that could be bought for a reasonable price, she wound the wire she'd used to frame it around her head. When Lillian was ready, she walked into the barn for a horse to pull a small buggy. She'd done it many times at home when she wanted to go off alone.

On the ride, she listened for any carriages that might come along. She'd not lit a lantern so as not to draw attention to herself, a woman alone.

Not long, she saw the lights and many carriages around a home larger than the Hammond's. Everyone for miles must be there, she decided.

Despite the lateness of the hour and the possibility of being recognized, excitement roiled in her belly. At last, she was going to see what should have been the highlight of her life to this point.

She stopped in front of the house where a hand helped her from the buggy. After a mere nod of acknowledgement, too afraid her voice might squeak, she went up the steps to the house. Music floated out through the windows. A man opened the door and motioned for her to enter. She followed him into a hall, letting the music guide her to a room to the right. Stopping into the doorway, her breath caught. The great room was more than she could have believed with its high ceiling and candlelit chandeliers.

She scanned the room, taking in the gowns of red, green, blue, even gold, silver and purple. They made her pastel pink dress feel drab. Stepping back to take her leave, her eyes landed on his. He came toward her and she froze. How was she going to escape?

He stopped before her and bowed. "May I make your acquaintance?" he asked. "My name is Samuel Wadkins."

Manners led her to curtsy. "Excuse me. I cannot stay."

He held his hand out to her. "I'd be pleased if you danced with me."

His eyes held hers when they met. Lillian could not deny him. With her hand in his, he led her to the dance floor and lay a hand on her waist. She followed his lead easily enough, having danced with her father many times around the house.

"I've not seen you before, have I?" he asked.

"Would it matter?" she asked, her eyes lowered, voice quiet.

"Who's your family?"

"Many questions. Am I to believe you're in training for service?" she asked, tilting her head to look up at him.

"Forgive me."

Samuel's hand tightened on her waist as he whirled her around the floor, stopping to spin and dip her. He held her bent over his arm longer than necessary, his eyes penetrating hers. She worried he might see familiarity in her depths. Part of her wished not, part of her was glad to be near him even if she must suffer another cold dip in the water to cool her wanting of his body. His eyes began to darken with desire and she shivered. If he laid her out now on the floor and loved her, the onlookers would be forgotten.

He drew her up, saying, "I feel I've seen into your eyes before. They're such a unique blue, between the sky and the night."

"It's the lighting, maybe the event," she murmured. Her heart pounded from both the dance and the desire steadily rising from being near him and remembering what it had felt like to have her body with his.

"I shall like to dance with you all night."

She didn't know what to say, but the change in the music tempo set them off on a waltz. They glided around the floor as if they were alone. For her it seemed so. When the music ended, he drew her close to him. She felt his breathlessness equal hers, from activity she would have believed had she not seen the growing need spread over his face. Was he so easily taken he couldn't control himself? This thought pricked her heart, but she wanted to believe somewhere deep within him, a particle of him knew she to be the Annie he was searching for. Wishful thinking or a way to save her heart for the moment, maybe?

The music ended and he led her toward a table and

handed her a glass of punch before guiding her through the nearest open door. She found herself in the night air, welcoming the breeze.

"I used to wonder about these affairs, but then I was sent off to school before I could attend."

"Is it everything you imagined?"

"Yes, and no," he said, closing the respectable distance between them. With a finger, he tipped her chin up. "There's something about you, something…familiar." His head bent near her ear and he whispered, "My body claims to know you in ways it desires."

She swallowed and took a step backward. "Did your school teach you to be so forward?"

"Pardon my bluntness. I'm not normally brash." He took her glass and set it down on the nearby table. "Shall we?" he asked, extending his arm.

Relieved to return to the dance floor, she wished for the normalcy the night should have had—one where she would have been open to talk freely, and maybe know Samuel in an accepted sense.

The chimes of a clock reached her. She listened and knew it to be the hour of ten. She must hurry home. Before the music began once more, she reached up on her toes and whispered in his ear. "Blessings to you, Samuel." Then she turned to leave, but he pulled her back, holding her to his body.

His mouth claimed hers, releasing a hunger she should have kept back. Instead, she drank, and gave as she'd done that morning many days ago. The quiet of the room disturbed her and she pushed at him to let her go. "I have to go." She ran from the room.

"Annie, wait!"

She heard him, but went for the buggy sitting beside the nearest carriage rather than wait for it brought up.

"Annie!" he called after her again.

She flicked the reins to hurry her horse along out to the road and headed back to the Hammond house as fast her horse would take her. Once there, she took time to care for the horse before rushing in to change for bed.

Breathless, she climbed under the covers on her cot and worked to calm herself. She must appear to be sleeping when the others came.

However, excitement over Samuel calling her Annie kept her heart racing and eyes unable to close. He hadn't fancied her because she was a woman, but knew it'd been her. Why hadn't he been forthright rather than suspicious? She'd like to ask, but did she dare attempt another appearance? A second look might ring the mind of those looking on, raising gossip about her father.

She flopped onto her belly and tried to settle in as the fact she had no other dress to wear sunk in, even if she changed her mind.

The clop-clop of horse hooves coming near told her the others were returning. At least those who must rise early as she did, she believed. Lillian turned to the wall and shut her eyes.

The door opened and instead of the quiet steps of the women who needed to be up in a few hours, Emma came over and bounced on her cot. "Wake up, Cappa!"

Lillian moaned, rubbed her eyes to feign waking. "What? Is something wrong?"

"Oh, Cappa, you should have been there. The women wore bright colored gowns. Oh, so pretty. One day, I'll have a red one. Master Waldkins was so handsome in his black evening suit. He danced with no one but this unknown girl. She was like a princess in her pink dress, her hair—"

"Emma, slow down."

Emma reached out and grabbed her hand. "Oh you shoulda been there. He kissed her in front of all. It put dancing butterflies in my belly. Then she ran and he ran after her, calling her Annie. You remember when he came to the house asking for her?" She sighed. "I'm sure he would have left the party if his father hadn't stopped him." Emma shook her head. "Sad in a way, but he refused all other dances after that."

"Seems rude of him," Lillian said, but inside, it warmed her to know he'd held no one else.

Mable came in. "All right girls. Off to sleep now. We have but a few hours 'til we get the day on."

"She shoulda been there, shouldn't she, grandmother?"

"Emma, let her get back to sleep."

"Tell her how Master Wadkins danced with a princess and no one else."

"Now, Emma!"

"Yes ma'am."

Snuggling down again, Lillian forced herself to sleep by convincing herself she had all day tomorrow to decide what to do.

* * * *

By the time the morning meal ended, Lillian wanted to scream for Emma to be quiet about the night before. The incessant chatter bothered her more than usual, giving pain to her head. Soon, Mable sent the girl and others who'd attended the event to rest, leaving the both of them to get on with preparing the mid-day meal. The older woman informed her, the house would then sleep until dinner.

Lillian's mind escaped the task of her hands set on coming up with a way to alter her dress, for maybe she'd attend the last dance. If only she had a sewing kit, she might remove the sleeves, the excess skirting, and make a sash for a different look. It'd take days to transform it into something presentable, even for a seamstress.

"Where's your mind, girl?"

Lillian jumped. She looked down and saw she'd put the peels in the with the potatoes rather than the potato. "I'm sorry," she said while picking out the skins.

"You're young, you should go tonight. If for no other reason than to keep Emma quiet so we may sleep."

"I've no real need to go."

"We none do, but it's time off."

"I've not earned the time."

"You work hard, you earn"

Lillian stood, lifting the pot of potatoes and set it in the sink to cover them with water before putting it on the fire. "I wouldn't want to shame Mr. Hammond," she said, wiping down the table. "Next year, maybe I'll have a dress to wear. I will stay and bake pies for tomorrow." She pulled over the bushel of corn to shuck, not expecting Mable to say more about it.

Later, when Lillian had reason to be outside, she sat on an old milk stool. She breathed in the air, hot and moist. A swim in the creek sounded good. Maybe later, once they all left, she could sneak away and bathe.

She closed her eyes and Samuel's handsome face appeared. His young, carefree smile framed with dark hair and gray eyes which darkened when he wanted her. The stutter beat of her heart drew a hand to lay over it. If only things were different.

Sighing, she decided there was no sense in feeling sorry to have lost the life she knew. The future, the now, is what needed tending, especially if she were with child, as her lack of monthly cycles indicated. Shaking her head, she told herself not to dwell on what to do. There'd be time enough when she learned for sure. Tomorrow when she went to town for supplies, she'd slip away to see the doctor in Littleton. There no one would know her to be the daughter Barrister Basford. For now, work needed tended. She rose to return to the kitchen.

"Lil, follow me," Mable said with sternness.

Lillian obeyed, wondering if she'd dawdled too long. She followed her into their quarters where she saw a dress laid out on her cot. Confused, she walked over and picked it up.

"I'm sorry, I don't know where this came from," she said, assuming Mable thought she'd stolen it.

Chapter Four

"I put it there. My waist outgrew it time back. If you

hurry to take it in, you'll go tonight," Mable informed her.

Lillian felt the sting of tears behind her eyes. No one had ever been so generous before. She gave the woman a hug. "Thank you. Thank you!"

The woman handed her a small basket. "Use what you need."

Mable left her alone and she hurried out of the dress belonging to Emma. Pulling on the larger dress, she whispered, "Oh, my." The dress needed much work to fit. She took it off and laid it out on the bed to study. Basic sewing and accessory projects she was capable of tackling, but this task…air whooshed from her lungs. Time was not on her side. However, it didn't need to be fancy, only to fit, she told herself.

By the time Lillian finished and stood with the altered dress on, she wished for a mirror to see how it really looked. Her stitches weren't perfect, but it'd have to do.

She gathered the fabric she'd cut from the dress and put Mable's sewing basket on her cot when an idea hit her. She could use the scraps to change the look of her own dress. The color wasn't too far off from the pale pink. It would compliment it. Spreading the strips out on the cot, she stood with her fingers pressed to her lips, pondering ideas.

Nodding, she pulled her dress from its hiding place and held it up. First, she looked at the front, then the back, before putting her vision to the fabric. She shortened the longer sleeves of the dress and edged them with a band of the servant fabric then, holding her breath, she cut a section from the back of the skirt to narrow it to conform with the current trend of evening wear.

Lillian worked as fast as she could, again, using small basting stitches. When she finished, she held the dress up. She smiled, thrilled with the outcome. The two fabrics rounding the waist to stream down the back was a good idea. Taking care to fold and return it to the hiding place under the cot, she wondered now about a mask. What could she do with the bit of scraps left?

The door opened and she closed her eyes for a moment, relieved she hadn't been caught doing her own dress. She turned around to see Emma.

"Grandmother said she gave you a dress so you could come tonight."

"Yes. I took it in some."

Emma kneeled and all but crawled under her own cot. Pushing herself out, she stood. "It's a masquerade, so you need a fan. No one pays us mind, so most don't wear masks."

Emma handed her a bamboo fan with floral artwork on it. "It's beautiful. I shall take care."

"It's going to be fun. You'll see."

She set the fan on the dress she'd wear in a short time. "We should return to the kitchen."

* * * *

The servants arrived at the Waldkins' home among a scurry of others. The enthusiasm filled Lillian with hope of an enjoyable night. She stayed with the servants of the Hammond household, hoping she didn't forget her place or happen across staff of her father's house.

In the great room, she went along the wall and stood as one of them, but with the fan covering most of her face while she scanned the room. Not many of the area houses had arrived yet. They'd want to make their entrances after the hosts. This, she understood from her sisters telling of previous events.

When the room quieted, she turned and watched their hosts enter. They were welcomed with respectable appreciation.

Emma spoke into her ear. "A looker, huh?"

"He's handsome, yes." She watched Samuel scan the room as he followed his parents across the floor they'd danced on.

Guests began to enter. Among them, her father, looking sharp in his black suit, escorting her sisters. Did he give her a thought tonight? Did he realize he would have had her on his arm for the first time?

She watched them greet their hosts while her stomach knotted at the way Elizabeth, her eldest sister, leaned into Samuel and held her hand out to him. He politely took the tips of her fingers and brushed his lips over her gloved hand. Gwen moved in, doing the same. The two were always competitive, and never had a problem boasting of how they were closer to his twenty-four years than she was. Still, this wasn't an affair where a wife was being sought.

Samuel's face reddened though he laughed at whatever Gwen had said then he leaned over and whispered in her ear. Giggling reached Lil's ears and she realized how much she'd missed her sister. An ache squeezed her heart and she looked around for an escape path to leave the show before her. If she didn't, she'd rush up to them, hugging her sisters and begging her father to forgive her. It could not be.

She left her group to follow others. Some who went through a doorway were from her father's house, so she went beyond and through an outside door. Finding a bench away from the doors, she sat. Gazing at the stars twinkling in the sky around the brightest moon, she felt moisture slip down her cheek and brushed it away.

Footsteps came near, but she remained seated. If she did not move, she might go unnoticed. A man passed her by to stand at the rail surrounding the outdoor sitting. Samuel, she saw in the moonlight. For minutes, he stood quiet, looking out into the night she supposed.

"Please come, my Annie," he said.

Lillian held her breath. She should slip away, but she couldn't. The sadness in his voice kept her still.

He sighed and gripped the wooden rail. "Why doesn't she come? Why don't I know where to find her?"

The frustration in his quiet voice tore at her heart. She sniffled before she realized she would. This small sound drew him around almost before she remembered the fan to shield her face. "I'm sorry, Master Waldkins. I did not mean to disrupt."

"You shouldn't come and sit where another is taking a

private moment."

"I would not, but I was already here, sir." She stood to leave. "I will leave you to your wishes."

"No. Stay."

She could not see his face, but didn't need light to know his eyes bore into her. What he could see in only the moonlight, she could not say, but tingles raced through her.

"Who do you serve?"

"The Hammond household."

"Hmm."

Scurrying feet rushed up on them. "Cappa, you must come. Grandmother's been huntin' you."

"Yes," she said as she rose.

"No, stay. She'll be along," he said to Emma.

"Yes, sir."

"I shouldn't…"

"Cappa, why does she call you this?"

"I mustn't bore you, sir."

"Please."

"It is not right for me to speak with you." She heard footsteps and wondered if Mable came for her out of displeasure.

"Do you not have a proper name?"

"I'm called Lil. Excuse me, I must return to my group," she said, turning to hurry off, but he grabbed her arm and she faltered. The warmth of his fingers stoked the embers that never died out where he was concerned.

"Please, do you know of an Annie in any service?"

She couldn't lie to him. "I know of her."

"Where would I find her?"

"I mustn't, it's not my—"

"Excuse me, sir, your father's requesting your presence," said one of the house's servants rushing up on them.

"I'll be along," Samuel responded. "Tell me where I can find her," he said, returning his attention to her.

"Sir, I cannot. I'd lose my place."

"Get a message to her to come tomorrow night."

"I'll try, but—"

"Excuse me. I must see to my father's request," he said when they heard a throat clearing sound. He walked off then returned. "I will have my father talk with Hammond and employ you here." Then he was off again.

She stood for a moment past his exit. It was clear things might soon fall in on them, causing a scandal for his family, and hers. She hurried back to where she belonged, enduring the stern look Mable gave her. There would no doubt be extra chores and the chances of needing to excuse herself from coming along with them tomorrow evening unneeded. Still, she must attend the final dance. She must have a moment with Samuel to set things right. To assure him he must give her up. She must be strong for them both.

A nudge to her shoulder brought her back from the plan of how the next night should be when boredom set her mind astray.

"It's time to go," Mable told her.

She nodded, realizing much time had passed, then turned to follow Emma toward the door.

* * * *

On the return trip from obtaining supplies in Littleton, Mable commented, "You took a while in Doctor Victor's."

Lillian didn't cast her a glance. "He was chatty." The truth was, she'd asked him to confirm or deny if Samuel's seed had blossomed. He did and she left with the medicine for Mrs. Hammond who was feeling poor.

"Your mind's been gone since. He didn't give you cause to be backward, did he? He can be abrasive."

"He's wasn't." Lillian didn't want to talk about it. For all her knowing, she didn't know what to feel, much less do. She wished her mother were around to tell her what to do. If things had been different—but in the back of her mind, she knew if they had, all this would be for naught.

For all her contemplating as the day wore on, Lillian left for the dance no better minded as to what to do. It would not be long for all to see she was with child, but what she should do about Samuel weighed heavy. No well-standing parents wanted others to know of a child between theirs and a servant, even if she came from standing prior.

Lillian prayed for guidance as she stood in the entrance of the room full of people, her nerves wreaking havoc with her belly. Eyes turned her way, bodies seemed to part and there he stood, handsome and proud. A slow smile came to his face and she went to him before she realized her feet had moved.

He took her hands in his. "I feared you wouldn't come this night as well."

"I don't think you'd have missed me with all the willing."

He laughed, a hearty sound, and pulled her into a waltz, smooth, practiced and familiar as it'd been the other night. The move, however, was no more than a ruse to take her across the room where he eased her out onto the terrace. The air filled with fragrant scents of the fall flowers and leaves wafting around her.

He caressed her cheek with soft fingers, easing over the corners of the mask she wore. "Please, may I remove it?"

"And spoil the mystery it serves?" she asked with a lightness she hoped he bought into.

"But I've seen you. I want to see you again."

"When the time is right."

"If this is your wish," he conceded.

His lips came down quick and brushed hers, then were gone.

She searched his face, and knew she could not leave without his knowing of their child and the reassurance she would ask nothing of him. "We must talk."

"Talk, yes. Annie…"

Samuel's arms came around her as his mouth took hers with tenderness, yet she sensed his hunger. Shivers swept through her.

They parted and he rested his forehead against hers. "Shall we go for a walk?"

"Please." A walk would not cool the fire he was adept at

flaming deep in her body, but it would it take them away from those who would watch and gossip.

He led her to the steps she'd not yet seen and they walked a path toward the gardens. Samuel stopped, turning to face her. "Annie, don't run out on me tonight. Stay. Stay with me through the night."

Chapter Five

"It cannot be," Lillian said, her voice carrying the sadness she felt.

"These snatches of time aren't enough."

He pulled something from his pocket and picked up her hand. She watched in stunned silence as he slipped a ring onto her finger. "I want to claim your hand."

"Samuel, you can't possibly."

"I dream of you. I wake and reach for you and you're not there. I think of you when I should be reading contracts. I search for you and no one knows you."

"It's as it should be," she said, now second-guessing her decision to tell him.

"I've heard when love strikes, you either don't recognize it or you know it. I know it. Annie, I love you."

"You mustn't." She yanked her hand from his and started to run away, but he caught up and turned her to face him.

Samuel let go of her arms and cradled her face. "You have feelings for me?"

"I do, but—"

"Then let them guide you."

"There's not been time to trust what came upon us. We aren't of the same stand. We don't know…there are consequences…" She hesitated, then continued, "Please let me tell you what might not be settling for you to hear."

"Annie, the only unsettling thing you can say is that you don't love me. And I'd know it to be a lie."

Lillian closed her eyes and opened her mouth to free him. "I'm going to have—" His mouth cut her off and she pushed against him, but he held her tight to his body. She gave in to the hunger, winding her arms about his neck. A moan slipped from her into him and his hands tightened.

On its own accord, her body pressed into him, her womanhood burning with need for his touch. A floating feeling came over her, but she hung onto the magic happening between them with only their mouths fused like a stud with a mare.

Samuel raised his head, causing her eyes to open. She saw the sky, the flickering stars as he gazed down at her. Caressing his cheek, she ran her tongue over her lips. His taste lingered and her belly quivered.

"I so want to see all of you, ravage every inch of skin," he whispered while his hand worked at her buttons. Her body lurched as he skimmed the undergarment covering her breasts. "We must talk," she said as her fingers defied her mind and undid the buttons of his shirt.

"We'll have time to talk, to learn the secrets of each other, after we're married."

"You have know what we've already done has consequences."

Samuel quieted her with his mouth once again as he pushed the fabric from her shoulders and her arms. Rising to his knees, he slipped her garments from her, leaving her bare to the night and to him. He flicked his tongue over her hardened nipples.

"You're a whirlwind to my heart," she told him as he bared his body before her. Reaching up, she ran her fingertips down his chest. There was not much hair over his firm smoothness. Boldness overcoming her, she sat up and ran her palms over the nubs before licking them.

He cradled her head as she felt lips brushing her hair. "Oh, sweet, sweet Annie. You'll cause my seed to spill if you keep doing this."

She looked up at him. "Is that wrong?"

"No, oh, no," he breathed. He leaned over and whispered in her ear, "I'm going to take you to heaven." She trembled, but he continued. "I'm going to lave your pussy with my tongue and make you beg for my cock."

Lillian fell into him while her heart fluttered, her belly jumped and sudden wetness came from her pussy. She reached for his cock, surprised at his heat. It moved and she looked down at it, feeling her face warm. She'd never ever thought about touching a man such a manner. It jerked and she let it go. He chuckled and she looked at him. "Teach me. Take me where you have before."

He laid his hands along her cheeks. "It will be better."

His lips brushed along her jaw as he leaned her back and lay alongside. Her hands moved over his damp, warm skin, kneading and filling with wonder at how right they seemed. Teeth grazed the flesh of her pale breasts and latched onto the pointed tip near him.

"Mmm." She sighed as her body floated upward and back down.

He skimmed across her belly and her skin tingled, but she had no time to ponder the feeling for he slipped his fingers into her pussy, deep inside her.

"Oh, feels good," she mumbled as she could no longer separate what he did from herself. Like leaf floating with the current, she let go and went with it.

Samuel kissed a trail lower to his fingers and she lifted her hips, her body seeming to know what to do, despite its lack of experience. His tongue entered her wetness and he moved between her legs. Her raspy breath vibrated on the air as he pushed her knees up and she could no longer see his face. She sought a solid hold with her hands and found the ground with her fingers, digging into the lush grass not yet browned for fall. Her body trembled and her legs wrapped around him.

"Samuel, Samuel," she breathed. He pressed more into her and she felt him circling her folds and pulling on them. "God, oh, please." Please what, she didn't know. Her body coiled as if it was a spring getting ready to fling into the air. His tongue came up and over a place so sensitive, she felt her lungs stop working. He sucked and pulled, as he'd done her breasts. Tangling her fingers in his hair, she stiffened and air whooshed from her chest.

"So wonderfully beyond..." she mumbled as her body quaked.

He rose over her and entered her with his cock. "Oh, yes." she muttered. The tips of her fingers dug into his arms as her body wildly convulsed. He didn't stop moving in and out of her even when it seemed her body finished.

Samuel nuzzled her neck, his breathing coming out in gasps. "Annie, my sweet Annie."

His body stilled but for a moment then he pounded her so hard and fast, new sensations rose and feeling of desire renewed.

"Oh, oh, never in the heavens," she panted.

Samuel grunted. "Oh, my love, I shall not wait any longer," he managed before his body shuddered and jerked with hers.

His breath coming out in harsh gasps, he lay beside her. "Wonderful," he managed and brought her hand to his lips.

Lillian closed her eyes and pressed his hand with hers over her belly. She inhaled, held it and let it out.

"Now, we talk." She patted his hand. "There's a baby beneath your hand." He remained quiet for so long, she looked at him to be sure he didn't sleep. Hesitant to say more, she bit her lip, then added, "The consequence of our previous act."

"A baby?"

It wasn't so much the question, but his harsh tone which had her edging from him. "Doctor Victor, in Littleton, told me this morning."

"Is that why you came tonight? To have me propose marriage—"

She sat up, looking down at him. "You do not know me," she retorted, his meaning quite clear.

"It's your word. You keep secrets. How—"

"That's a vile thing to accuse!" Lillian spouted and rose

from the ground to pull her dress on and gather her undergarments. "Love accepts, it doesn't accuse," she said, running off before tears came.

Rounding the far side of the house to get to her buggy, she slammed into someone lurking in the darkness. "Excuse me, sir. I did not see you."

He grasped her arms, holding her away from him. She looked up into eyes the same as hers. Her father stared at her, but she could not tell if he knew her. Movement drew her attention to another man.

"My son is foolish. Take your leave. I will see he does not follow."

Shaken by the collision with her father and her need to go, Lillian didn't ponder the words until she was well away from the place. Samuel's father, her father, too, saw and heard them. They'd given no thought to the sounds they made. Her breath hitched. If they only knew what hadn't been loud enough for others to hear. There'd be no worry his son would come after her.

Chapter Six

Weeks passed and the weather turned dreary with chilling cold rains. The talk of Samuel's indiscretion with the woman had been crude, but dwindled as days went. Still, the occasional word caught as she served the dining room informed her Samuel pined and searched for his Annie. It would have set heavy on her heart, if she hadn't decided it'd the be ring he wanted back.

"Lil, come with me," Mable said when she reentered the kitchen, coming from a summons to Mr. Hammond.

"Yes, ma'am," she said, wiping her hands down her dress. She followed the woman through the house to a room. Inside, behind a large mahogany desk, sat Master Hammond.

"Sir, this is the young servant spoken of."

"That'll be all, Mable."

He studied her. "My wife says you know when a position

came open elsewhere, you'd be placed there. The Wadkins' household is in need of help."

"Yes, sir." Turmoil began to rumble about her belly. Once in the house of the Wadkins, the game would be up the moment Samuel saw her. He'd know she was both Annie and Lil. Would he then listen to what she had to say?

Mr. Hammond set coins on the edge of the desk. "Your pay."

"Sir, I work for no pay. Only food and shelter." She took leave and saw Mable waiting in the hall. Without a word, she followed her out to their quarters.

"I will not tell Emma until you've left."

"I will miss her...all of you."

"Mr. Waldkins is harsh, but he's fair."

"I'll change and take leave round the house so as not to be seen."

"You will need the dress. Emma would want you to take it."

"Thank you."

When left alone, Lillian took her hidden bundle from under the cot and pulled on her cloak. Hurrying around the house, she met the stare of a thin, elderly man whose gray hair looked as if it hadn't been combed in weeks.

"Come on, girl. The mister has need of the carriage."

Lillian climbed up, but before she settled in the leather seat, he sent the horse down the road, toppling her forward before she righted herself.

Once they arrived at the Wadkins home, he let her out near the backside. "Alice waits you in the kitchen," he told her and went on his way.

Walking up to the door, she knocked.

"Get on in here, girl."

She stepped inside a room, larger than the Hammond's.

"What's you wearing?"

Dark eyes under a scowl looked her over, making her feel like bark on a tree.

"What'd you wearin' rushes for, girl? Are you without

senses?"

"No ma'am."

"Get it off and leave your things outside the door."

Lillian left a pile near the step and returned.

"Wash up and get the meat cut!" the woman ordered.

"First, I want her to come with me."

Chills spiraled down her spine. Mr. Waldkins' voice was no friendlier today than it'd been the last night she saw Samuel.

"Don't keep her long. With the young'un taken to his bed, I can't tend his needs and get dinner on too," the woman spoke, rather forthright.

He did not respond but turned back into the hall and Lil followed as expected. Lillian assumed she'd meet the misses of the house and hear her duties. Instead, she found herself in his study, much like her father's, with mahogany furniture and shelves of books.

She stopped before his desk while he sat behind it. "My wife bid for your service in hopes it will raise our son from his bed. He insists you have knowledge to help with his search."

Lillian couldn't believe Samuel would take ill over a ring. Unless it was a family heirloom—did he gave it to her without the knowledge of his parents?

"I do not want him to find her," he told her.

She looked across the desk into blue-gray eyes, wondering why then she'd been brought over.

"Return to the kitchen!" he ordered.

She scurried off. Alice put her to work making gruel, all the while mumbling about the extra work of trudging up and down the stairs with food the young'un wouldn't touch. This settled like a pit in Lillian's stomach—concern both for his state and what was to come fought.

When Samuel's offering was ready, she ladled it into a cup and set it on a tray ready on the table. "Shall I take it up?" she asked.

"No."

While the back of the woman was to her, Lillian reached into her dress, yanked the ring from its nesting place, and dropped it into the cup. With her eyes closed, she prayed it would bring him from his bed and he'd not search out the servant hired to help—but not help.

Alice came to take the tray. "Get the meat on. The guests will be arriving. Mr. Whitzer likes his near raw, Mr. Basford has his not quite done, but five others are cooked through."

Lillian froze at the mention of her father as a guest. Could things become more uprooting? Seeing the beef slab set out, she cut seven thick pieces and laid them out for seasoning.

As she worked, her thoughts were on her father and the night she'd been banished. Her sister's responses to his question of how much they loved him were, to her, shallow and selfish, while hers had been both selfless and truer than she could have expressed. Why did he toss her out over it? The question had come to her many times, yet never with any clear answer.

As she waited for the time to put on her father's beef, a thought occurred to her. She cut the curing from the edges and did not add salt to it as she had the others. It was a risk to serve it this way, but she hoped it'd be worth it.

Alice returned without the tray, but she said nothing. It seemed a good sign to her.

When it came time to serve the meal, Alice had her help serve. With much care to avoid direct vision or eye contact, Lillian took comfort in her father's attention toward those more worthy than those who worked for the house. This gave her courage to serve him herself.

She didn't breathe until she reentered the kitchen, where she waited with her ears perked. It wasn't long when she heard his, "Oh, surely this isn't the wares intended to be served. There is no salt on the meat to…" He stopped and she stiffened her back.

"Certainly not," she heard Mrs. Wadkins tell him.

She rushed across the room and started on the pots and pans. The door opened and she listened while Alice made apologies for the error and set to fix the meat straight away. Once the misses left, Alice came up to her.

"Go to your quarters!"

Lillian stepped back from the sink, wiping her hands on her apron. "Yes, ma'am. If you'll show me where they are?"

Alice pulled her by the arm and shoved her out the door. "To the left of the barn!"

She saw it, gathered her belongings and started to go, but then she heard her father's voice. He sounded sad and it pulled her closer to the window. Sneaking nearer, she heard him.

"Such an intelligent child, my Lillian," he said.

"I'm sorry, Louis, we're not understanding your mumblings," the misses told him.

"I did not understand her words, the meaning of them until now. The unsalted meat is unbearable, but salt gives it flavor. The way she loves me…"

She heard a scraping of a wooden chair across wooden floor.

"I must make my leave. I wronged a daughter whom I thought did not love me. I pray she's not met harm in her wanderings."

Lillian didn't know what to do. If she revealed herself now, what would happen? His daughter, a servant who served him in front of his friends, would bring undue shame.

Her heart heavy with uncertainty, she ran toward the barn and into the servant quarters. An unmade cot sat in the far corner. She laid her things on it and sat with her hands in her lap. Her mind went this way and that, trying to decide what would be best. She hadn't perished in the elements of outdoors, but was a servant, and with child. Would his relief and love allow him to accept what she'd become?

The door banged against the wall, startling her. Alice's face was scrunched with fierce anger while her black eyes pierced her like a sword. Never before had such fear filled her. Lillian scooted back to the wall, drawing her knees up and buried her head into them.

Something hit her back again and again. She realized the woman used a whip.

"No one messes my kitchen!"

Another lash came across the searing pain of those before. Lillian's body shook with sobs and pain she never dreamed possible.

"No one gives my kitchen a bad name!"

"Stop!" a male voice ordered.

The whip came again.

"I ordered you to cease!"

"It's not your concern, Master Samuel. I handle those who work the kitchen," Alice talked back.

Lillian dared a peek at her savior. Samuel stood wearing only a robe and stockings, his face unshaved and rough. He'd taken the whip from Alice and stood glaring at her.

"It's no wonder we can't keep staff on. If I hear of this happening again, I shall use the whip on you. Do you hear me?"

"Yes, sir," she replied through gritted teeth.

"Get back to kitchen while you have work!"

Alice gave her a threatening look that sent ice through the burning sensations covering her back.

Samuel kneeled and cupped her face. "Annie, my Annie."

Lillian flinched as he looked at the welts on her back. Wiping her face on the skirt of her dress, she then rested her forehead on her knees. The shaking of her body would not cease.

"Come, let me tend you." He scooped her up and muffled her whimpers in his shoulder.

"The ring is where it belongs. You mustn't acknowledge me," she managed.

Samuel took her into the main house, up the stairs to the second level and set her down on the bed of a room not far down the hall. A glance around at the rose and white colors told her it wasn't his room.

He disappeared and reappeared with a handful of supplies and dropped them on the bed. "I'm afraid your garments have been ruined."

She nodded. With no hesitation, she began to unbutton the front. He reached out and helped her when her fingers fumbled.

"It was smart to put the ring in the gruel, but what if I hadn't found it?"

"I didn't think of that. I wanted you to have it so you'd you stop searching to regain it."

In silence, they bared her to his eyes. She watched him look her over through tear-blurred vision as the pain from having the fabric pulled from the wounds intensified. He reached out and touched her belly, which was no longer flat.

"My son grows within you," he whispered.

Lillian met his eyes when they rose. She could not tell if it pained or worried him. He was going to have to start the talk this time.

He wiped a tear from her lip. "I wasn't after the ring. I had to find you to make apologies and beg you to forgive me for my ignorance."

Afraid to trust the sincerity in his voice, she waited for more.

He brought her hands to his lips, brushing them with a kiss. "I see love even through the pain of your beating. How can you love me when I was horrid to you?"

"My news was a shock, but had you known me…" Stinging pain shot down her back, causing her to stiffen her back.

"I'm so sorry," he said, reaching for a cloth. "I will try not to add to the pain, but I'm afraid the attempt will be unsuccessful."

She nodded and turned to angle her body, giving him access to whip marks.

"You might want to grip the post."

The sudden thickness of his voice gave her an idea of how ugly her back must be. Scarred for life, she imagined. She turned toward the foot post of the bed and wrapped her fingers around it. When the cloth touched the raw flesh, she bit down on her lip to hold in the scream, but a moan escaped.

"Try to be brave, my love. This one broke through the skin."

Lillian nodded, holding her breath. He pressed in with the cloth. "Samuel, stop for a moment." Warm, gentle lips brushed over her back. It helped ease the pain.

"Why would she beat you like this?"

His voice sounded sullen as if he, too, was close to tears. "I served unsalted meat to a guest—my father."

"Your father?" he urged when she stopped.

"It was not for meanness. I set to clear up a misunderstanding." She winced as he resumed the tending. "I once told him I loved him as much as food loves salt. He now knows what my words meant and regrets banishing me. I cannot let him find me now. His daughter, Lillian Ann, a servant and with child, would bring scandal and shame."

Prying her hands from the post, he turned her to face him. "Hold no shame for what we feel. For the child we made." He returned the ring to her finger. "We will see your father, then marry. If you'll forgive me for all I've brought on you."

"I never thought ill of you, Samuel. My love is deeper than pettiness."

He kissed the palm of her hand and drew her against his chest. "My love," he whispered.

About Bekki Lynn

Bekki Lynn is a multi-book published author who resides in the Midwest surrounded by her family, friends and small petting zoo. Included in this mix are the characters writes, lives and breathes. They keep her on her toes while taking her on a roller coaster ride of emotions. She'd have it no other way.

When she's not glued to her laptop-is there a time when she's not? There is, but we won't go into much detail there. She loves to shop period—music, movies, the works, go to baseball games and to dinner with her husband of more than thirty years.

Bekki listens to music and watches sitcoms, movies and sports as writes. She needs the noise after raising four sons and being used to their sounds. The quiet frightens her.

To learn more about Bekki Lynn feel free to visit her website:

http://home.mchsi.com/~bekkilynn

RE-WRITE
By Marshall Ian Key

I had always assumed that it was a rule of hackdom that we did not receive invitations to the Palace. It was nothing formal, of course. Nobody said anything at the monthly meetings, but nobody ever mentioned getting an invitation, either.

When I was thirteen, I had dreamed of going to the Palace. The Queen had invited me, because she was young and gorgeous and soft and sexy, and I was young and manly and virile and quite full of myself. There was no way that the King, who was none of those things, could possibly satisfy her. Just look at him, for crying out loud: short, jug-eared, bug-eyed, and with a nose that preceded him like Diogenes's lantern. So she invited me. I was more than willing to pitch in, of course, for the overall happily-ever-afterness of the kingdom. There were thousands of other thirteen-year-old boys who would have been equally willing.

I was forty now, the Queen an elegant sixty. She had grown older gracefully, given birth to a single child, Prince Christian, when I was fifteen. He appeared to have inherited nothing from his mother—proof, in my mind, that she had washed her hands of the whole thing. She appeared content. If not actually satisfied.

I had grown older somewhat more clumsily, having finally settled into a career as a hack. When I graduated university, some fifteen years or so ago, I had dreams of becoming a novelist. A famous, best-selling novelist was what I had in mind, but any sort of novelist would have done. I had no sooner entered the "real world," though, when I realized I was completely bereft of ideas. I had no story to tell, not even a short one, let alone a entire novel's worth. I wrote some magazine articles and a few primers on gardening. I still wanted to tell stories. I just didn't have any.

Fortunately, other people had stories. So I took to telling them. The name Joe Boston started appearing on plenty of books, always preceded by "as told to." *Britney: A Nightingale's Story*, as told to Joe Boston. *The Shaq Attack*, as told to Joe Boston. I had made decent money over the last few decades. It was a living.

It just wasn't a living I ever expected would bring me to the Palace. When my agent called to forward the invitation, I accused him of a prank. Up until the moment they opened the gate to let me in, I was ready to laugh the whole thing off when my friends popped up to let me in on the joke.

I parked on one of the streets that surrounded the courtyard that surrounded the moat that surrounded the palace.

The guard at the gate raised an eyebrow at my approach.

"I have an appointment?" I suggested.

The eyebrow went further up.

"Seriously, pal. I was told to come."

"Name?"

"Joe Boston."

He retreated into his guardroom, eyeing me all the while. He returned with an ornate skeleton key.

"Most of the visitors use the car entrance," he said, nodding further west toward a larger gate.

"I'm fine," I said. "I got two hours on the meter."

He shrugged and unlocked the gate. I passed through and made the long trudge to the Palace entrance. One of the reasons their other visitors no doubt used the car entrance was the half-mile or so between the gate and the Palace proper. It was a nice day for a walk.

I was greeted by an equerry, the sort of guy who would have been tending horses a hundred years ago and whose job managed to survive both the introduction of the automobile and the elimination of the King's Royal Stables. He appeared to be more of a doorman now. I followed him down a long corridor that echoed with the sounds of our footsteps. Paintings of former kings and queens filled the walls on both sides.

By this point, I had rejected my first idea—that some disgruntled courtier wanted to tell a salacious story about the King and Queen or, even better, at least from a sales viewpoint, about Prince Christian and Princess Valerie. The idea had never been more than half-baked anyway. For one thing, wouldn't he or she have wanted to meet in some out-of-the way tavern? "Excuse me, your Majesty, can I use one of the meeting rooms to spill the beans about your son and daughter?" For another thing, it was a fairly gruntled staff. Everyone always had the same smiles on their faces. Like they'd managed the happily-ever-after thing despite the lack of my sexual participation. Still, it was the best idea I had come up with.

The doorman silently showed me into a room, his expression making it quite clear that I was to wait and touch nothing. I had seen pictures, of course, but I was still unprepared for the garish opulence—the gilt chairs, the lush tapestries, the ancient books lining the shelves, the ocean of silver occupying the tables.

"Would you like some tea?"

I had been so wrapped up in the furnishings, I hadn't heard the door. I turned and froze. Princess Valerie was far more stunning in person than in the papers or even on TV. The change over the past five years, when the prince had first introduced her to the kingdom, was astonishing. The waif of that time, the girl who appeared to have spent the previous year wandering the forest eating roots and berries, was completely gone. Now—her bosom full, her skin a beautiful pink, her eyes a flashing, happy blue, her brown hair brushing her shoulders—the woman who had taken her place was as perfect as a flower in full bloom.

"Your—your Highness," I stammered after a pause that threatened to last into winter.

"Mr. Boston," she said with a delightful smile. "Tea?"

"Thank you, your Highness. I would love some."

She opened the door, said something and then closed it before walking toward me with her hand extended. I took it and, with no idea what to do with it, bowed deeply.

She laughed, a hearty rumble of sound that seemed wholly disconnected from her regal bearing. "Mr. Boston, if we are going to be working together, you will have to learn to treat me with a little less deference. Pray take a seat."

"Work together, Highness?" I asked as I parked my butt on a plush red couch. "You want to work with me?"

"I do, Joe. May I call you Joe?"

"Certainly." I shrugged. She could call me anything she wanted.

"And you shall call me Valerie."

I thought that very unlikely. I gave her a half-smile.

"I must confess to being somewhat still overbowled by your suggestion that we work together on anything at all, your...eh...Valerie...ness. I am a common writer. A mere amanuensis as of late. Well, and as of early as well. Pretty much as of all my life, really. I earn my living by writing other people's stories."

"Precisely," Valerie said. "And I should like very much if you would agree to do the same for me."

"Tell your Highness's story?"

"Yes."

"The palace, the parties, the footmen, the whole thing?"

Another hearty laugh. "God, no, Joe. I can't imagine anything more boring."

"Than your Highness's life?"

"Than reading about my Highness's life—the parties, the clothes, yada yada yada. It's boring enough living it sometimes. Even I couldn't stand reading about it. No, I'm talking about my previous life. From before all this."

"Seriously?"

"Why do you ask like that, Joe?"

"Well, I mean the gossip about your past has finally died down. Why do you want to bring it all up again?"

Her eyes flashed. "What was it?"

"What was what?"

"The gossip! I'm shut up here in this palace and I can't get any of the really good magazines—*Star, National Enquirer*. All we get here is *National Geographic*. So what did they say?"

I hemmed and hawed but eventually it all came out. She was a whore. She was a hippie. She was raised by wolves. Or sheep. Or wolves and sheep, taking turns. She worked as a maid for her ugly stepmother and equally ugly stepsisters.

"And then I was transformed into a princess by my fairy godmother?" she said, clapping her hands in delight.

"Something like that. That was the one for the kids. But now, everybody loves you. You have higher favorables than the prince, higher than the King and Queen."

She leaned forward, her silk brocade gown offering a tantalizing glimpse of what Penthouse had offered ten million dollars for a better view of. I stared, unblinking, into her eyes.

"Can you keep a secret, Joe?"

"Certainly."

"You won't tell a soul?"

"Nobody," I said, crossing my heart. I promised with the full knowledge that if I failed to keep my word, I would be drafted into the army and posted to the disease-ridden swamps of the south.

"I'm pregnant, Joe. With twins."

It was delightful news. The entire country was waiting for their Royal Highnesses to start producing little Highnesses. Although there were thousands of thirteen-year-old boys who would be crushed.

"Congratulations," I said.

"Well, between us, Joe, it was my pleasure." She added a wink that rendered me speechless once again. Was she talking about Prince Christian? A man as short, jug-eared, bug-eyed and nasally challenged as his father? I was saved by the arrival of the tea. As we sipped from the delicate china, she explained that she wanted her children to know all about her life.

"I was very impressed with your bear book."

Ah, yes. *The Blond in the Baby Bear's Bed*, as told to Joe Boston. My first and only foray into children's literature.

"Thank you," I said.

"So when I decided on this project," she continued. "I decided to ask you to help. Are you in?"

"Of...of course," I said.

"All the proceeds will be yours, of course."

"All of them?"

She laughed again. "I have little need of the money, Joe. I've done quite well here, particularly considering where I started."

"Perhaps," I suggested, "we could donate your half to some sort of charity. The Princess's Trust for..."

Tears welled up in her eyes. "I knew I had the right man. Orphans, then. The Princess's Trust for Orphans. I'll have the lawyers draw one up. How fitting."

"Your Highness was an orphan?" I asked.

She glared at me.

"You were an orphan?" I rephrased it. "Er, Valerie?"

She smiled again.

"As good as," she said with a sigh. "Let us say it was an unusual childhood. As my name indicates."

"Your name?"

"Valerianella Locasta."

"It's lovely."

"It's a plant, Joe. They named me after a plant."

"Sorry."

"Anyway, what with doctor's appointments and royal appointments, I'm not sure I can block off a big amount of time for this. It's going to kind of be a couple hours here, then a week off, then a couple hours there. Is that a problem?"

"Not at all," I said. "Maybe the best thing to do would be for me to take notes when we can get together, and then write up what I have before I come back. We can spend some time going over what I've written and then move on. How does that sound to your...you, Valerie?

"My Valerieness approves," she said with yet another laugh. I loved this woman. I pulled a notebook and pen from my jacket pocket.

* * * *

Hezekiah and Rebekkah Stonewort were among the least ordinary people in the kingdom. Hezekiah scratched out a living making chalk drawings in the park, while Rebekkah gave lessons in yoga and meditation on a schedule that was apparent to her alone. As a result of their lack of business sense, they lived in a neighborhood described as "transitional" by local authorities and as "edgy" by those who lived nearby. Many of the houses were old and in need of repair; the trees were even older, their gnarled branches casting strange shadows in the moonlight.

Their neighbors were equally strange. On the one side was a witch, or at least a woman who was widely rumored to be a witch, and on the other side, two young women who appeared to have foresworn the company of men and whose arguments and reconciliations filled the area with all sorts of interesting sounds.

Five years into their love-filled marriage, Rebekkah became pregnant, and it was during the course of that pregnancy that she developed a craving for field salad. It was unfortunate, perhaps, that the only place it grew was right next door, in the garden of Mrs. Stranglemeister, the putative witch. Rebekkah was expert at sneaking in and out, at cutting just so much that it went unnoticed during the first seven months. It was at that point, however, that her physician, or more properly her herbalist, put her on a strict regimen of bed rest. It fell to Hezekiah to obtain the plant.

He succeeded, for a while. But on the two-hundred and sixty-seventh day, as Rebekkah lay in her bed, awaiting his return, the phone rang.

"Hello?"

"Mrs. Stonewort?" Mrs. Stranglemeister's voice was both silky soft and brittle hard.

Rebekkah felt a cold chill run up her spine. "Yes?"

"I found your darling husband stealing my field salad, and he confessed the two of you have been doing so for the last nine months."

"I have no idea what you're talking about," Rebekkah said. It was always better to deny everything.

"Then I shall deal with your husband," the witch said, a cackle in her voice suggesting she was not using "deal" in its ordinary sense.

"No, wait. Oh, shit."

"Your pains are beginning. No doubt you would like your husband at your side."

"Please. Let him go."

"I shall be happy to, let us say, exchange him, my dear."

"Exchange? For what?"

"You have no idea what a constant diet of field salad will do to an as yet unborn infant, do you?"

"Oh my god, what?"

"Let us say she will be a special infant, and will need special care. The sort of care you will be unable to give her."

"You want my daughter?" Rebekka asked in a horrified tone.

"And you want your husband. You have my number, my dear. Pray call me back when you have decided."

"Oh, shit," Rebekkah cried again as she hung up the phone.

In the end, faced with a cruel choice, Rebekkah knew she could not leave her darling Hezekiah in the witch's hands. There would be other children to raise. Her hands trembling, she called Mrs. Stranglemeister and agreed to the deal. Her husband would be freed immediately; the babe was to be delivered no later than one day after her birth. The witch warned her that any attempt to flee with the baby would result in the couple's demise.

The girl to whom Rebekkah gave birth nine hours of painful labor later was a child of unimaginable beauty. Her golden, almost platinum hair framed a face whose deep blue eyes bespoke not so much intelligence as a remarkable capacity for trust, a naïve faith that everything in the world was good.

Her parents spent a sleepless night, wondering whether they should test the witch's threat by running away with the child or stand and make a fight. In the end, their fear made the decision for them. They bundled up the girl and prepared to take her next door. As they stepped onto the front porch, however, Hezekiah had a thought.

"We cannot leave this block with the babe in our arms, and it will break our hearts to turn her over to the witch."

"Very true, my love. But I see no other choice."

"There is but one that I see. Suppose we step off the porch and turn not to the left but to the right?"

"Then we shall be going the wrong direction," Rebekkah said, "for Mrs. Stranglemeister lives to the left."

"Very true, my love. But suppose that we leave this beautiful girl not in the care of that horrible witch, but with our other neighbors? And in the meantime, we will flee to avoid the witch's wrath."

"Ingrid and Susan? But they are...lesbians, my darling."

"You would rather give her to a witch?"

"I guess when you put it that way, no."

And so the child, hastily named for the plant that had been the source of so much trouble, was abandoned to the care of Susan Prosser and Ingrid Fleckham.

* * * *

"Abandoned seems kind of harsh, doesn't it?" Princess Valerie asked. It was two weeks since our first talk. I had pretended to sip at my tea while she read the first chapter of what would one day be *On the Road to Ever After*, as told to Joe Boston. "I mean, you make them sound heartless. They were scared, Joe."

"Of a witch?" I responded, my tone of voice suggesting witches belonged to that category of objects the fear of which should be tempered by their non-existence.

"Yes. And yes, I know there are no witches. But can't you find another word?"

"Sure," I said, pulling out my notebook. "So when we left off you were about to be raised by lesbians."

"That's right," Valerie said with a laugh. "Not wolves or sheep."

"And the so-called witch? She must have been a little upset when she found your parents gone."

"I was told she stormed over and demanded that I be handed over at once.

"'Because you traded some fucking plant for her?' Ingrid demanded. 'Look, bitch, you may have fooled everyone else in this town, but you know you're not a real witch and I know you're not a real witch. Now why don't you just crawl back to your fucking hole in the ground and leave us alone?'"

"That's a great story," I said. "So the Prince ended up rescuing you from the lesbians?"

Valerie laughed again.

"I'm not sure rescuing is the right word," she demurred.

"Okay. So tell me about Susan and Ingrid."

"Oh, they were wonderful. Ingrid was a good deal older, maybe forty at the time. Susan was twenty-five. Ingrid was much more the parent, the responsible one I guess you'd call her. She worked in some sort of finance business. Susan was just sort of my older friend. She made pottery and Ingrid used to show her how to sell it.

"Then when I was about ten, Ingrid died. We didn't realize how much debt she had. And that was right when the market tanked. So all she really had to leave to Susan was this place in the country. And since the other house was a rental, and Susan couldn't afford the rent, Susan moved us there."

"That must have been difficult."

The princess shrugged. "It's not like I had any friends in the city. There was a lot of prejudice against Susan and Ingrid."

"Against lesbians in general back then," I agreed. "I remember."

"So Susan kept on homeschooling me after we moved."

"Still, it must have been very lonely."

- 181 -

"There was Susan..." she said, her voice trailing off.

"But nobody your own age. And no, um...well, you know, there weren't any boys, I imagine."

"No," Valerie said, but she was blushing a deep scarlet.

I thought for a moment. "Wait a minute, you mean you...? You and Susan?"

* * * *

The ancient farmhouse to which Susan Prosser brought her ten-year-old was a ramshackle dwelling of rooms that had been added, one upon the other, like the slightly off-center blocks that might be assembled by a child. Valerie was delighted with it, as it created a crazy quilt of hideaways and retreats. Her particular favorite was the tower that had been added to the northwest corner. It was only three stories high, hardly a tower in the castle sense, but it was tall enough to allow Valerie to pretend she was the princess of all of the land she could see. And it was private, accessible only from an outside door. It was a perfect bedroom.

She was a gawky girl then, all arms and legs, as wild as a feral cat. She would run in the woods every day, making friends with the trees, the animals, the flowers. She would return with her ever-present jeans a mess, her fingernails dirty, and her long hair, now a sun-drenched blond, matted with sticks and leaves and burrs. Susan would brush it out each evening, always afraid one of the smaller animals might have crossed the line between woodland plaything and hair ornament. Finally, in exasperation, she cut it short.

Valerie's education, such as it was, took place in fits and starts. She seemed wholly uninterested in art, music and history—in anything, in fact, that she could not relate to her beloved woods. For three desperate years, Susan despaired of the little girl's becoming anything except the ignorant wife of one of the itinerant woodsmen who passed by the house, offering to cut firewood or do other chores in exchange for a hot meal.

The change was gradual, although it began with a single event. It was raining—not the light or even moderate rain

Valerie had trained herself to ignore, but a driving heavy rain that kept even the animals in their dens. She stared out the window, trying to will the rain to end and the skies to clear. Finally, with a sigh, she slumped onto the couch and reached toward the table. Her fingers betrayed her, finding not the comic she sought but a book. Her thumb drifted across the cover, brushing the ridges in the leather with which the book was bound. It felt like luxury, as if the people who had published the book had considered it worthy of richness. Against her inclinations, she opened it. *Pride and Prejudice.* Stupid name for a book. Still. "It is a truth universally acknowledged, that a single man in possession of a good fortune...." It might not kill her to look at it.

By the time she reached fifteen, Valerie no longer spent all her free time in the woods. She still visited her friends, but now there were others, friends who lived between the two covers of books. They were friends who lived in far-off places, friends who were old and young, men and women, heroes and villains.

By the time she was seventeen, she was wearing dresses nearly every day. Susan had stopped chopping off her hair once a month and it had started to grow. And once it started, it seemed to make every effort to make up for lost time. The eighteen-year-old Valerie was a woman with luscious, long, golden hair, conscious of herself and equally conscious of the attraction she held for the husky young woodsmen whose visits were becoming more and more frequent. She loved to have Susan comb it for her.

She had also become conscious of just how much Susan had sacrificed to make it possible. Susan was still only in her late thirties and the move to the country, although obviously the perfect choice for raising Valerie, had been difficult. Just as Valerie's appearance reflected her growing acceptance of her womanhood, so did Susan's attest to the effect of the last ten years. At twenty, her clothes had been loose and free-spirited, her eyes shiny, her hair a wild aureole of black. She still wore jeans when making her pottery, but she had become much more serious about selling it. Her sales trips found her in suits that Valerie found severe. Her eyes were narrower, as if the forest held more danger for her than freedom. Valerie was most taken, though, with the older woman's hair. It was cut far shorter now, and to the extent it had any length at all, Susan always kept it in a knot at the back of her head.

One evening, shortly after her nineteenth birthday, Susan had just returned from one of her trips. Valerie had cooked her dinner after searching far and wide in the forest for special ingredients.

"That was wonderful," Susan said. "Perhaps you should cook every night."

"I'd love to."

"But maybe you could use some store-bought ingredients. You look like a rat's nest. Come here. Sit in front of the mirror and let me comb your hair out."

As Susan ran the comb through Valerie's long tresses, she couldn't help but think to herself how much the young girl had grown. For her part, Valerie just smiled.

"What?" Susan asked.

"Nothing."

"Tell me."

"It's just nice to have you back."

"Well, thank you."

"I've never told you that before, have I? How much I appreciate your doing all the work you do, all the trips to sell your pottery, so we'll have a place to live, clothes to wear, food to eat."

"Valerie..." Susan demurred.

"Do you, um, see anyone when you travel?"

"See anyone?"

"You know," Valerie said. "I used to listen to you and Ingrid in the old house."

By now Susan was in full blush.

"I'm past eighteen," Valerie said. "We had our little birds and bees talk several years ago. Plus I watch the birds and bees all the time."

Susan giggled.

"Well?" Valerie persisted.

"No," Susan answered. "There's been nobody since Ingrid that I've really..." She had paused in brushing Valerie's hair and the brush suddenly slipped from Susan's hand, dropping into Valerie's lap. She reached down for it and felt Susan's fingers wrap around her wrist.

"What are you doing?"

"I'm not your daughter, Susan. You're not my mother."

Susan pulled back, but the young girl's strength surprised her. Valerie drew Susan's hand closer, pressing the palm against the soft skin of her exposed torso. Susan fingertips slid down to the even softer skin of Valerie's upper breast that was hidden beneath Valerie's gown,

"Valerie!" Susan gasped. "We can't."

Valerie's answer was a soft, low hum that vibrated throughout her chest, tightening the nipples of both women. "Methinks the lady doth protest too much. If she could with her cousin, there's no reason she can't with me."

"You knew?"

"I used to listen through the closet," Susan said. "I learned quite a lot of interesting vocabulary. Shall we have a quiz?"

Susan made one last attempt to put Valerie off, even as she felt the rhythm of her heart begin to match the beat of Valerie's, a strong, quickening pulse transmitted through Susan's fingers and seemed to go straight to her soul. "But Ingrid and I..."

"...were in love," Valerie finished. "Whereas with us, it would just be sex. A little vacation. You haven't taken a vacation in ten years. I do love you, Susan, but not like Ingrid did. All we would have is the passion...the tenderness...the press of lips and flesh and softness."

As Valerie spoke, Susan felt her breath grow shorter and quicker. She became conscious that Valerie was caressing her fingers. That meant that the younger girl wasn't holding those fingers in place on her chest. That meant that those fingers were staying there of their own volition. Or of Susan's. She pulled them back.

"You have read far too many books, girl."

Valerie stood to face Susan. "And lived far too little life." As Susan opened her mouth to respond, Valerie reached up and put a finger across Susan's soft lips.

"I couldn't bear to hear you tell me no, but I understand if that's the answer. I'm going back to my tower now." She pulled out the pins holding Susan's hair in place. "The door will be open. Maybe if you just need to let your hair down a little bit, you might stop by." She bounced once on her feet and walked away quickly, leaving a stunned Susan standing there in silence.

Valerie was lying in bed later that evening, her hands working furiously between her legs, small gasps of breath bursting from between her lips. The knock was almost too quiet.

"Is someone there?"

The knock came again, louder this time.

Valerie smiled. "If someone is out there, and someone is ready to come in and let their hair down...I'm waiting."

* * * *

Over the next half a year, whenever Susan returned from a trip, she would find the house deserted, the only lights those in the tower. She would find a small snack in the refrigerator, but she was usually far too anxious to waste time eating it. Instead, she ran to her room and changed into a soft peignoir. As autumn approached, she would throw on a long coat, knowing that it would not be on for very long.

After a quick look in the mirror, she would hurry out of the house and knock on the door to Valerie's tower. Their routine was always the same—the tentative knock; a louder knock and Valerie's invitation.

Susan would close the door behind her and drop her coat on the floor. She would walk slowly upstairs. Valerie would be on her bed, sometimes wearing a white or powder blue negligee, sometimes not. In either case, she would be wearing no panties. Her legs would be spread, exposing her soft, already moist golden curls to Susan's eyes. Valerie's eyes would be closed. She would purr as Susan mounted the bed, and when the older woman moved between her legs, she would reach down and find the pins holding Susan's hair. She yanked them free and then entwined her hands in Susan's hair, pulling her closer, pulling her lips into her cleft.

"Fuck." Valerie would growl the instant Susan's tongue touched her pussy, a long, guttural rumble that served as a mere introduction to the music that would follow. Susan was a quiet, almost sedate lover. Valerie was just the opposite. Her voice rising to an inarticulate keen, she would pant, moan, groan, gasp and scream her passionate submission. Her thighs would tighten around Susan's head, her legs locking across her back. Her cries would take flight in a crescendo of sound, always stopping just short of the climax that Susan withheld.

And then it was Susan's turn to be pleasured, and suddenly the night would be filled with quiet. Between the owls and the wolves, the whippoorwill and the wind, only the most sensitive ear could have picked up the liquid sound of Valerie's tongue inside Susan's wet, swollen cleft. Susan would appear to hold her breath for minutes at a time, her body rigid, her muscles tense. Valerie would back off just a bit, Susan would relax, and breathe. And Valerie would start in again. It had taken the younger girl several months to learn how to deny her partner an oral climax. But she was gifted, and her skill developed quickly.

The two women finished one atop the other, rubbing body parts together, pinching, rubbing, slapping, and wiggling as they egged each other on. Valerie's climax was no less explosive for being delayed, and the two were now able to ensure that it arrived simultaneously with Susan's.

It chanced, however, that one day Susan was delayed in the city. And it chanced further that a young man noticed her absence. Most of the young men of the forest had heard the sounds of Valerie's pleasure and walked home in disappointment and disgust. They knew precisely what the sounds meant, and knew that if they were not their cause, then someone else was.

Christian, however, had no idea what the sounds meant. He was a prince, the only prince of the land, and his parents had impressed upon him the need for saving himself for marriage. The last thing the kingdom needed, they claimed, was a horde of little bastard princelets. And whereas most young men would have agreed with their parents and then run off to rut with the next available girl, Chris was different. Even when he turned twenty-one and went off to explore the kingdom he would one day inherit, he remained a naïf in the ways of women.

He thought Valerie the most glorious singer he had ever heard. He had tarried several weeks in the area, watching Susan knock on the door and seeing her invited inside for the concert. He had imagined her sitting there listening to the beautiful young girl, whom he had glimpsed one day as she strolled the woods. Imagine, such a lovely girl and such a melodious voice. If only he could meet her.

The day Susan didn't return, he screwed up his courage and decided to take a chance. He knocked once on the door, softly.

"Is someone there?"

He knocked louder this time.

"If someone is out there, and someone is ready to come in and let their hair down...I'm waiting."

It was enough of an invitation for Chris. He closed the door behind him, threw off his cap and walked slowly up the stairs. The sight he beheld stopped him in his tracks. The blonde girl was naked, her eyes closed, her legs open. Her hands reached for him. He shrugged and approached the bed. He moved atop it and the Valerie wrapped her fingers in his long hair. She pulled him down to her sex and he instinctively began to lap and suck at the wet opening.

The singing began again. Until finally she made him stop.

"No more, wait," Valerie gasped, her eyes still closed.. "No more. You promised you'd bring me a toy tonight. Where are you hiding it, you naughty? In your clothes?"

Chris leaned back. There was something hidden in his clothes, come to find out, harder and longer than it had ever been before.

"Give it to me," Valerie demanded with a petulant pout.

Chris obediently pulled down his pants and leaned forward again. Valerie reached down and found it with her fingers.

"It's fucking huge!" she whispered. She guided it toward her opening and felt its massive head part the folds of her pussy. "Fuck a duck! This is—who the fuck are you?"

* * * *

"This is where we left off last time?" Valerie asked me with a frown.

"You were telling me the story and said you needed to go see your husband about something."

"Oh, right." A soft smile and a distracted look spread across her face. "I remember."

I rolled my eyes.

"See, this is the part that just doesn't work," I said. "Everybody likes the prince. Fine fellow, good egg, all that. But this part about him and the giant cock..."

"You do know he's not the most physically attractive guy in the kingdom?" Valerie asked.

"Well, yeah."

"Like his dad, right?"

"Right."

"And you never wondered how King Hollingsworth had managed to get himself a hot wife like Queen Kristal?"

"Of course, I have. Shit! You mean the King has a...This is really more than I want to know, Valerie. So that's it? You and the prince found true love, he brought you home, happily-ever-after, fucking you with his big dick?"

She shrugged. "Almost. Chris left the next day but promised to return. Meanwhile, Susan had a shit fit when she found out and tossed me out of the house. I headed off in what I thought was the direction of the city, but the forest was a lot bigger than I imagined."

"And the prince searched for you."

"For a whole year. So did Susan."

"Do I want to know how they found you?"

"I found this perfect piece of ebony and spent every night carving it and sanding it," she offered. It was a perfect non sequitur.

"To make a fire?"

Valerie nearly fell out of her chair laughing.

"You do have a lovely way with words, Joe Boston. Yes, to make a fire. I was a skinny little wretch by then, living off berries and roots. I was dirty—what little hair I had left was completely black, *all* my hair. I was very dirty. But I kept remembering that first night with Chris. And when that ebony was perfectly smooth and exactly the right shape, I—"

"Started singing again." I finished the sentence for her. "Okay, to recap. Your parents gave you up to a two lesbians. You ended up in the forest, and the prince heard you making love to one of them. He snuck in, made love in her place, she threw you out, and he found you by tracking the sound of your orgasm. Is that about right?"

"Exactly."

"See, Highness. That's just not going to work. Nobody's going to believe that."

"They believed your bear story."

"Nobody believed the bear story, Valerie. It was a fairy tale. There were talking bears, for God's sake. Who lived in a house. And ate porridge. They just liked the story. Ya gotta be able to go one way or the other. Fairy tale or real-life. And as real life goes, this story goes too far."

"So fix it up," she implored me. "Make it a fairy tale."

"I'd have to re-write the whole thing," I said.

"Like what?"

"Well, I'd have to take out the lesbians, for one thing. Your parents would have to give you to the witch. That also gets rid of the sex. We can keep the tower—"

"—and the long, blond hair?"

"Sure. But maybe make the prince attracted by something other than your, um, orgasms. Do you sing?"

"Sure. A little."

"Excellent. We'll have him come to your singing. Well, not come, but..."

I was blushing now.

"I get it, Joe," Valerie rescued me. But it'll still end happily ever after, though, right?"

"Oh, sure, sure. You could even read this to your twins when they're a little older. Unlike the real story, which..."

"I get it, I get it. Oh, Joe, it's perfect. I knew you were the right man for the job."

"There is one final thing, though. I don't think we ought to use your real name. Chris can just be 'the prince,' but Valerie makes the whole thing too real. What do you think about a name like…I don't know...How about Rapunzel?"

About Marshall Ian Key

Marshall Ian Key, who also goes by the alias Marsh Alien in order to avoid certain creditors related to the gaming industry, is a writer of comic romances. Some of them occasionally contain sexual material. Not so frequently that you would actually want to read them for that purpose, but often enough they you might not want your thirteen-year-old reading them at all. Up to you, though. Mr. Key worked as an organ grinder, an itinerant peddler, and a fishmonger before finally discovering a career suited to the present century. He currently resides outside a large Eastern metropolis in the United States. He enjoys skiing, fishing and white water canoeing. He can't actually do any of them; he just likes the idea of them.

THE LOTHIAN FARMER
By Willsin Rowe

In the Lothian region of southern Scotland, there lived a young farmer called Jack. He shared his tiny cottage with his beautiful wife, Lucy, and his three tufty-headed sons, Henry, Ian and Michael.

Jack worked hard every day, watching his sheep as they grazed, then he whiled away his evenings before the fire, smoking his cow-bone pipe and contemplating the week's upcoming weather. From time to time he would catch sight of his Lucy, who gazed lovingly at her master as she spun wool, cleared the scullery, bathed the children and prepared the next day's meals for the four hungry men in her life. Jack would gaze back at her and nod approvingly.

"Idle hands beg the Devil's influence," he would say to his wife and his sons. From his place at fireside he would supervise Lucy as she embroidered his wisdom on a banner.

"You shall hang this fine banner above the fireplace, good wife, and each time you stoke the fire you may take comfort that you are worthy."

He would keep his own hands busy tending his pipe as he pondered the elements.

One evening Lucy interrupted his reverie.

"My darling husband, 'tis Saturday tomorrow. Do not forget that I must be away into town. Callum is done patching our kettle."

"Aye, wife. Do go and see the blacksmith. You can have a good brew of tea boiling when I'm back from the fields."

But the next day, Jack arrived back home to three squealing boys and no wife. His mouth hardened in the certainty that she was still in town, dilly-dallying with the other wives. He removed his belt, ready to remind her of her duties to the men of the house.

When the sun dipped below the hills and Lucy still had not returned, Jack's annoyance turned to anger. Henry, Ian and Michael sat, beating their bowls on the table and bleating for their supper. Jack silenced them with a sharp look and sent Henry to bring back Lucy's mother.

Grandmother Regina arrived, dressed in her nightgown, her eyes heavy with sleep.

"What the dickens is the matter, boy?"

Jack pierced her with a glare. "Your flibberty-gibbet daughter is away who-knows-where. We need our supper, old woman."

"Aye? And are your fingers broken?"

"Och, ye old witch. Just be gettin' to your duties," he barked. He took his customary seat by the fire and lit up his pipe, his scowl easing only when dinner was served. When they had eaten, Jack returned to the fire.

"Old woman, I have weather to contemplate. The boys need washing and then must be put to bed."

"Perhaps they'd like their father to do it."

"'Tis not my place. Children are a man's blessing to his woman. Only when their voices grow deep shall they become my duty."

He turned back to the fire and tried to fathom the weather for the coming week. After a day of greater hardship than usual, he drifted to sleep in his chair, and woke to the clattering of Regina fixing breakfast.

"D'you have to be so noisy, woman?"

"We will be late for church, Jack. 'Tis time you boys all rose."

After a quick breakfast they all hurried into town and scuttled into the back pews. The service was augmented by the parson's plea for help on Jack's behalf.

"If anyone knows the whereabouts of lovely young Lucy, please would they tell us? She has duties to her family."

Jack scowled, angry that his private business had been made so public. When the service finally ended he stormed out, caring little if his boys were following. He was half-way home before he heard the call.

"Farmer Jack!"

'Twas the tall, young blacksmith calling out.

"Farmer Jack! Heed me! You must wait!"

"Och, what has your apron in such a whirl, Callum?"

"Jack, 'tis your bonnie wife."

"My Lucy? Where?"

"She was in among your boys, outside the church. I saw her with my own eyes, worrying at the lads' hair with a beastly big comb."

"Aye, that sounds like her, no doubt."

Jack turned back toward the churchyard, a steely look in his eyes, preparing to address his wife about her waywardness. The blacksmith called him again.

"Jack."

"Yes, Callum? What now?"

"Dinnae rush," said the blacksmith.

"I've missed her? She has scarpered again?"

"No, Jack. I saw it with my own eyes. One minute she was there, the next she just…vanished."

Jack frowned. "That cannae be. That sounds like…"

The blacksmith nodded. "Aye, laddie. Witchcraft."

Jack ran back to the churchyard, where he found his boys but, as Callum had said, there was no sign of Lucy.

Henry was holding his younger brothers in tight headlocks, making short work of any grooming their mother may have achieved.

"Boys!"

Henry quickly loosed his brothers and beamed his innocence. "Aye, father?"

"Your mother was here, was she not?"

"Aye, father. She was."

"Did she say where she has been?"

"No, father."

Michael, the youngest spoke up. "She said she's off with the fairies, dah."

Henry quickly cuffed his brother around the ear. "Shut it, you little pillock. She told you not to say."

Jack crossed his arms and scowled at his sons. "What is this nonsense, boys? Fairies?"

Henry looked at his shoes. "That's what she said, father. I made sure I didnae believe her."

Jack ruffled his eldest boy's hair. "Aye, lad. Dandy. There's nae such thing as fairies."

Michael and Ian glanced at each other. Ian pulled softly on his father's sleeve.

"But dah...ma wouldnae lie to us. No' ma."

Jack gazed into the hurt expression on his son's face. "Oh, yes she would, lad. If it were smoother than the truth. That's a woman's way, and it's time you learnt it."

Ian's sniffling caught on with young Michael, and before long the two boys were bawling. Even Henry's lip began to quiver. Jack stood abruptly and stared at them each in turn.

"Wee jessies," he spat and then turned on his heel, steaming homeward again. "Come now, babbies. There is work to be done."

The boys scurried after him, still wailing. Jack lifted his pace, driving his sons so hard that soon their crying was pushed aside by the need to breathe.

When they reached home, Regina, who had rushed home from church to fix lunch, swept straight past Jack and pulled her grandsons into an enormous hug.

"What's the matter, wee ones?"

Jack watched with disgust as eight-year-old Henry erupted in a babble made incoherent with breathlessness and caterwauling. Disgust turned to anger as Regina gave comfort where there should have been discipline.

"Shush, shush. Och, my lad, calm yourself. Let me put on—"

"Old woman!" Jack bellowed from the front door. "Put on the kettle. I need a strong cup of tea to aid my thoughts."

Regina gave them all a quick squeeze and went into the kitchen. For the sake of her grandsons, who she loved more than anything, she did her son-in-law's bidding.

"Here's your tea, boy."

Jack grunted and took a long sip. "Och, there's nae sugar in it."

"You don't take—"

"I take it when I take it!"

For the rest of the day, Jack sat in his chair and wondered what had become of his good and loyal wife. Why had she shirked her duties? Why was she not here to keep his house in good order, and his children out of trouble? He was a busy man, with sheep to watch and weather to contemplate.

Every day began and ended the same way. He would wake to the clattering of his cursed mother-in-law and his unruly boys as they worked together to make his breakfast. He would trudge out to watch his sheep, then stagger back home to a hot meal, which he would eat but not truly taste. He would retire early but spend half the night awake and cursing the shame his wife had brought on him.

The next Sunday, he took his sons to church, to pray for the swift return of his indolent wife. In the churchyard, he once again encountered the blacksmith, whose strong arms were barely contained in the sleeves of his good Sunday shirt.

"Any news, Callum?"

"Not a lot, Jack. Hello, boys."

Jack's three sons leapt and cavorted with the blacksmith, who always seemed happy to see them. Callum twirled them around to make them dizzy and then sent them off to play together.

As he watched them totter away, the young blacksmith smiled. Then, suddenly, his face grew white.

"Jack," he said. "Look."

Jack turned to behold his sons huddled on the grass, and in their midst, his Lucy, wielding her comb as a highlander wields his claymore.

"Och, look at you all. Like ratty old scarecrows, the three of you."

"Ma! Ma! Pick me up!"

"I cannae, Michael. You're too big."

"Pleeeeease?"

Jack had never seen Lucy resist Michael before, but she stood firm this time.

"Mikey, I'm so sorry. I truly cannae."

Suddenly, Jack found his voice, and even he was surprised with its strength.

"Lucy!"

His wife's beautiful face shot up like a startled hare. She stood, slowly and gracefully, her hands seeming to skim across the ragged tips of the boys' hair.

"Hello, husband. You look tired."

"Aye, wife. I've been doin' the work a two since–"

"Oh, aye? And you're keeping ma around for her looks?"

Jack gritted his teeth and stared into Lucy's eyes. "Your sons have loose lips. No doubt they get it from your side."

Lucy smiled weakly as she shook her head. "My love, we have so little time. Must we spend it quarrelling?" She brought her hands up to his face, but stopped short of touching him.

"So little time? You forget your place, girl. Where have you been?" He shrugged away his own question. "No matter. You're coming home now."

"No, love. I cannae."

"Why not?"

She closed her eyes, her sadness seeming to grow every second. "Och, if I explain it, Jack, 'twill seem even more ridiculous."

Jack suddenly became aware of the chill which seemed to cascade from Lucy's body, as if she were carved from ice. A ball of fear rolled down his throat and into his stomach, landing with a thud that threatened the integrity of his knees.

"Lucy...you're not dead, are you? A spirit?"

"Nae, my Jack. I've been taken from this world, but I'm no' dead." She seemed unable to look him in the eye as she spoke. A moment passed and then she drew in a sharp breath.

Jack turned to see what it was she was looking at, finding Callum the blacksmith leaning easily against a yew tree, a gaggle of young women all begging for his attention. Jack frowned deeply and turned back to his wife.

"Lucy, you must tell me what's happened."

"Love, if I tell you, you will only try to save me. I cannae let you."

"Woman! Tell me!"

Lucy sighed heavily and turned to the boys with a great show of reluctance. "Lads, would ye no' like to go and climb a tree or somethin'?"

When they'd left, Lucy turned back to her husband. "It was nothin' really, Jack, just...bad timing."

"What was?"

"'Twas when I went to see Callum. To get the kettle."

"Aye?"

"Well, I walked straight into his workshop, rather than the shop front. We've known each other all our lives, I saw no trouble."

"Aye?"

"He was working very hard, pounding away with his hammer, his skin glistening with sweat and I had...an impure thought."

"About Callum?

"Aye."

"But...he's a blacksmith. He's beneath you."

"Perhaps. But I had a vision where...he was above me. And working just as hard."

"Wife, are you trying to shame me all over again? First you leave me alone with your spawn, now you wish to tell the town that I'm no' good enough to have had you in the first place?"

"I'm no' sayin' that. And it's *you* who's tellin' the town. Keep your voice low, Jackie."

"Dinnae call me that. Harlot!"

Without another thought, Jack swung his arm to slap his wife, but fell heavily to the ground when his hand passed straight through her.

"What devilry is this?"

"I told you, love. I'm gone from this world. I'm with the Wicked Fairies. At that moment, when I had...that thought...I was clutching my moonstone pendant. It brought them straight to me."

Jack crossed himself automatically. "The Wicked Fairies? But…no, that's just a tale to scare the bairns, stop them from…bein' impure before they wed."

Lucy shook her head. "No, love. 'Tis true enough. And 'tis a strange level of Hades in which I now dwell. I must beg you, love, to forget me. Leave me here and raise our sons."

Jack felt anger in his heart, even greater than when he lost a sheep to a fox. Did these Wicked Fairies believe they could steal his wife from him?

"I will no' be defeated, Lucy. I will come for you and take you back."

"Love, you must not. 'Tis simple enough to enter, but to return you must pass tests. Tests the like of which you have never endured."

"I am man enough. Or do you doubt your husband…again?"

"Quite honestly, Jackie, I do. You know not what will be asked of you. And if you fail, you must remain here and…do as I do."

"Wife, I will do what must be done to bring you back. Then I will…remind you of your place." He patted the buckle of his belt.

Lucy held Jack's gaze for a moment, then sighed. "All right. There's but one chance. At midnight on All Hallows Eve, you must come to Green Meadow, alone. On that night, and that night only, can a man pass into the anteworld between where you are and where I am."

"To bring you back, wife, I would climb the highest mount."

Lucy began to fade. "Aye. Keep that thought in mind, husband."

"Ma!"

Henry and his brothers ran back.

"Where did ma go, dah?" Michael asked.

"I dinnae quite know, lad. But soon you can ask her yourself."

Time flew by until the day of All Hallows Eve. For the first time in memory, Jack bid his sons good night. Then, without a word to his toiling mother-in-law, he wrapped himself up warmly and slipped away from his cottage. The full moon's blue-white light gave the world a ghostly hue and Jack's breath clouded before him as he stamped from foot to foot to ward off the chill air of Green Meadow.

On the stroke of midnight, the wind died, leaving the world utterly silent. Jack felt his heart jump in his chest but he stood still, his eyes searching the meadow for signs of danger. He saw nothing but could hear voices, just whispers at first, then cries of pain. He felt his knees weaken and he turned to flee, stopping only when he remembered his wife's impudence.

He turned back and walked toward the middle of the meadow. The voices grew louder, and he believed he could hear Lucy in amongst them. Then, with one final step, he was assaulted by a warmth that put the Scottish summer to shame.

Jack tore off his overcoat and threw it to the ground. He glanced around himself and saw shapes beginning to form.

People. And they were writhing in pain.

But as the shapes became clearer, he realized that they were not people...and they were not in pain.

Most were tall and slender, with hair the color of sunset and wings the size of pillows, covered with downy white feathers.

The Wicked Fairies! And scattered among them, real people, all being forced to do...unspeakable things. Jack found Lucy, naked and on her knees, her hands caressing the belly of a beautiful youth while her–

"Lucy! Get that...thing...out of your mouth!"

With a sound like a cork popping from a bottle of whiskey, Lucy's lips pulled away from the flesh she'd been feasting on. She glanced around her but seemed unable to see past all the smooth male skin.

"Lucy! By Jove, when I get you back home, I swear I'll–"

"Who dares disturb my festival?"

Jack spun quickly and was confronted by a tall flame-haired woman.

She had beauty to rival a summer's day, but her eyes, like her voice, were pure ice. Jack found his own eyes seizing on the full redness of her mouth, her lips so tempting that he barely noticed her nakedness.

She crossed the meadow without taking a step, staring at his gaping form, studying the farmer as he would examine one of his flock.

"Oh, dear. Standards are slipping. Which one of you peasants brought this creature to me?"

Jack felt a surge of indignation at being addressed so dismissively. "I am no creature! I am a man, and I've come to take back what belongs to me. Och, I've never known a woman to address her masters in such a fashion!"

The woman seemed to glow with raw power as she rose on her wings. "I am the Fairy Queen, you filthy ape. For your insolence I should have you pulped right now."

Jack's anger dissipated as quickly as it had peaked, and he dropped to his knees. "Please, good Queen. I am here only to bring back my wife, who your people have kidnapped."

"Your wife? Oh...the lovely young Lucy." A winsome smile curled across the Fairy Queen's lips. "So you must be Jack."

"Aye, your majesty. I am."

"Lucy has told me much about you, farmer."

Jack beamed with pride as he looked over at his adoring wife. Even when subjected to the torturous attentions of one of—no, three of—the most beautiful fairy males imaginable, still her thoughts were only of him.

The Queen waved a delicate hand and two fairy males grasped Jack by the arms. They squeezed his limbs with fingers that stroked like silk but pressed like iron, and they wrenched him backwards, holding him still against a fallen tree. The Queen coasted across to him on her powerful wings.

"You wish to take Lucy back?"

"Aye, Queen."

"To come here, to risk your life and hers…that is not a matter to be treated lightly."

"Queen, I am strong, brave and proud, and my wife has forgotten herself. I will take her back to my world. My sons need care, my house needs cleaning, my belly needs feeding."

The Queen drifted, looking him over again from head to toe, a grin curling across her full lips. She nodded curtly to the two guards who held Jack's arms. In seconds they had torn the clothes from his body.

"All you've told me, farmer, is that you need a servant. Why should Lucy be that servant? Why should I give her up?"

"Och, she's mine. A dutiful wife's place is in her man's home."

The Queen crossed her arms, pressing her breasts together, drawing Jack's attention away from her lips. Her eyes squinted as she studied his face. "And what of Lucy's desires?"

"She could want nothing more than to serve her man and his sons."

The chuckle that bubbled up from the Queen's slender throat held all the darkness of a well in winter. "I meant her bodily desires."

"Och, dinnae be daft. She doesnae have any. The conjugal times are for a man. Women dinnae enjoy it, but the dutiful wife shows her devotion by accepting her man's…presence."

The Queen floated aside to allow Jack full view of his voluptuous young wife, now pressed warmly between two willowy fairy maidens, her lips exploring the firm breasts of one as her feminine fancy was caressed by the other. There was no mistaking the expression of ecstasy on her face.

"She has no man with her right now, yet…"

Though she left the sentence hanging, she noticed Jack's manhood no longer was.

Jack coughed gruffly. "She's…er…under the 'fluence."

She gripped Jack's face, squashing his lips together. "Young Lucy has been the brightest catch we've ever had. Desire is a strange flower, farmer. The more it is neglected, the stronger it grows. She would not be here now, had you...tended her flower properly."

"I beg your pardon?"

"You must do more than beg to receive *my* pardon, ape. Little wonder that Lucy was so...*captivated* by the young blacksmith."

"That's a lie!"

"We fairies may be wicked, brute, but we only pick those who are...ripe. And I can tell you...we've had none riper than lovely Lucy."

The Queen rose again on her diaphanous wings and drifted around Jack's naked body. She pressed at the meat of his shoulders, trailed her fingers across his neck, pushed him forward so that she could assess the tautness of his buttocks. The corners of her mouth curled up as she breezed around. Presently, she lit atop the fallen tree, her knees pressing against Jack's hips from behind.

"Turn around, beast," she growled. Sensing his hesitation, she nodded again to the fairy men, who lifted Jack bodily and spun him to face their Queen.

Where Jack's eyes had been drawn to her mouth before, now he found them falling to the patch of fiery hair between her long legs, and the sliver of glistening flesh therein.

"You foul, stinking beast," spat the Queen. "All meat and sweat. So high and mighty in your domain, yet here, in my land, you are worthless. Any one of us here could snap you in pieces with only one hand. Kneel before me, swine!"

Dreading the soft steel fingers of his guards, Jack fell immediately to his knees, finding himself wedged between the sleek thighs of the beautiful Queen.

"If you truly wish to return to your world, and to take Lucy with you, you must pass three tests. Fail any one test and you will take Lucy's place, serving us here for eternity. Do you accept these terms?"

"Aye, Queen. I do."

"Then your first test begins now." She curled her fingers into Jack's hair and drew him forward. "You must learn that the female has far more capacity for pleasure than you steaming brute males ever will."

Jack blew a raspberry, but his derision was cut short as his mouth slipped against the soft, wet opening of the Queen's glory.

"Mmm…very nice touch, beast."

Jack held still, the scent of the Queen's arousal made robust by proximity. It tickled at his nose and throat as her down-soft fur tickled at his lips and nostrils.

His mind was frozen by the sin of the moment. His tongue, however, seemed to think independently as it stretched out, sneaking between the curly hair and fleshy lips, sinking deeply into the warm heart of the Queen's quim.

"A little deeper, brute."

The only way for Jack to dig deeper was to press his mouth up against her, and he did so without hesitation. He rolled his tongue inside her as he explored her essence, part oyster, part ocean, just a hint of rich forest soil.

His curled his hand around his rigid member, scarcely aware what he was doing. He had barely begun to stroke himself when his hand was pulled away from his crotch by the now-familiar fingers of his guards.

The Queen's voice had become less bark and more moan. "You must learn how to give without receiving, primitive. A little higher."

With his goal clear in his mind, Jack did as he was told.

"Do you feel that, farmer? That little lump?"

"Aye," Jack murmured between mouthfuls.

"Put it between your teeth. Now, bite it, gently."

Jack attacked the Queen's pleasure button with the fervor of a starving man. Only the twisting of her long fingers in his hair made him stop.

"Animal! When you see nought but the destination, you are blind to the journey! You will pass this test only when you bring me to the highest plateau."

"I dinnae understand."

"Dunce! Let me put it simply. How do you know when you've finished...conjugating?"

"Och. I squirt my juice. It's obvious."

"And the feeling you have when you...hmm...*squirt*?"

"Aye, it's wonderful. Like I'm a lemon that's been squeezed dry."

"Lovely," the Queen murmured through curled lips. "That is the feeling you need to create in me."

Jack frowned heavily as he looked up at her face. He started to talk, then stopped and shook his head.

"I still dinnae–"

"Just put your mouth back on me and do as I say."

Her tone suggested immediate harm, so Jack pressed his mouth back against the scented wonder between her thighs and awaited instructions.

The Queen placed her hands either side of his face. "First, brute, make circles with your tongue. Trace the shape of me, top to bottom, side to side. Mmm...that's it."

Jack continued following the Queen's directions, licking where he was told to lick, sucking what he was told to suck. He ached to pleasure himself, but the heat in his groin was suppressed by the fire in his heart; the desire to bring his wayward wife to heel.

"Mmm...farmer, for someone so obviously inexperienced, you are doing a very good job. Indeed, the only novice better than you was your lovely wife. But then, *she* knew where to find everything."

Jack dared not let his surprise register, lest he break the rhythm of his mouth. Instinctively, he sensed that his goal was near.

"Brute...what is that trite saying you use all the time? Lucy told me it...oh, yes. 'Idle hands beg the Devil's influence'."

Jack hummed his affirmation.

"Then it is perhaps time for you to ward off your Devil. Release him, guards. Now, animal, bring both hands up to where your mouth is."

Under the Queen's impatient direction, Jack licked his fingers and slid two of them firmly, deeply into the tight, moist fissure before him. Amazed by the heat that clutched his fingers, he gasped.

"Now lick your thumb and press it there…that's right, on that little bump…ohh…"

Jack ground away at the apex of the Queen's slit and watched her skin growing pink all over. He almost lost his place as she fell back gently onto her wings and opened herself up completely.

"Now, brute, it is your mouth that is idle. 'Tis time to put it back to work."

Automatically, Jack gushed his tongue back inside the Queen's warmth, moaning anew at her spicy flavor.

"No, brute. Not there. Down."

Jack crept his mouth downward.

"Oh, for pity's sake, you dunderhead! Right down! To the other one!"

Jack quailed at the Queen's fury. "But…that's where you, er…let out your…uh…"

"I am a Fairy Queen, you animal! I do nothing of the sort! But that little spot gives me pleasure…and isn't *my* pleasure what you are striving for right now?"

Jack hesitated. This was a notion that had never occurred to him, something that seemed should never be done. A quick glance at his errant wife, writhing beneath the attentions of so many wet mouths, gave him back his steel, and he pressed his tongue to the Queen's rippled rosebud.

"Good work, creature. Don't stop…yes, fingers and lips…and tongue…oh, my…"

Jack had sensed in the Queen the avarice and brutality of a starving fox. In one moment, it seemed she lost any pretence of civility, as she curled her body tightly and then stretched out, shooting up from the fallen log, bellowing her ecstasy with such power that the trees around them shook. A dozen feet above Jack's moist face, she rolled like a tongue through the air, her slender fingers tracing the points of pleasure which Jack had only moments before been tasting.

Slowly she returned to the ground. She placed her hand on Jack's shoulder.

"Rise, brute. You have passed the first test."

"As I said I would."

Jack stood, his member still rigid and aching for release.

"Do not get cocky, boy. The second test is a far greater challenge."

"I fear no test. I am man enough."

"You will need to be." She nodded to the two males who had held Jack so firmly. "Brey! Kale! Prepare this...*man*...for the second test."

Jack was seized again, but this time the fingers lost their steel, keeping only their silk as they fluttered across his skin. As the hands crept searchingly all over his body he tensed, jumping like a shot arrow when the clenched mounds of his buttocks were bisected by Brey's strong hand.

"What kind of lunacy is this, Queen? Men do not commune with other men!"

"These are not men, brute. These are fairies."

"I'll not do it! It is wrong!"

"Then your Lucy is lost to you." Leaning forward, the Queen pressed her red lips against the side of Jack's face. She drove the scent of her body into his nose as she breathed honey into his ear.

"Do you forget how you wish to take her home, to stretch her across your knee, to slap her bare, round bottom raw? To remind her who her master is?"

The image of Lucy's bottom danced behind Jack's closed eyes. He imagined using his hand, and not his belt, to teach her, and a strangled moan escaped his throat.

The Queen continued. "Do you not recall how sweetly she held you between her legs? Or how beautiful her face is when you hold her down? Oh, how delicious her fearful expression as you force yourself into her."

The images and memories flooded Jack's mind. Brey's hands began to work at the insides of his thighs, and if he kept his eyes closed he found that it felt quite…acceptable.

"Lust is like making tea, farmer. Men are fire, hot in a heartbeat. Women are water, and need time to simmer. The fire must lick at the kettle for some time."

"Uhhh…"

The Queen continued her murmuring. "Do you wish to learn of the second test?"

"Aye…uh…" Jack moaned as a strong hand grasped his manhood and began to massage it.

"Brute, you must learn how it is to start cold…and to be made to finish just as you are beginning to steam. You must learn how it feels when you are the weaker partner. In short, you must learn how it feels for Lucy."

"Uhhh…"

"Brute, I would make a suggestion to you. While ever it is *you* being pleasured, your chances of passing the second test are slim. Two men must climax…if one is you, then you fail."

"But…no, I cannae do that!" He indicated Kale, who was running his closed hand around the fattened peak of Jack's lance.

The Queen sighed heavily. "Beast, you came into my world with intent. Would you falter now? Think again on your lovely wife. Look across at her. Watch as her beautiful pink mouth slides easily up and down the hardened spear of that male. See how the male behind her is driving smoothly into her."

Jack groaned with desire as he watched Lucy being pleasured in ways he had never dreamed about. "But she is a woman. Everything being done to her is sinful, but still she is built for it. Women receive what men give."

The Queen's voice turned cold. "Farmer…look closely. She is using nothing that you do not possess."

Jack stared intently, and realized that the male behind her was plunging heartily in where no babies would ever be made. He felt the blood drain from his face as the Queen continued.

"Two males to please, two holes with which to do so. I'm sure you can find a way. Watch your wife for inspiration."

Jack watched Lucy for a moment, the heat of his jealousy thawing out the cold fear in his chest. He studied her mouth, the hunger with which she drew the meaty length in, the abandon as her lips fattened against the hardness, the whirling of her tongue around the sightless head.

With every passing moment he found more and more that he needed to punish his wife for. He closed his eyes and steeled himself for what was to come. A last moment of bluster escaped him.

"Well, Queen, I always say anything a woman does can always be better done by a man."

Working as a farmer had, over the years, brought Jack in close contact with his sheep. On occasion, there had been need to work a ram over in its nether regions, either for docking or cleaning. He gritted his teeth and prepared to picture the two smooth fairy males as nothing more than rams needing a thorough cleaning.

He knelt between Brey and Kale and grasped their prongs. He studied them for a moment, compared them to his own and felt pride when he realized his was both longer and thicker.

Slowly at first, using just his thumbs, he rubbed at the sensitive undersides right near the tiny mouths of the rods.

"Farmer, you are going to need to work harder than that. Did I not mention that you must pass these tests before daybreak?"

"You most certainly did not!"

"Whoops-a-daisy."

Jack turned his attention back to his work. The two fleshy rods were only inches from his face. He caught the same earthy essence from them that he had found between the

Queen's thighs, though with undertones more of the sand than the sea. He felt Brey's hands come to rest on the back of his head. With his eyes closed, the young farmer murmured darkly to all around him.

"Any uh you...*fairies*...tell anyone about this..." His words were knocked aside as Brey's manhood dived between his lips. Jack felt as if his eyes were being forced from his head as the meaty lance tickled the back of his throat.

Jack tried to pull his head back, but Brey was far stronger, driving forward and back, treating the farmer's mouth as if its sole reason for existence was to swallow the fairy's sword.

"That's it, beast." Brey's voice was almost musical. "You know you want it. Just relax...yeeessss..."

Jack found wisdom in the words, easing his muscles, letting the juicy sliding motion lull him. He even began to hum.

The Queen sat back atop the fallen tree, her long fingers exploring her own slit as she watched the action before her.

"Look boys. Seems our little farmer here has found a way to...take his medicine."

Jack hadn't realized until then that his own rod had stayed very stiff. He desperately wished his right hand was free.

Kale grasped Jack's hair and pulled the farmer backward, popping his mouth wetly off the end of Brey's lance. "I am here too, animal. When is it my turn?"

Jack turned to Kale and began to take the other fairy's flesh in, having learned very quickly exactly what to do.

"Do not forget me, brute."

Jack tried to work Brey's manhood with his left hand, but it was too difficult while ever he was sucking on the lance before him. Brey slapped Jack's hand away.

"There is only one way we will achieve this, beast."

Already on his knees, Jack sensed Brey kneeling behind him. Distracted by the strange feeling of having a male inside his mouth, Jack didn't at first realize what was about to happen.

He felt Brey's long finger, wet with spit, press against his fundament. To cry out in protest would be a sign of weakness, and Jack suspected that would only excite these fairy men further. He reconciled what was to come by picturing Lucy in his place. Indeed, he fully intended to pass on all his new learning to her when he got her home.

In truth it was not an unpleasant feeling to have a slender finger nudging into him, and he had used that hole all his life, after all…other than the direction of motion, what difference was there?

Very soon, Jack knew exactly the difference. Brey's lance was smooth and slender, reflective of the fairy male himself, but was still much larger than a finger.

Jack groaned, more from surprise than pain, as Brey drove himself deeply into the untried cavern. It hurt, most assuredly…but in the same way as alcohol stings on a cut. It was a necessary pain, and it created warmth that would smooth the sharp edges off any further soreness.

Brey and Kale began to work in harmony, pressing forward and drawing back in unison, pumping Jack as if he were a sailor's squeezebox. The motion became rhythmic, like a cradle being rocked, and Jack found himself warming all over.

Jack squeezed his eyes closed as fingers burrowed into his hips, mimicking the lances that were digging into his body. Never had he felt so powerless.

Suddenly Kale grasped Jack's head and thrust two, three, four times, so deeply that Jack could barely breathe. Behind him, at the same moment, Brey grunted heavily. The two fairy males pulled noisily from either end of Jack's body and rose gently on their downy wings, their juice bursting from their lances and gushing onto the grass.

Jack drew in a long breath and tried keep from collapsing. He had always believed that pleasing a man in bed was as simple as laying back and letting him have away at you. He looked across to Lucy and considered their time together, years where he had never gone without his desires being fulfilled. Of course, 'twas true she had had only *one* male to contend with. He took pride in his strength, having proved once again that men were the superior beings.

His efforts suddenly weighed heavily on him, his elbows and hips loosening as he fell to the grass. He felt himself drifting away when the Queen's voice cooed into his ear again.

"Farmer Jack. That was but the second test. There is little more than an hour until daybreak. You must prepare yourself."

Jack dragged himself to his feet, his lips stiff with grim tension, his manhood stiff with relentless provocation. "After what I've just done, Queen, I am ready for anything."

With a surprising tenderness, the Queen placed her hand on Jack's shoulder. "You do not know how wrong you are, boy." She switched her attention to a small gathering of fairies at the edge of the meadow. "Laika, Kyrna and…Triskelle. Here, now."

Three fairy maidens disentangled themselves from their various partners and flitted across to kneel at their Queen's feet. The Queen touched each on the head in turn and they stood fluidly.

"I have chosen you three for this creature's final test. Do not disappoint me." She turned her cold green eyes to Jack. "Do you think yourself ready for your final test, farmer?"

Scanning the tall and slender fairy maidens before him, Jack hesitated.

"Am I to…to bring each of these maids to that same plateau that you reached?"

The Queen's laughter was less cruel this time. "No, brute. Their pleasure is not your concern. You shall learn the art of endurance."

"Endurance? I am to…keep my juice?"

"Poetic as always, but yes. There is but an hour until daybreak. You must last until the first slice of sunlight catches the tops of those trees. No matter what is done to you."

His lance already bellowing for release, Jack doubted he could withstand the attentions of a bearded nun for more than a minute, let alone three of the most comely lasses he'd ever set eyes upon.

The Queen clapped her hands twice and the maidens, Laika, Kyrna and Triskelle, floated across to him.

The young farmer glanced from one to the next in quick succession. Their hair was red, like their Queen's, though not quite so vibrant, and it tumbled in gentle curls over their wings and shoulders, reaching to the bottoms of their tender breasts. Save for the Queen herself, they were the most beautiful lasses he had ever seen, easily as tall as himself and with slender limbs and pale, faultless skin.

Triskelle spoke first, her voice as musical as a mountain stream. "This shall be so easy."

Laika continued. "Oh, yes. The work is already done. He is beginning to weep."

Jack touched his cheeks, wondering if that were true, but found them dry.

Kyrna knelt before him. "No, not there, farmer." Her mouth felt like damp silk as she drew his pole inside it, sliding it back out with a comical popping sound. "There."

Jack clenched his hands into hammers and beat at his own thighs, trying to put from his mind the sensations of pleasure that threatened to end his challenge. He thanked his God as Kyrna stood up without feasting further on his manhood.

Laika pressed in against Kyrna. "How did he taste?"

Kyrna licked her lips and closed her eyes. "Raw. Beastly."

"Mmm. That sounds…naughty. May I?"

Laika slipped her pink mouth over Kyrna's and kissed her with the slow tenderness of a flame melting a candle. Their tongues, even pinker than their lips, curled over each other and danced like smoke.

Jack felt his skin growing tight all over his body as the two maidens embraced before him. He was aroused beyond any point he could have imagined, but took comfort that while ever they were embracing each other, they were not touching him. It was a very cold comfort.

As he watched, Kyrna pulled her lips from Laika's and swept her tongue down the other maiden's willowy throat, stopping only when she had the cherry of Laika's nipple between her teeth.

Jack groaned with desire, then grunted with shock as Triskelle curled her long arms around him from behind, pressing her palms against his chest and her breasts against his back. Her sweet breath, an intoxicating floral scent, gushed through his hair.

She swept her hands down until she had one on his prong and one around his sack. Her skin had the softness of a baby lamb's ears, her hands the same steely strength as the rest of her kind. She squeezed, just softly, and it stole the breath from Jack's chest.

He ground his eyelids together, trying in vain to remove from his mind the image of Kyrna suckling sweetly on Laika's breasts. When he opened them again the maids had dropped to the soft, cool grass and Laika was delving her tongue into Kyrna's navel. Kyrna's moans were like birdsong and they grew in volume as Laika slipped her mouth down to tickle at the pink velvet between her lover's thighs.

Just as Laika's tongue slipped into the juicy slit before her, Triskelle released Jack's rod, for which the farmer again thanked God. His respite was short-lived, though, as the supple maiden flitted around in front of him and pressed her breasts against his mouth.

In his frenzied state, Jack couldn't resist the temptation, and he drew Triskelle's raw pink nipple into his mouth, gnawing at it like a dog gnaws at gristle.

"Ohh…" Triskelle's voice was even more musical as she moaned. "You truly are a beast, farmer…ohh…" She twirled her long fingers into his hair and held him against her, then pushed his face skyward so she could kiss him. "Mmm…you *do* taste coarse."

She flitted aside and allowed Jack to once again watch Kyrna and Laika. He felt an almost physical jolt as he watched Laika devouring her companion. Where there had been the tenderness of a candle flame there was now an inferno of tongue, lips, teeth and fingers. Jack tried to look away, fearing he would shoot his juice simply by watching.

Triskelle hovered, her back to the aching farmer as she, too, watched her fellow fairies. "Mmm...how does that feel, Kyrna?"

"Ohh...it feels as good as when you do it, Triskelle."

Jack moaned again. Hearing him, Triskelle looked over her shoulder, a sly smile curling her beautiful mouth. She lit before him, just inches between her wingtips and the farmer's body. She made sure she did not impede his view of the two maidens as they made love.

"Are they not beautiful, beast?"

"Uhhh...aye..."

"Do you not wish to join them?"

"Uhhh...aye..."

"Or would you perhaps rather...join me?" She allowed her wings to spread slowly, revealing her long, toned back, all soft muscle and snowy skin.

To Jack, it could not have been more arousing had she been drawing her thighs apart to reveal her feminine glory. The fluid motion, and the gentleness with which she controlled her strong wings, left his throat clutching for air to breathe and sounds to make.

He turned his attention back to Laika and Kyrna, who had rolled a little closer to him. Now Kyrna was on her hands and knees and Laika was resting on her wings, still delving her tongue into the silken slit of her lover. The beautiful roundness of Kyrna's bottom was pointing directly toward him, and he felt his pole quiver like a divining rod, aching to delve into the moisture it had found.

He jumped again with shock as something began to caress his manhood. He looked down to find Triskelle on her knees before him, still watching her companions, while the feathered tips of her wings stroked lightly up and down the length of Jack's rod.

He had thought her skin soft, but he had nothing in his life's experience to compare with the softness of her wings, the downy feathers seeming to move like tiny fingers, each pressing and releasing, clutching and biting, drawing ever more blood into the already straining flesh.

He feared he would be finished, and he pulled back. He recalled the rules as the Queen had said them. He had to resist shooting. Nowhere had she said he must involve himself with the maidens at all.

Sensing his determination, Triskelle dropped into a crawl and swayed across the grass to plant her mouth in the moist heat of Laika's ripe orange bush. For what was probably a minute, but felt to Jack like an hour, Triskelle's tongue drew hearty moans from Laika's throat, moans which quivered against Kyrna's quim.

Her face covered with Laika's wetness, Triskelle looked back over her shoulder at Jack.

"Are you sure you do not wish to join us?"

He wanted it beyond wealth, beyond power, beyond all the sheep in Scotland, but he had to stand firm. He coughed out a grunt of frustration, his rod slapped against his belly and he wondered how he could stand any firmer than he already did.

He eyed the lightening sky. His farmer's experience told him he had at most a quarter hour until the final test was won. He turned back to the writhing maidens, unable to resist the splendor of their love-making.

The Queen floated in beside him, also watching the maidens intently. She only whispered, but it was as clear as a shout.

"Farmer, we have had none who has lasted so long before."

"I told you I am strong. I am growing tired of this now." He tried to sound convincing.

The Queen's laughter blew the bravado from his heart. "Do you really think we have done all we can?"

Before he could answer, she again clapped her hands twice. The three maidens uncurled from each other with a series of delicious sucking sounds. Kyrna flew across and landed straight before Jack, immediately drawing his hardness deep into her mouth. Triskelle rolled onto her back and Laika flowed like honey over her body until they each could drink from the other's flower.

Not content with simply suckling at Jack's prong, Kyrna embedded her teeth into the fleshy tube and began pulling back on it. Fearing the strength in her jaws, Jack allowed himself to be drawn along until he stood within a desperate, searching arm's length of all three gorgeous maidens.

Slipping his spear from her lips, Kyrna began to bark out orders. "On your knees, brute!"

Jack fell instantly, his rod resting between the upturned cheeks of Laika's heavenly derriere. He jolted as Triskelle took his satchel into her mouth and gnawed lightly.

"Put it in her!" Kyrna grasped Jack's moist rod and pointed it at Laika's quim. With all his might, the young farmer tried to resist, but Kyrna pushed him forward until his lance was dipped deeply into the boiling heat of Laika.

He could resist no more, and grasped the young fairy's hips, thrusting like a ram on heat. Triskelle's tongue danced all over his sack and he turned his face to the sky to bellow with pleasure.

His roar was cut short as Kyrna planted her velvet flower down over his mouth. He opened his eyes to see her hovering on her wings, her thighs wrapped around his head and her lip squeezed between her teeth.

Lucy called out to her man. "Remember, love, you do not have to finish them. You only have to avoid finishing yourself."

He pulled his mouth free for an instant. "If I finish them, though, they'll not have time to get their steam back before daybreak."

Lucy sighed heavily and shook her head. "Oh, husband. Has this night taught you nothing? I fear it matters not whether you win or lose."

Jack had no time to ponder her words. He bit insistently at the hard little lump at the peak of Kyrna's lips and slid his tongue all over the softness around it. In seconds he felt her thighs grip him as the Queen's had done and suddenly she burst upward like ocean spray and twirled across the meadow, humming with the release of climax.

"Right," said Jack. "One down."

He continued grinding his hips against Laika's rump, sensing in her a quake which had nothing to do with fear. The heat of her body rose, bringing a scent of pollen and honey with it.

A moment later Laika popped off the end of his prong like a cork from a bottle, and flew upward, entwining with Kyrna in a sensual embrace. He watched as the two maidens caressed each other's wings and body. The cold night air bit into his soaking wet rod and he drew comfort from it, hoping it would suppress his climax.

Triskelle rolled onto her front and took in the deep sensual aroma of his lance, coated as it was in the nectar of Laika's womanly flower. Her huge green eyes looked up into his and she smiled archly.

Jack stood up and glanced at the sky. Less than five minutes remained. He was nearly done. A heavy flapping sound drew his attention to Laika and Kyrna, who landed beside Triskelle and formed a wall of temptation.

The maidens looked at each other and seemed to reach an unspoken agreement. Triskelle swept her tongue all the way along Jack's manhood, from root to tip, then, as if it were a piece of rock candy, she handed it across to Laika.

"My lovely, your flower tastes even better when 'tis mixed with beast," said Triskelle.

Laika swirled her tongue all around the brazen dome of Jack's rod, then passed it along to Kyrna.

"Hmm...but I taste better on your fingers, Triskie."

Kyrna grabbed Jack's rod with both hands, swooped them along its length and then licked her fingers. "You're both wrong. What tastes so sweet is…victory." She opened her mouth and poured Jack's meat into it, clamping hard with her tongue and cheeks, her lips and fingers.

"Oh…God…help me…" Jack whimpered, and in a fleeting moment, he thought back on the night's events. The things he had done tonight that he'd never even thought could be done. No wonder Lucy had warned him away! The wanton harlot wanted to keep this all for herself!

Suddenly, he didn't care if he failed…he wanted never to leave this.

He whimpered and felt his bones shudder as the tension in his belly mounted.

Triskelle pulled away from him, leaving him anchored achingly close to the point of no return. His eyes shot open as if he'd been thrown from a horse.

"I think he's about to come, girls."

Triskelle lifted lightly from the ground and began to circle Jack's body, sliding her wings and her infant-soft skin all over him. As her tight breasts buffeted his face, her hot quim slid across his hip. She circled and danced, pressing herself to every sensitive part of his body.

A moment later, Laika and Kyrna joined her, until there was barely an inch of Jack's body that was not covered with heavenly flesh.

As they danced all over him, they took turns moaning smut into his ears.

"Oh, farmer…come on my breasts."

"No, no, I want it on my face, brute."

It was Triskelle who finally defeated Jack's resolve.

"Oh, beast," she hummed. "I need you to come in my mouth…please…"

The aching need in her voice, and the notion of filling her licentious mouth with his fluid drove Jack plummeting over the edge. He grasped his rod, ground it hard and roared with desire as he pumped his juice out into the meadow.

With the reflexes of frightened birds, the three maidens recoiled, no longer able to disguise their distaste.

"Eurgh. Didn't he taste awful?" muttered Kyrna. The maidens flitted back across to their partners and slipped back into the warm embraces they had abandoned to do their Queen's bidding.

In his post-climactic haze, Jack heard none of what was said. He collapsed onto his belly. His breath was raw in his throat, and he could barely lift his head. An elegant pair of feet landed on the grass before him.

"That is too bad, farmer. Look, if you can...the sun has just begun to kiss the trees. You had but a handful of seconds to last and you would have been free."

When his breath slowed and his strength returned, Jack rolled into a sitting position.

"Aye, Queen. And I could ha'e done it. But why would I leave this? To go back to whining bairns, a witch of a mother-in-law and a disobedient wife who, while pretty enough, is no match for three fairy maidens."

The Queen nodded slowly. "Brute, if you are typical of your kind, then 'tis no mystery why Lucy's desires brought her to us." With all her might she grasped Jack by his jaw, lifting him bodily from the ground. "Guards!"

Brey and Kale swooped in and grasped Jack's arms, this time without a hint of silk.

"Put him with the other slaves."

"Slaves? I dinnae under–"

"Of course you don't. You are but a foul, stinking beast. Did you think this an ordinary night? 'Tis Hallowe'en. The one night when our slaves, like your lovely Lucy, are given freedom to experience the life of the Wicked Fairies."

Jack glanced across at Lucy, his fear turning instantly to anger. "Why did you no' tell me, wife?"

"I warned you not to come for me. I foretold the danger. But you saw only your loss, and you came here with a heart burning in envy."

The Queen scratched her nail down Jack's chest. "'Twas with love and devotion that Lucy tried to keep you safely in the human world. Though I'm sure she now wonders why." She turned to Jack's selfless wife. "You are now free, Lucy. Enjoy your young blacksmith. I'm sure he will be a fine father."

Lucy began to walk away, turning back at the edge of the meadow. "Fare thee well, husband. The work is not too hard, 'tis just dirty and neverending."

She stood still and looked into her husband's eyes for the last time. The moment the sun's rays touched her hair she vanished, back to her own world.

The Queen dropped Jack heavily onto his feet. "Now, slave. Remember how I told you I don't use that hole you were licking?"

"Aye?"

"I was lying. Open your mouth."

"What?"

"You don't expect me to just drop it on the ground, do you? I *am* a Fairy Queen."

About Willsin Rowe

Willsin Rowe falls in love with a scent, a playful expression or an act of casual intimacy more easily than with physical beauty. When confronted by both he is a lost cause. He has done many things over and over. He has done even more things only once. He has half-done more things than he cares to admit. He visited Europe with the aching need to see Scotland, and succumbed to the clichés when he fell in love with Paris instead. He doesn't yet know if he can ski, speak Italian or keep calm in a life-threatening situation, but he has his suspicions.

He plays bass in a swampy blues band. He loves to sing and doesn't let his voice get in the way. Since he became a parent the crises of employment have paled. He commutes to and from work on a motorbike. When he rides he is a lone wolf, a hunter. He is primeval, and for twenty minutes at a time, he is in control of his destiny.

He loves the complications of English and the naturistic charm that results. He fears that streamlining it allows function to usurp form. Nature is beautiful without adherence to symmetry or consistency. He is intelligent but not sensible. He is polite but inappropriate. He is passionate but fearful. He is honest but reticent. He is not scruffy enough or stylish enough to be cool.

A LOVER FOR CACHÉ
By Dakota Trace

Chapter One

Caché Ululani stood in front of the wall of glass and stared down at the bustling street below. It was a surprisingly warm spring day and many were taking advantage of the nice weather after a long cold winter. But not Caché! She hadn't left her penthouse suite in years, and though her exile was self-imposed, with the Internet and online shopping, there'd been no reason for her to leave. Everyone and everything else came to her.

As the CEO of Ululani Beauty Products, she preferred to stay behind the scenes. So far behind, at times, most of her people mistakenly took her twin sister Thalie, for her. She smiled softly at the thought of her younger and much more beautiful sister. Even though she'd been born seven minutes ahead of Thalie, her younger sister had stolen the show from the moment she was born. She didn't begrudge her sister the attention. Thalie couldn't help the fact that the beautiful features that allowed her to be the chief model for Ululani Beauty Products had been significantly lacking on Caché. Her features were a softer, plainer version of her sister's incredible beauty. Not to mention her sister was a lot sweeter and nicer than Caché could ever be. She had earned the name 'The Beast of Ululani' honestly. She was a tough competitor and astute businesswoman despite being almost a recluse.

A knock on the door had her turning around. The only person who'd dare breach her 'inner sanctuary' was supposed to be thousands of miles away. Frowning, she walked over to the big plush desk chair where she oversaw the running of the entire Ululani empire. Sinking into it, she bade the person enter before spinning the chair around. She was in no mood to be stared at this afternoon. They had better have a good reason for the most unwelcome interruption.

"Ms. Ululani?" The hesitant voice of her sister's executive assistant was a surprise.

"What is it, Lori?" Her brisk tone was impatient.

"I'm afraid there's an issue that's arisen with Ms. Thalie's schedule. There's been a mix up and the reporter who was supposed to come next week is here now."

Stroking the scar on the side of her face, she prayed for patience. "Then simply reschedule the appointment, Lori. Problem solved."

"I tried that, Ms. Ululani, but..."

"...I wouldn't take no for answer." The dark masculine voice had Caché cringing.

"Oh, for the love of god!" Softly but not quite under her breath, she began to mutter. "This is the last thing I need today. All I wanted to do was curl up with Casey Addington's book which I've been waiting for so impatiently, but now I'm stuck dealing with some intrepid reporter my sister's dumped in my lap."

"Well the last thing I've ever been called is an intrepid reporter but I suppose I can play the role if you want." As the masculine voice drew nearer, Caché had to close her eyes. There was no way she was going to give into the flirtatious offer she heard in his voice, even if it did have her nerve endings tingling.

"I'm sorry, Mr..."

"Stone. Caleb Stone."

"Well, Mr. Stone, I'm sorry but my sister is out of town. You'll simply have to reschedule your appointment." When silence grew longer, she thought he'd taken the hint and left.

"You know, sweetheart, it's terribly rude to kick a guy out without even looking at him."

"I don't need to look at a person to tell them to leave. In fact most people I know would've cleared out already. Evidently you're either denser than most, or more obstinate. My bet is you're just more stubborn than most normal men would be, even when it's obvious you're not welcome."

"Well I wouldn't have gotten as far as I have if I weren't a persistent ass."

Rubbing the bridge of her nose, Caché mentally went over her options. It was quite obvious the man wasn't going to be run off by her fabled 'charm'. Perhaps once he got a good look at her face, he might high-tail it out of her office. Spinning around, she reached under the edge of her desk to press the security button. It couldn't hurt to have Enrique come up.

"Listen Mr. Stone, I…" Watching his face for any disgust or pity, she was surprised when he cocked his head and seemed to examine her.

"It's Caleb, and you must know you look incredibly like your sister."

Gritting her teeth, she continued, "So I've been told. Caleb, I really don't have the time or inclination to cross swords with you. The best I can offer you is rescheduling your missed appointment when Thalie's returned. She's the one who gives interviews. Although I'm surprised she granted you one. She's notoriously bad about talking to the press under the best of circumstances."

"Yeah, she once referred to my job not being fit for a cockroach, but a guy's gotta eat." As if on cue, his stomach rumbled. "I missed breakfast this morning, so why don't you join me for a late brunch? We can get to know each other and you'll find out I'm not that bad a guy despite my dubious job description. Besides it's beautiful outside. I know this perfect bistro where they make the most delicious Mimosas."

"I don't drink Mimosas." Keeping her tone flat, she tried to deny her most surprising desire to join him.

"Well then you can have a Mint Julep, or if alcohol isn't your thing, they make a killer espresso. From what your sister tells me, you don't ever go out. Don't you get tired of being cooped up in this building?"

A light bulb lit up in her head. Now she knew why her sneaky sister had granted Caleb an interview. He was the 'yummy' reporter that lived across the hall from Thalie. No wonder she'd broken her own rule and granted him an interview. His tawny hair shone with gold highlights and he had the most unusually colored eyes. They reminded her of wet pewter, but it was his crooked smile that had Caché's heart racing. It promised all kinds of wicked things. Steeling herself to resist his 'golden boy' appeal, she shook her head.

"Whether or not I leave my building is of little importance, Mr. Stone. Rest assured I'll be talking to my sister about her discretion concerning my personal habits..." A knock on her outer door made her pause as Enrique, her personal security guard, who'd been with her family since Caché had been a small child, walked in.

"You called, Miss Caché?" Despite the silvering at his temples, Enrique was a huge bear of a black man who'd never failed to make Caché feel safe.

"Yes, Enrique. Mr. Stone here was just leaving and I don't want him to get lost in the process. Would you mind showing him the way out?"

"Of course, Ms Caché."

When Caleb looked like he was about to protest, Caché smiled at him sadly. "Thank you for the offer, Mr. Stone, but I'll have to decline. I have a date with a book which I intend to keep. I'll have my sister call when she comes back to reschedule your appointment."

"Don't think this is the end of it, Caché. I'd like to see you again." The look he gave her matched the determination in his voice. Caché couldn't help but shiver with sudden awareness.

"I don't think so." She nodded to Enrique who hustled the man out of her office. She was going to ignore the tugging in the pit of her stomach which told her she hadn't seen the last of the delicious Mr. Stone.

* * * *

Fuming as he rode down in the elevator with the security guard, Caleb tried to cope with his unusually intense reaction to Caché Ululani. While she wasn't a stunning beauty like Thalie, she appealed to him on a deeper level than any woman ever had. Even her waspish tone had turned him on. He'd wanted nothing more than to turn her stinging words into hisses of pleasure. It'd taken all of his considerable control to keep from dropping to his knees in front of her and giving her something to really scream about while he ate her, forcing one orgasm after another from her until she couldn't berate him anymore.

While she had the same dark hair as her sister, her jade eyes were a shade darker than Thalie's emerald ones. Her features had been softer too. But it was the loneliness in the smile she'd given him before the brute of a security guard had escorted him out, which had made him realize what Thalie told him earlier about her sister being a recluse had been true. *"My sister refuses to come out of her tower even though I can tell she's lonely, Caleb,"* had been her exact words.

He'd been so sure Thalie had been trying to set him up. She seemed to take his bachelor status as an insult. Besides, the way he saw it, there was no way in this day and age an attractive woman in her late twenties would willingly sequester herself, when she had the famous New York City nightlife at her fingertips. He'd thought he'd neatly escaped Thalie's matchmaking attempts until she'd tempted him with the one thing he'd had his eye on since he'd met her—her one-of-a-kind espresso machine.

Unlike most models, the one Thalie possessed made large quantities of the heavenly brew at once as opposed to the tiny four ounce serving his made. He'd been drooling over it since he'd helped her set up it up. When she offered it up in exchange for a date for her sister as part of a wager at their last poker party, he'd been unable to resist. He'd taken a chance with his pair of aces and kings, never realizing the conniving little witch across the table had a royal flush in her hand. Despite his protests, Thalie had held him to his word and set up the mock interview as an opportunity for him to ask her sister out.

"Which miserably backfired, Stone."

"Excuse me, Sir?"

Looking over at the guard, he shook his head. "Never mind, just thinking out loud."

The guard chuckled. "Ms. Caché has that affect on people. Most don't know how to take her."

Caleb nearly groaned at the man's words. He knew how he wanted to take Caché—*hard and fast while she's writhing and screaming under me and begging me for release.*

"You don't say?" Caleb couldn't help himself. He had to know more about the woman.

"I don't talk about Ms. Caché to just anyone, Mr. Stone."

"It's Caleb."

"Ms. Caché is off limits. She's been hurt enough."

"Aw, come on, Enrique, I'm not going to hurt her. I'm harmless as a fly. Thalie trusts me. Doesn't her approval count?"

"I know—or you would've never made it up to Caché's penthouse."

Caleb's jaw almost hit the floor.

"She told you?"

Enrique turned and smiled at him. "Of course she did. She knew I would never let a strange man within a hundred yards of Caché without checking him out. While I don't agree with the way she got you to do it, I know Thalie loves her sister. Plus I happen to agree with her about Caché's self-exile."

"I just can't believe she told you after swearing me to secrecy."

"There are few secrets in this family which I don't know about, Caleb, or about anyone who happens to enter their inner circle. I told Thalie having you meet Caché as a reporter would do nothing more than get her sister's back up. She doesn't do interviews and damn seldom sees even company people."

"Unfortunately it's what I do. I can't change the fact I write for a living." Caleb knew he sounded defensive but he didn't care. Whether it was writing for the paper or writing his novels, he loved his job and wasn't about to apologize for it.

"I never said that. If you're still serious about taking Ms. Caché out, I have an idea which just might work."

Caleb grinned. "Lay it on me. What do I have to lose?"

"Only an arm, if Ms. Caché finds out." Enrique kept his face solemn.

"I'll take my chances."

"Good, a man who doesn't mind risking a woman's ire is a 'rara avis' these days. You'll do." The elevator doors opened and Enrique escorted him to the door before pitching his voice low enough only Caleb could hear him. "Meet me around the corner at LaGarnia's in fifteen minutes."

Nodding, Caleb stepped out into the sunshine.

* * * *

"Did he give you any problems, Enrique?"

Caché was still sitting where he'd left her before escorting Caleb downstairs. Spying the book on the edge of her desk, he knew he'd have to be smooth, but it wouldn't be an issue as long as he could distract his sharp-eyed employer.

"No problem whatsoever, but I do believe he's smitten with you, Ms. Caché."

Arching an eyebrow at him, he could tell she didn't believe him. She rarely did when it came to her appeal to the opposite sex. No, she wasn't as beautiful as Thalie, but she was no dog and he'd like to shove his foot so far up Mr. Ululani's ass he'd have been tasting leather for weeks for implying even before her accident that Caché was dull as dish water. He could still remember his employer's horribly hurtful words when Felipe had turned away from his daughter after seeing the carnage the accident had left on her body. *"Pathetic. You were barely passable before the accident. No man will want you now."* The terrible accident had killed his wife and left his daughter broken and needing the father who betrayed her with his words. If the heart attack caused by the same accident hadn't taken Felipe Ululani mere hours later, he'd have hunted the man down himself.

"You're always nice to me, *un ami,* even when it's not warranted. I'm comfortable with my lack of appeal to the males of the species."

He nearly cursed when she reached for the book on the corner of her desk. "I'm going to LaGardina's for lunch. What you would like? My treat."

She glanced up at him and he knew he had her. She absolutely loved their quiche lorraine and tiramisu. While her eyes was focused on him, he slipped the book into the deep pocket of his suit coat.

"I'd kill for some quiche lorraine." Her smile was contagious.

"Quiche lorraine it is." He grinned back at her, turned quickly and left the room before she realized he'd just snatched her new book right out from under her nose.

* * * *

After a filling dinner and relaxing conversation with Enrique, who'd just left, Caché was ruffling through the papers scattered on her desk and looking for her book. Surely she hadn't misplaced it already. She hadn't even read it yet! After

looking for a third time, her eyes narrowed. The only person who'd been in her office today, other than herself and Enrique, had been Caleb Stone. Enrique had never expressed any desire to read it and even if he had, he would've simply asked her if he could borrow it. That ruled him out. So why would Caleb Stone take her book? Caleb was as masculine as they came and she couldn't see him reading an erotic romance novel. Playboy maybe, but not Casey Addington's newest book, especially an advanced copy.

Pressing the button on her intercom, she barked at her secretary. "Samantha, get Caleb Stone on the phone. Immediately!"

"Yes. Ms. Ululani."

A few moments later, her phone chirped. "Give me back my book! Do you realize what I had to do to get an advanced copy of it?"

A warm masculine chuckle filled her ear. "No, but I know what you're going to have to do to get it back."

His smooth tone had her seeing red. "Excuse me? Are you blackmailing me, Mr. Stone? Do you want your interview so badly you'd stoop to such lows?"

"This has nothing to do with any interview. You want your book back. I want to see you again. Surely we can come to an agreement."

"Fine, meet me here at six o'clock. Bring the book. I'll have Enrique escort you up."

"It's not going to be that easy, Ms.Ululani. I want to see you on my terms—not yours. I'm not a lowly peasant you can command to attend you. You may be the Beast of Ululani but I'm no Belle."

She hissed. "I see you heard about that. I assure you, I realize I'm not the lord of some fictitious castle. I am merely a woman who values her privacy and prefers not to be stared at."

"Fine, then come to my place."

Her heart racing, she tried to reason with him. "Do you honestly think I'm going place myself at risk by going to a man's home unescorted?"

She heard his sigh of frustration. "Listen, Ms. Ululani, despite what you think of my chosen profession, I've never once physically harmed a woman. If you don't believe me, ask your man. I'm sure he's already checked me out."

"All right, Mr. Stone. What time?" Her icy voice froze the phone lines.

"Eight is fine. I'll tell the doorman to expect you. I live directly across the hall from your sister, so you know the address."

Before she could even reach for a pen to jot down his address, the phone clicked in her ear.

"Damnit." Setting down the pen, she pressed the button on her intercom. "Samantha, get me my sister's address and ask Enrique to have the car ready at seven-thirty."

"Yes, ma'am."

Caché barely noticed the absolute shock in her secretary's voice. She had more important things on her mind than to worry about how totally she'd astonished her secretary. How the hell had one persistent reporter managed to do when others had tried and failed? She was leaving her tower for the first time in ten years, albeit reluctantly and under pressure.

Chapter Two

Staring down at the cover page of his book, looking at his own signature, Caleb finally realized why his reaction to Caché had been so potent. A thrill raced to his groin. It was hard to imagine the uptight Miss Caché was the sexy tease who'd been tempting him online for the last six months. He'd been surprised when he'd gotten her first email and before long they'd been instant messaging each other sometimes several times each day. In fact, they'd gotten so close he'd chosen to pull some serious strings to get her an advanced copy of his latest book, which he'd personally signed and had hand-delivered. No wonder she was adamant about wanting it back.

Sinking down on his couch, he took a few deep breaths. Now that he realized who the little minx was, it was going to take all of his considerable control to not toss her over the nearest hard surface and fuck the life out of her. He'd given her a very dangerous weapon if she ever figured out he was the Casey Addington. Through the anonymity of the Internet, they'd confided in each other things he knew they'd never even thought about confiding in any other person. He knew her secret fantasies as well as she knew his. If he even hinted at the fact he knew her secret identity, one of two things would happen. Either she would storm out of his life or they would both go up in flames. Despite the fact his body would love it, he knew he wanted more than hot, sweaty sex with Caché, and if the latter happened he knew he'd be missing out in something more important than sating his raging hard-on.

A brisk knock on his door had him surging off the couch. The book fell to the floor unnoticed as he rushed to the door. Jerking it open, he wasn't surprised to see Enrique standing behind Caché.

"Good evening, Enrique. Thank you for escorting Caché up, but I think I can take it from here." Drawing her into his apartment, he closed the door before Caché could catch the wink the other man had tossed his way. The last thing he needed was for Enrique to give away the game now.

"Can I take your wrap?" Gesturing to the hooded jacket and silk scarf around her head, he waited for her answer.

"I won't be here long enough to remove them, Mr. Stone."

Folding his arms over his chest he leaned up against the closed door. "We'll see about that. I said I wanted to see you again, not just give you the book back."

Sighing she placed her hand on her hip. "I've about had it with you, Mr. Stone. Consider yourself lucky I came over to get it. I simply could've let Enrique fetch it for me."

"Fat chance. It was either you or nothing. Now hand me your coat and scarf. I'll make it worth your while."

"Excuse me?" Her protest was muffled as he quickly stripped her out of her coat and pulled the scarf off.

"Come with me." Taking her hand, he led her into his kitchen. Pulling the dish from the refrigerator, he placed it on the island in the middle of the room. Cutting a sliver of tiramisu, he placed the rich dessert on a small china plate next to a fork before handing it to her. His breath caught in his throat when she licked her lips and stared hungrily at the dessert.

"You made me tiramisu?" Cache's voice was breathless with surprise.

"Yep, a little birdie told me you absolutely loved this. I figured if I pressed for dinner, you'd shoot me down, but what woman doesn't like dessert?"

"I really need to talk to my sister about how loose-lipped she is about me." Even as she protested, he couldn't help but nod with satisfaction as she reached for her fork. He wasn't about to tell her she'd been the one to tell him about her fondness for the Italian dessert. He'd let her think it was her sister for now. That dessert wasn't her only secret vice, just the most fattening.

A low moan of pleasure escaped her as she slid the fork out of her mouth. Leaning over the island, he couldn't help but watch her savor the creamy taste and fight his own need to taste her.

"Good?" His voice came out huskier than he intended.

"Yes. It's absolutely delicious. You have hidden talents, Mr. Stone. Are you sure you wouldn't rather be cooking for me instead of reporting? I'd offer you a competitive wage."

Even though he knew she was joking, he found it hard not to take offense. Every woman he'd ever dated had tried to change him. "Nope. Not a chance in hell. I'd end up being fired for sexually harassing the boss, so it's better I stick to my writing."

Her eyes widened and she left a smear of cream at the corner of her mouth as she jerked the fork back out of her mouth. "You have an issue with working for a woman?"

He reached out and captured it with his finger before popping it in his mouth. "Nope. I'd have a real problem keeping my hands to myself if *you* were my boss."

"Really, Caleb, you can turn the charm off anytime now. I'm here and you accomplished your goal."

"And what goal would that be?" For a moment he panicked. How had she found out about his wager with Thalie?

"You obviously wanted me to leave my 'tower' and here I am."

He relaxed. "Yes, you are. So why don't you relax and enjoy the rest of the evening with me? I promise I won't bite until you ask me to."

Setting her fork down, she tilted her head. "You really are a rascal, aren't you? You just can't resist flirting with every woman you come across."

Clutching his chest, he pretended to stumble backwards. "Ah darling, you wound me."

A laugh escaped her and she shook her head at his antics before sobering. "I'll admit the attention is flattering and good for my ego, but I really wish you wouldn't try to lull me with false sentiments."

Crossing his arms over his chest, he had a feeling he knew where this was heading and he didn't like her implications in the least. "What exactly are you implying, Ms Ululani?"

"I'm aware of my appeal or lack thereof. I'd much rather you'd be honest with me than lie. Pretty, little social white lies are still lies."

"So you think you're unattractive, Caché?"

Shooting him a mocking look, she pushed away from the island. "I own several mirrors and despite the fact I don't spend time studying myself in them, I know I don't have much to offer a man physically."

"That's bullshit. So you're not as beautiful as your sister. Almost no woman in the world is that beautiful, but why should it matter? There is more than one kind of beauty—both outer and inner—otherwise this world would be awfully boring."

"It matters when she's my twin and every second of the day, I wasn't allowed to forget the attributes I was lacking. *'Study harder, Caché. You'll never land a man with your looks. You'll need to know how to support yourself.'*"

"That's bullshit!" He grabbed her hand and yanked it against his dick. Under the denim of his jeans, his cock jumped in response, before hardening even further. "If simply watching you eat dessert has this effect on me, what do you think is going to happen the first time we kiss, or I see that luscious body you're so set on hiding from me?" He held her hand firm as she tried to jerk her hand away.

"Caleb!"

"Relax, I'm not going to attack you. I want you to understand reality. *This* is the reason I wanted you to come over. It has nothing to do with any interview or anything else. I find you attractive and, as a single man with a very healthy libido, I feel the urge to pursue the object of my lust."

It was his turn to groan when her fingers tightened around the solid shape of his erection through the denim. "You really want me?" The amazement in her voice had him opening his eyes to look at her. The look of awe on her face had him flushing. Exactly what kind of lovers had she had? Obviously men who'd never taken the time to show her how thankful they were to have her sexy little body under theirs.

"Hell yeah, I've wanted you since the moment you tried to throw me out of your office today. Do you know what I thought of while you were chewing my ass?"

A self-conscious laugh escaped her. "What a bitch I was being?"

"No. I had the most erotic fantasy of dropping to my knees and finding out how loud I could make you scream while I explored your pussy with my tongue."

He watched her face flush deepest rose, while her nipples pressed against the fabric of her silk blouse as she tried in vain to control her rapid breathing. "Unbelievable. You were thinking about sex during the middle of the day inside a business setting? What are you? A satyr? A lecher?"

"What can I say?" He shrugged his shoulders. "There is something about you which tempts me beyond what is acceptable. Believe me, if I ever get the chance to fuck you in your office, I can guarantee I'm going to take it."

Leaning closer to her, he backed her up against the wall with his arms braced on either side of her head and let his lips brush the shell of her ear. "Can't you imagine what it would feel like to be sitting in your plush executive chair behind your desk with it turned around, so no one other than me could see the pleasure on your face while I drape both your legs over the arms of the chair and prepare to eat your pussy? The arms would spread you so wide, you'd be a veritable feast for a starving man and that's exactly what I'd be. I wouldn't be able to resist. I would explore every fold with first my fingers and then my tongue. I'd be finding out exactly how velvety your outer folds are, while suckling on the tender and slippery inner ones until you're filling my mouth with your cream." His response ended with a deep, heartfelt deep groan.

She lifted her head with her lips parting on a gasp, and found he couldn't resist her offer despite the fact he'd promised himself he wasn't going to do this tonight. He captured her lips under his with an intensity he was sure would scare her away, but now found he couldn't control. He needed to sample her sweet taste now—he wouldn't wait one minute longer. His tongue shot inside of her mouth, intent on exploring every crevice. Rubbing his tongue against hers, he savored the lingering, sweet flavor of tiramisu mixed with her unique taste. It made him ravenous for more. Slanting his head, he searched for a better angle and couldn't help but growling as her arms wrapped around his neck and held him tighter. Hot damn if she couldn't kiss, he thought as he cradled her head in his hands.

When he finally jerked his mouth free of hers, his body was throbbing with the need to claim her. Forcing his desire down, he rested his forehead against hers. "Promise you'll see me again, Caché. I can't let you go without finding out where this will lead. Don't make me beg, baby."

She opened her eyes and searched his face. "I…ah hell, if I say yes, will you kiss me again?" Her voice was raspy with unfulfilled need, her lips were soft and wet from his kiss.

He nodded "Hell, yes. Wild horses couldn't stop me from sampling your sweet lips again." He moved to release her. He was surprised when her arms tightened.

"No. Now! Kiss me now." Her face was flushed and her eyes closed.

He drew a harsh breath as he heard the desperation in her voice. Her arms tightened around his neck. His breath rumbled out of his chest and he prayed he had better control than he thought he had. That last kiss had nearly done him in, but there was no way he could resist the plea in her voice.

Picking her up, he fastened his mouth over hers while holding her tightly against him. Each moan which escaped her made his body tighten further. He finally couldn't stand anymore and yanked his mouth away. "Please, baby, you're driving me insane. I'm trying not to rush this."

"Caleb." His name came out as a soft exhale. When he went to lower her back to the floor, her sex brushed over his and she stiffened in his arms. Her eyes flew open. "Caleb!" Her response came out as a muffled scream as she bit down on her lower lip.

"What the hell?" Shock rolled over him as she began to peak helplessly in his arms. The sight of her orgasmic pleasure nearly sent him over the edge after her. He continued to hold her as she trembled through what was obviously an extremely intense orgasm.

When she slumped breathlessly in his arms, he carried her out of the kitchen and into the living room. He sank onto the couch and held her as her breathing returned to normal. When she finally stirred in his arms, he pressed a chaste but longing kiss against her forehead.

"Better?"

"I…" A flush filled her face.

"Shh, there is nothing to be embarrassed about."

"But, I…"

"Found pleasure in my arms and I don't think I've ever seen anything as hot as watching you come for me, even if I'm not sure exactly how it happened." He brushed a piece of her dark hair away from her damp cheek. She flinched away and ducked her head.

"Don't, please?"

"What are you afraid of, Caché?"

"I have scars…"

"You mean these faint lines?" He traced his fingertips over the silvery lines which ran along her jawbone.

She nodded.

"They're barely noticeable. They're from the accident right?" Her sister had mentioned an accident which had caused Caché's self imposed isolation.

She nodded.

"Then they are badges of honor, living proof you're a survivor."

She sighed and laid her head against his chest.

Chapter Three

Biting her lip, Caché stood in the hall outside of Caleb's apartment. He'd called earlier to let her know he was back from his trip. He'd been out of town for only a few days, but she'd missed him dreadfully, much to her surprise. Tonight would only be her fourth visit in as many weeks to his apartment since the night she'd climaxed in his arms.

There had been no repeats of that particular night to her great dismay. He seemed to be keeping his libido on a tight rein no matter what she did. If it weren't for the fire in his pewter eyes, her already battered self-esteem would've taken even a larger blow than the one her father had dealt her. But every time she saw him, the desire he felt for her was clearly apparent despite his reluctance to take their physical relationship any further.

Looking down at the paper in her hands, the latest email she'd received from Casey Addington, she wondered what had possessed her to bring it with her. First and foremost, Casey would always be a close confident of hers. He was a nonjudgmental man who'd taken the time to listen to her deepest desires and not scoff at them. He'd even role-played with her online on several occasions since she'd met Caleb. With his valuable input, she was slowly coming out of her cocoon and she had both Casey and Caleb to thank for it. She'd be lying if she said her self-image no longer bothered her, but she was much more comfortable with herself than she'd been in many years.

She wanted to take the next step with Caleb, but first she wanted to see if he could accept the other man's presence in her life. She wasn't about to give up her friendship with Casey for Caleb no matter how hot he'd made her. In fact Casey had told her any man worth his salt wouldn't feel threatened if his woman had male friendships outside of their relationship. The only part which bothered her was that while Casey still remained her friend, their online banter had become even hotter and more risqué. There'd been several times in the past couple of weeks, she would've attacked the tease if he'd been in the same room with her. She thought perhaps he felt the same way about her.

But how could she be lusting after two different men? Sure, they had similar interests. Both were writers and, despite the subject of his writing, Casey was just as masculine as Caleb. They both called her 'baby', even though she was a long time out of the school room. Amazingly enough, rather than feeling belittled by the endearment, it gave her a special thrill to think each man wanted to care for her. It'd been years since anyone other than her sister had tried to baby her.

As wonderful as both men were, she was deeply torn. Each man had the same effect on her libido, they were driving her crazy trying to decide between them, and possibly having to give the other up. Too bad she couldn't have both. Pushing the thought away, she knew she couldn't stand in his hallway forever. Someone would come and wonder why she was loitering.

Deciding to get it over, she took a deep breath, knocked and waited for him to answer the door. She hadn't called before coming over and knew he wasn't expecting her. When she received no answer, she tried the knob and much to her surprise found it open. Pushing the door open, she called out but received no response. Hearing nothing, she wandered further into the living room. A quick tour of the rooms he'd shown her had revealed he wasn't in the public areas of his apartment.

Approaching the closed door at the end of hall, she put a trembling hand on the knob. Slowly turning it, she opened it to only hear the water running in the adjacent bathroom. Feeling braver than she'd ever felt in her life, she walked up to the ajar door and slid inside of the steamy room just as the water shut off. A squeak caught in her throat as Caleb stepped out of the shower in all his wet naked glory. While water ran down his impressive chest, she found her eyes hopelessly locked with his. A flaring of his nostrils was all the warning she got before she found herself pressed against the tile wall with over six foot of wet, aroused male so tight against her, she could feel every inch of him soaking through her light spring dress.

"Baby, where the hell did you come from?" His voice was hoarse, but he gave her no chance to answer before his mouth covered hers. A feeling of homecoming washed over her. She speared her fingers through his damp hair while their tongues tangled together, then arched against him as his thumb brushed over the pebbled surface of her nipple. Tearing her mouth away from his, she panted and tried to bring her 'out of control' desire under control. It was a futile battle though as his mouth slid down the length of her neck to sweep across the exposed swell of her breasts.

"Oh god, Caleb!" Her cry echoed through the bathroom as he nudged aside her neckline to get better access at her breasts. A loud ripping sound filled the room as he jerked on the bodice of her dress. His muttered apology barely registered as he took one lace covered nipple into his mouth. The erotic contrast of heat and lace had her moaning incoherently. Pleasure sharper than the last time she'd been in his arms filled her. Her womb clenched as his mouth left one nipple to attack the other. "Please, Caleb, I need you!" Her cry had him tearing his mouth away from her heaving breasts. His eyes dazed with passion met hers.

"God, you're so sweet. I've missed you, baby." His voice was deep and roughened when she reached in front of her and snapped open the front catch on her bra, spilling her diamond-hard nipples into his view.

"Suck them!" Her plea seemed to snap whatever leash he'd had on his desire. A low rumble came from his chest before he inhaled sharply.

"Fuck! Wrap those legs around me." His words were barely audible but she did as he ordered. A sharp moan escaped her as the only thing separating his hard cock from her creaming pussy was the moist crotch of her panties. Keeping his eyes on the hard nubs in front of him, he shouldered open the door of the bathroom and stumbled the remaining few feet to his bed before coming down on top of her.

Keeping his weight braced on his elbows, he rocked against her as he licked his way down her chest. Licking and nibbling at her nipples, he paid them homage before ripping her dress the rest of the way down.

"Caleb?" Her voice was weak with need when he pulled back to examine what he'd exposed. Heat raced over her as he took in the peaks and valleys of her body and the faint silvering of scars along her right side. Using his tongue to trace down her torso, he slid lower across the bed until his wide shoulders were nestled between her thighs. Without waiting for her to protest his actions, he yanked the crotch of her underwear to the side and gave her wet sex a long stroke with his tongue.

Crying out, she sat up in surprise only to have him press a hand against her stomach to hold her in place. "Don't move." His growl was deep and fierce. She fell back to the bed with a whimper. What little protest she'd thought about voicing was washed away as the hot glide of his tongue over her swollen folds sent pleasure skittering over her already strung tight nerves. As the tension built, she rocked, instinctively wanting the sensations his mouth was offering. She'd die if he didn't fill her this time. She needed more than his talented tongue. She needed his rock-hard cock all the way inside her.

"More, Caleb. I need you to fuck me!" She tugged at his shoulders hoping to convince him back up her body. His warning rumble had her hands falling away. He wanted his fill and wasn't going to stop just because she wanted to feel him inside of her. A choked scream escaped her when two of his thick fingers thrust inside of her and his tongue lashed at her clit. Her hips rose off the bed as her orgasm crashed over her and she bucked against his mouth.

Before she could return to Earth, Caleb scrambled to his knees, took her ass in his hands and lifted her hips to meet his downward thrust. A full-fledged scream filled the room as he sank to the hilt inside of her. She was unbelievably tight—almost virginal. The scream had been of pleasure but was there some pain? Had that been her very first time?

"Yes! Scream for me, baby. Tell me about it. Take your pleasure." His words escaped through gritted teeth as he began to move almost violently against her. The sound of wet skin smacking against wet skin mingled with the rising grunts from him and escalating cries from her.

Digging her fingers into the bedding below her, it was all Caché could do to hold on as the pressure inside her built to astonishing heights. She whimpered with both need and fear. She wasn't going to survive this. He was going to kill her with pleasure. Closing her eyes, she tried to fight this driving climax off.

"No you don't!" Caleb's voice, harsh and demanding, had her eyes flying open. "You are not going to hold back—fly, baby, fly!

"What?" Her dazed reply had him baring his teeth as he forced her knees up and over his arms to rest on his sweaty shoulders.

"Quit fighting it! I want it all, baby. No more teasing looks or scorching online innuendo. I want the woman behind it all and you're going to give it to me. I don't care who or what or why—there's only us and right now."

Her shocked eyes locked with his before she lost focus under the onslaught of his desire for her. A muffled shriek left her tortured body when his hand slid between their smacking bodies. His thumb pressed down on her clit and rotated with deadly accuracy. She couldn't do anything other than obey as her world exploded around her.

Intense, overwhelming orgasmic pleasure rocked her and her tremors would've thrown him out of her if he hadn't had such a firm grip on her sweaty hips. A wail escaped her as she thrashed around him and incredibly grew wetter, her fluids now coating both her thighs and his groin. To her dazed mind, she was afraid she'd lost control of her bladder, as she kept on leaking her own come while a hoarse shout escaped him.

"Fuck yes. Soak me, baby. Come with me!" His hands tightened on her until she knew she'd have bruises left from his hold. Moments later his wetness joined hers and he sank down on her trembling body barely catching his much heavier weight on his forearms. Even bent in half under him, she was sated right down to her toes. She was barely aware when he gently lowered her sore and stretched legs back to the bed. The orgasm she had felt in his arms almost a month ago had paled beside the intensity of her first real experience. Yes, she was an adult, but self-isolation had been an overwhelming barrier to ending her virginal state. Now, there was something nagging at her mind she needed to tell Caleb, but exhausted sleep beckoned and she couldn't resist its lure. She was asleep before he even separated their lower bodies.

His heart thundering in his chest, Caleb tried to catch his breath. She'd literally blown him away. The control he'd prided himself now laid in tattered remains around their sweat covered bodies. When she'd shown up in his bathroom all thoughts of resisting had flown from him. He'd wanted her right then and there. Her teasing innuendos to Casey had him half cocked for the past couple of days and her sudden appearance had sealed their fate.

For the past month he'd treaded a very fine line. Even as he was courting her as Caleb—he'd pursued her online as Casey. He knew it wasn't the right thing to do, but he couldn't help it. Whether talking with her online or in person, the moment she opened her mouth he'd forgot about anything other than claiming her as his. He'd almost found himself being jealous of himself and his guilt for his ruse grew each day, until he'd decided he had to tell Caché the truth even if he lost her. All he could do is pray that she forgave him.

"Caché, baby, we've got to talk."

When he got no response, he lifted his head. His heart softened as he realized he'd exhausted her and she was already asleep under him. Brushing the tangled hair away from her cheek, he traced the scarring on her face. She hadn't thought of hiding it from him tonight as she had when they first met. His little butterfly was spreading her wings and he only could hope she'd let him go with her when she decided to fly away, because he didn't know if he could survive without her.

Dragging the coverlet up and over them, he wrapped her in his arms and yawned. Even though it was only one o'clock in the afternoon, a nap with his lover sounded like a fine idea. Great sex wore a person out even more than travel. Holding her snuggly against his side, he joined her.

* * * *

Waking with a start, Caché tried to figure out what had woken her. Glancing over at the clock, she realized it had been two hours since she'd appeared at Caleb's apartment. Pushing herself up off the bed, she smiled at the picture he made with one arm thrown above his head. The peek of hair in his underarm lent him a vulnerability she'd never seen before. His features were relaxed in sleep. She had the overwhelming urge to brush a kiss over his sleeping lips but the urgency of her bladder reminded her she needed to assuage one need before the other.

Slipping out of the bed, she padded into the bathroom. After using the facilities, she snagged one of Caleb's oversized shirts and slipped it on over her head. She giggled as it fell to her knees. Her lover was a monster of a man. No wonder she always felt protected by him. His size was comforting, especially when she'd knew he'd never hurt her with it.

Checking on him, she decided to let him sleep. The poor baby looked exhausted. Wandering out into his kitchen she fixed a cup of coffee for herself and grinned at the shiny espresso machine sitting on his counter. It was obvious he was an espresso aficionado, like her sister. She herself preferred imported teas from Ireland and England over coffee any day of the week, but since he had no tea, she settled on plain old Columbian Coffee.

Sipping on the cup, she wandered around his apartment. Seeing another door ajar across the hall, she wandered in, thinking it was either a spare room or perhaps an exercise room. With a body like his, he surely had some kind of gym routine. Much to her surprise, she was surrounded by a home office. In the corner sat a teak desk with a sleek laptop. It was closed but next to the laptop and scattered across its surface were papers and sticky notes. Assuming it was his home office for his writing, she wandered over.

The phone in the corner of the desk rang. Rushing over to grab it before it woke Caleb, she lifted the phone as his answering machine picked up. Lowering the phone back into its cradle, a contract sitting next to the phone caught her eye. She listened to Caleb's voice instruct the person to leave a message as shock washed over her. A contract bearing Casey Addington's name and Caleb's signature was patiently waiting for him. As if she were watching from a distance, she saw herself picking the document up. Tears filled her eyes as she realized the two men she had been agonizing over were one and the same.

She was jerked out of her daze as she heard a familiar voice. *Thalie.*

"Hey Caleb. It's just me. I was calling to thank you for fulfilling your end of the wager. I never thought I'd see the day my sister would willingly leave her tower. I can't thank you enough. Anyway, give me a call when we get back. I'd say you earned yourself a cup of espresso. Ciao."

The tears, on the verge of falling moments ago, dried up as violent anger and absolute fury replaced them.

* * * *

Caleb jerked awake when the phone rang. He knew the machine would pick it up. Rolling off the bed, he was looking around for Caché when Thalie's voice came from his office. Scrambling to his feet, he didn't even bother to grab a towel. He raced into his study as he listened to Thalie's message condemn him to a life without his lover. Caché looked up at him with the contract in her hands that he'd been going over before getting in the shower. From the death grip she had on it, he knew he was doomed and her words proved it.

"You rotten son-of-a-bitch!" The glass paperweight sitting on his desk came flying at him. Ducking, he winced as it shattered when it hit the wall.

"It wasn't bad enough my sister had to use a bet to get you to go out with me." When the stapler was the next victim of her rage, he surged across the room. He caught her as she reached for his laptop.

"Calm the fuck down, Caché!"

She glared up at him before kicking him in the shin. "You weren't content to just fuck me over as Caleb, were you?" You had to take the one friend I thought I had and use him against me too." Doubling up her fist, she swung at him. He swore under his breath and yanked her up against him, so she couldn't pummel him anymore. It broke his heart to hear the sobs coming from her now as she continued to chew his ass out in her rage.

"You're a real fucking asshole! You, Mr. Addington or Mr. Stone, or whoever the hell else you want to be, can go straight to hell!" She continued to smack at his chest as her sobs became harder. "Do not... pass go... do... not... collect... two... hundred dollars!"

"Shh, I know, baby. I'm a total asshole." He rocked her in his arms, cuddling her and totally uncaring that he was standing naked as the day he'd been born in his office with his sobbing lover in his arms.

She finally stopped, her voice quiet. "Let me go."

He leaned back to look down at her. "Why?"

"Because it's time for me to leave."

He raised an eyebrow at her. "Do you honestly think I'm going to let you go? Especially now that you've discovered *my* secrets?"

"I don't care what you think you're going to do or not. I'm done." She jerked out of his arms and turned to leave. His heart sank as he realized he was still going to lose her. Or was he?

"So you're gonna run back to your tower to lick your wounds? The Beast of Ululani wouldn't run from a fight. She'd give me hell for deceiving her and probably call Enrique to come and kick my ass." He prayed his gamble worked.

She gave him the sad smile he hadn't seen in over a month. "It wasn't the Beast who you deceived, Mr. Stone. It was the woman underneath, and she no longer wants the two-faced charlatan who stole her heart."

"You claim to be so innocent in this mess we're in. I wasn't the only one who used an alternate identity—Ms. "Hiddenbeauty". What the hell do you think I went through when I realized the woman I wanted with every fiber of my being was online flirting with Casey Addington?"

"You knew it was me?" Ashamed shock washed over her face.

"From the night you came back to get your book." Grabbing her signed copy of his book, he opened it. "This isn't just a signature stamp, baby. I signed this after going through hell to get an advanced copy for you. I wasn't going to let my publisher use that damn rubber stamp. You deserved the real deal. You got my own hand-written signature."

"The real deal?" Her sneer was lost on him.

"Yes. Let me introduce myself to you Ms. Ululani. My name is Caleb Casey Addington Stone, the third."

She stared at him before blurting out the first thing that came to her mind. "Dear Lord, did your parents hate you?"

Caleb laughed ruefully. "Hate me, no. Disappointed in me? Yep. Every day of my life. I love to write, baby. Whether it's as Caleb Stone, the intrepid reporter or as Casey Addington , the hopeless romantic."

"But that doesn't explain the wager, Caleb. You still went out with me as favor to my sister."

He sighed. "You've got to understand something, baby. Your sister is a matchmaker from hell. I wasn't looking for a woman when I lost that bet. You see, there was this feisty but vulnerable woman online I wanted to get to know better, even if she was elusive as hell and wouldn't even tell me what part of the country she lived in."

Hope grew in her eyes. "You wanted me before…"

"Yes, baby. I fell in love with you as 'Casey' online and then I met you as Caleb and I couldn't help myself. He fell for you, too. Frankly it doesn't matter which one you take, Ms. Ululani, because both are going to love you 'til the end of time, whether you're the Beast of Ululani or the woman who resides inside the Beast. That's why I won't let you go. Both the Beast and the 'Hiddenbeauty' love me and I can prove it."

She arched a brow. "Really? How can you do that?"

A devilish grin crossed his face. "Go sit down in that chair and I'll show you how I know."

She glanced at the chair, then back at him. "Excuse me?"

"Remember what I told you about the first time you gave me hell, baby? I'm going to use those tactics right now and keep on loving you until you admit you love me." Picking her up, he easily carried her over to the chair.

"Eeek!" Her eyes widened as he dropped her onto it.

Without pausing for even a moment, he draped her legs over it. "Before I'm through, I'll have you screaming it." Lowering his head, he smiled. He'd hear those words many times before the night was over. He knew how to tame his little Beast and damned if he wouldn't love every single moment of it.

About Dakota Trace

Dakota is a simple Midwest girl, who has found her passion in storytelling at a young age. Her father was always saying she was making up the craziest stories. Most remained unwritten though as writing wasn't Dakota's strong suit. That all changed in junior high when she took her first typing class. Problem solved for the dyslexic Dakota. There was no stopping her after that. She wrote her first novel her freshman year about a girl who could speak to animals on an old electric IBM typewriter and never looked back. Writing in several different genres, she is now a published author with multiple books under belt. When Dakota isn't writing she's a crazy mom of three wild Indians who are posing as children, a loving wife to the man of her dreams and a full time student.

To find out more about Dakota visit her at <u>dakotatrace.com</u>.

THE SLEEPING BOOTY
By Ava James

Captain Bartly, William P. Bartly, stepped foot on the sandy soil, his boots splashing through the water as he pulled on the wet rope in his calloused hands. The small dingy he'd loaded down weighed more and more.

How in the hell did he think he would make it out of this one? Sure, Corsican merchants were a hard group to steal from, but he couldn't resist the bounty that awaited him. When he learned that only three men manned the ship over night, he couldn't help but steal the gold. And the jewels. Who knew such fat men had a penchant for rubies?

Will pulled the taut rope and the wooden boat scrapped against rock. Finally!

He tugged as hard as he could, leaning back with all his weight to get the dingy well stuck on the shore. He glimpsed up at the sky. In a few hours it would be dawn.

Not too far off in the distance, the black outline of a ruined tower blocked the stars from view.

Home sweet home.

Lucky for Will, no one knew of his noble family history. If it weren't for his lecherous ancestors, that castle tower might stand proud and tall. But the glory of the MacGilroy clan faded centuries ago. Some said it began as a feud between his family and that of another, when a distant ancestor of his refused to marry his betrothed. How his family came to ruin didn't matter much to Will now. They'd been reduced to living on this lone island in the Hebrides raising sheep to survive. If his father hadn't deserted them, Will probably would have stayed on the island. And then what would his life have been? Sheep shit and rocks, that's what it'd be. No, pirating was far more interesting and lucrative. Too bad that last guard on the ship had seen him. If it weren't for the Corsicans searching after him, he might be in Venice enjoying all of the cultured comforts such a fine city could offer a wealthy pirate.

With the amount of booty he'd accumulated, he could retire comfortably and live a life far beyond his humble beginnings. But, for the foreseeable future, that life of comfort would have to wait.

He fought hard to pull the small boat further onto shore and once it was securely away from the time, Will sat down to rest before he went to fetch the hand cart. In the past ten years, he'd returned to the island a handful of times. He'd come here to deposit his loot before heading out again to search after his fortune. Rested for the moment, Will followed the winding path—more like an overgrown weed trail—which led to the old cottage.

The cottage, more than rundown, stood like a pile of rocks against the overgrown greenery. A small tree now sprouted up through the hole in the roof. Its skinny top stood only a few feet over the old cottage walls. Beside his old home, a small wooden barn harbored his hand cart. Will pulled the door open only to have a small bat come flying out at him.

"Damn vermin," he muttered before entering. A large tent cloth lay draped over his cart. He pulled it free and wadded it up before tossing it in the corner. The rickety old cart had two ill-matched wooden wheels. The left wheel had a particularly flat side to it that made turning it rather troublesome when carrying a loaded trunk. Will grabbed the handles of the cart and made the fifteen minute journey back to the shore. There were three trunks for him to haul to the ruined castle and he didn't want to be stuck doing this all day. He reached for the metal rings on either side of the first trunk and pulled.

Snap!

The ring on the right side of the trunk broke away just as he had lifted the trunk clear of the side of his boat. The trunk swung downward and landed square on his left foot.

"Son of a bastard!" he shouted. Will tried furiously to pull the cargo off of his damaged foot. He yanked and yanked again on the good metal ring that remained. Finally, he freed his injured appendage, but as soon as the pressure was removed, the pain tripled.

Will bit down on his lip, longing to kick the trunk, but that wasn't going to help him. He fell backward to the ground and fisted his hands in the damp sand. If he didn't have bad luck, he'd have no luck at all. Hobbling back to the castle while dragging the damned cart wouldn't work. He tried to rotate his ankle and pain shot up his leg like scalding liquid that went straight to his gut.

"Damn."

His foot had to be broken. This was just great—everything about his life could be summed up in this scenario. Just when things were looking up, they always went terribly wrong. Will laid flat and shut his eyes. With each heartbeat, he could feel the swelling. The pain thumped steadily through him. While he laid silent, he tried to focus on something other than his foot. He could hear the waves as they hit the shore, the subtle rumble of the building wave just before the whoosh of water drawing back. The air smelled wet, rich with minerals and the salty scents of rock and ocean. If he listened very closely, he could hear the beat of his heart. He tried to concentrate on those senses rather than the ache.

"Excuse me?" A soft voice broke through his meditative thoughts. Surprisingly, it did not cause him alarm. Odd..."Are ye well?"

Will opened one eye to a slit. Long blonde locks hung down as if reaching for him. Light green eyes, set in a pale face, stared with concern. He frowned and opened his other eye to be sure she was there.

"I say, are ye hurt?" She leaned closer, her hands flat against the blue gown she wore. The woman stood just behind his head, leaning over him.

"Aye," he replied. "But who are you and what are you doing on my island?" Other questions buzzed in his head too as he lay there staring up at her.

"Yer island? Beg yer pardon, who do ye think ye are? I came here to help, but if ye intend to be rude, help ye I will not." The woman blew a huff of air down on him before disappearing from his limited view.

Will rolled over on his side but the woman was gone. One moment she'd been there, right above him, and then she vanished. A thin mist hung over the ground and the sky held dawn's light. He pushed up off of the ground, up onto one knee, and then stood. He placed most of his weight on his good foot. Still, not a trace of her could be seen. Will looked down the shoreline and then in the opposite direction. Nothing.

He ran his hand through his hair and stood confused. "A dream?" It could very well have been. He shook his head and dismissed the odd occurrence. After all, no one lived on this isle. This was what happens when one was exhausted and had a run of bad luck.

After an hour and a half of agonizing labor, managing to get the trunks to the castle, Will decided he'd get some much needed sleep. He unloaded each trunk into the old solar of the castle. The once great hall had a gaping hole in the roof, but at the back of the room, off to the right in a nook, stood the door to the one room in the building that was not touched by the elements.

His great-great-great grandfather, Lord Ewan MacGilroy, commissioned a single window into the room, stained glass for his lady wife. The gentle hues of amber, blue and red cast against the plastered stone wall—a reminder of the past glory of his family. In the glass was a simple family crest, a badge with waves meeting a setting sun in the center. Someone long ago abandoned an over large wooden bed frame in the room, and Will took advantage of it, creating a straw mattress for himself to lay upon. He pulled the thick blanket from the bed and shook it out. Dust floated up like golden bits of nothing in the air. Next he grabbed up the pillow and beat it with his hands a few times before laying it back on the mattress.

With his bed made, Will crawled beneath the blanket and laid on his back waiting for sleep to claim him. On the ceiling, a faint Celtic cross was painted. The green outline and the intricate design were visible best when the morning light shone in. His eyelids felt heavier with each passing thought. Sleep claimed him quickly and Will hoped it would help alleviate the ache in his swollen foot. He closed his eyes and breathed deep until the warm fingers of rest claimed him.

Click...

Will frowned. His tired eyes were slow to open. His throat felt dry and his stomach grumbled.

Scrape...

A sixth sense, more than a notion, told him he wasn't alone. Then again, the noises were a good indication as well. He slid his hand beneath his pillow stealthily, but his dagger wasn't there. In his pain and exhaustion, he'd forgotten to place it under his head. *Damn!*

He opened his eyes to slits. The room was pitch-black and only a lone shaft of moonlight penetrated the darkness. Could his luck get even worse?

Will tried to keep his breathing normal and listened. He waited for any sound that would alert him to his intruder's location. Past that, he wasn't sure what he'd do.

The person in the room was not silent for long. He heard the soft slides of the sole of a shoe against the stone floor. At first, they sounded as if they moved away, but then they became louder and he knew they drew near.

If he was going to stop this person, he'd have to do it with his bare hands.

He listened, his heart beating faster in anticipation of the confrontation. Closer and closer, he now felt the warmth of their nearness.

Will snapped his hand up and caught the invader by the wrist.

Splash!

Cold water came crashing into his face and went right up—or down—his nose. He choked on the liquid, his senses in shock. Will instinctually leaned up. *Whack!* He knocked his head into something decidedly metal. Falling backward, he groaned, bringing his hands to his now aching, wet head. His shirt and the blanket became wetter by the moment.

"Goddamnit!"

"Don't ye go swearing when 'tis all yer own fault," a woman's voice chided.

That voice! The woman at the shore?

He opened his eyes and saw her face against the shadows. Her lips were set in a hard line of disapproval and she shook her head.

"Stay here while I get a torch."

A torch?

She disappeared into the darkness once more, but as promised, she returned almost immediately—torch in hand.

Who was this strange woman?

He could now see her features clearly. She wore the same dress as before, the edges of it tattered and worn.

"Who are you?" he asked.

"I live here," she replied after setting the torch in a ring hanging on the wall. "A better question would be, who do ye think ye are? Ye lay in my marriage bed and ye are not Angus MacGilroy."

"No, I am not."

"Then why are ye here?"

The lilt in her voice was far more pronounced and appealing than any he'd ever encountered. And what was with all of the 'ye's'?

"I own this pile of rocks. Captain William P. Bartly, at your service, ma'am." He gave a slight nod and asked, "And you are?"

"Lady Aurora FitzStewart."

From the look of her attire and the fact that she was here, the lady part made no sense at all. But then, neither did her claim to live in this ruin, or the fact she said this was her marriage bed. Either he was dreaming once more, or someone played a foul joke on him.

"Now listen here, *mi'lady*, you don't live here, and Angus MacGilroy sure as hell doesn't live here either. Since I know no Angus in my family, I am going to guess you made that part up. So why not be honest with me before I lose my temper?" He neglected to point out that she'd dumped water on him, and he hadn't even asked what her intention for having the water was in the first place.

"Ye get all high 'n' mighty just like Angus and ye said yer name was Bartly not MacGilroy." She folded her arms across her chest, and he noticed the gentle swell of her breasts above the neck of her gown.

"MacGilroy is my name." He looked into her doubting face.

"Aye, and ye would have me believe ye after ye just said yer name was Bartly?" Her eyes narrowed beneath her thick lashes. "What are ye a captain of anyhow. I do not see men about to serve beneath ye." She looked over her shoulder as if confirming her suspicions.

"My real name is William Patrick MacGilroy. This island is all that is left of MacGilroy lands and I am the sole MacGilroy on this earth." He now sat up in his bed and folded his arms across his chest, returning her glare.

"And I am to believe that when just two days passed, I saw the whole lot of the MacGilroy clan myself?" She shook her finger at him and stepped closer to the bed.

Was she daft? He put his hand on the bed and leaned toward her, speaking in a clear, unquestionable tone. "There has not been more than a handful of MacGilroy's for some time now. I assure you, I am all that is left of that once proud clan."

"Ha! Get out of yer bed." She grabbed his arm and pulled him. Her hands were cold on his skin and he quickly came out of bed before she made him fall out. He followed close behind her as she grabbed up the torch and pulled the solar door open. "See?" She said casting her hand out over the empty hall.

Her brow knitted in confusion and she released his arm. The space looked the same as it had when he entered this morning. Small vines climbed the barren walls and weeds grew between the stones in the floor. She swung the torch from left to right, her features conveying her disbelief. Lady Aurora took a few steps away from him and spun around, the light of the torch creating a shadow of light around her.

"What magic is this?" She demanded, pointing to the ground. "What have ye done?"

"Me?" he replied to her accusing tone. "I've not done a thing. I come here but once a year. Never before today have I seen you."

His words did nothing to calm her. If anything, she looked more agitated than before. He waited for her to say something, but she held her tongue. From the look on her face, several thoughts whirled through her mind—none of which gave her solace.

Aurora stepped closer to him until their bodies were separated by a mere hands width. She smelled of lilies. Her lips looked full and pink in the torchlight. Her steady gaze bore into him and he felt eternity in a moment. There was something deep, unwavering and demanding within her stare.

"Where is Angus?" she asked in a whisper.

"Dead?" he replied as honestly as he knew how. If there was an Angus MacGilroy, he certain did not exist in this time.

"Dead...actually and forever dead? Never to return?" Her eyes fair shined. Was she going to cry?

"I believe so..."

Then Aurora did the most unexpected thing of all, she hugged him. Her arms wrapped tight around his neck, her cool check pressing against his. She laughed and for some strange reason the sweet sound brought a smile to his lips. He felt stupid in sharing her joy for the death of an ancestor, but then again, nothing had made sense since he returned here.

Once her grip loosened, she leaned back and smiled wide. Aurora's expression brought a warmth to him that her skin lacked. Then the light in her eyes changed. Her brow wrinkled, she stepped back, and asked, "Why are the others gone?"

That he had no answer for. "No one has been here in a year."

"But that is not true—I saw them, just before I came in here this night. I saw them as I see ye." She pinched Will, and not too gently either.

"Ouch," he said.

"Well, ye seem to be real."

"If you wanted to see if you were dreaming, you should have pinched yourself," he muttered wondering what Aurora would do next.

"That wouldna' done me any good. I pinched ye because I thought ye might not be real, but ye are flesh and blood."

"Of course I'm real. Have you had a bump on your head? How did you come to be here?"

Her features changed as she thought. Aurora looked over Will's shoulder as if she were watching a scene play out in her memory. "My father brought me to Angus MacGilroy and the bans were waved two days ago. We are to be married in a few short weeks. He gave me the solar for my own until our wedding night." She walked passed Will and into the room she'd referred to. "But my trunks are missing." He followed her and watched as Aurora ran her hand over the tops of the treasure trunks. "I do not recognize these."

"No, those are mine."

"Oh," she replied absentmindedly. "My comb—'twas here this morning." She pointed to a spot beside the bed. "And the flowers I picked, they were there." Aurora looked across the room at another one of his trunks. "I don't understand." She ran her hand over the mattress. By the look on her face, his blanket was not what she remembered to be there either.

A single, unbelievable thought popped into his mind, and as he watched her look about, it made more and more sense. She talked about people who could not exist, things that had never been, and the way she talked...Lady Aurora was a ghost. It explained how she'd vanished this morning and then reappeared this evening. In an odd way, this answer made sense. But how does one tell another that they are a ghost?

"Um, Lady Aurora?" He walked over to stand before her. At first she did not acknowledge him. When she did look up though, he wished she hadn't. She looked lost and what he was about to say to her would certainly not be welcome news. "Aurora, would you sit down?"

She did as he asked without taking her eyes off of his. He didn't have much experience with imparting bad news to people. Usually his interactions with women were dalliances that lasted a few hours or less. "Would you like something to drink?" Okay, call him a coward, but he stalled.

"No, I'm not thirsty," she said as her gaze fell to her lap.

He tried to think of a nice enough way to say what needed to be said. Will took her hands into his and rubbed his fingertips over her knuckles. Her hands felt even colder now.

"Aurora, I think that you're lost." He danced around the truth a bit.

"No, I know where I am." She looked into his face again. Her gaze unnerved him. The woman appeared terribly vulnerable.

"I mean that…you have lost your way home."

"William, I don't understand ye at all. I know where my father's house is."

He wished she'd pick up on his subtle way of saying the obvious. "By home, I mean to say, that you have lost your way to heaven." That made even less sense—he could tell by the look on her face. "I think you did live here…a very long time ago. And…well…and you are no longer living."

She did not react but sat calmly gazing at him as if he'd just said it was night time. "You're dead," he said plainly, squeezing her hands tight to emphasize his point.

"That's rubbish. I can't be dead. I'm here." She shook her head. "Don't ye think I'd remember dying?"

Aurora slid her hand free of Will's and reached up, rubbing her palm against his bearded cheek. It felt good. There was a bit of heat in her touch.

"See, do ye not feel me? I feel ye."

"Aye, I do," he said, inhaling deep. Calm came to him as her soft skin rubbed against him.

"How can a dead person feel and be felt?" She stared deep into his eyes. Something sparked there and he felt a pull towards her. Will leaned in to her touch, her face now inches from his. "How can the dead kiss?" she asked before touching her soft lips to his.

At the subtle brush of lip upon lip, he felt a tingling sensation. "Did you feel that?"

"Oh, aye," she replied with a sigh. "Are ye sure Angus is dead?"

"Why?"

"Because if he were not, ye and I would be in great danger." Aurora pressed her forehead against Will's.

He closed his eyes and savored her nearness. They sat in the dreamlike silence of the moment. Was she a ghost or was this a cruel dream? In Aurora's presence, tranquility seeped into his soul. How could one person do this to him in so little time? Nothing about this situation made sense and reasoning it out proved even less sane.

"Hold me," she said and he obliged without second thought. Will held her close and tucked the top of her head beneath his chin. He ran his hand through her long blonde locks and admired the silky texture.

"A Bean Nighe, an evil witch, told me Angus would be my death." She spoke in a soft tone. "The old woman came to me at the shoreline and said I would fall in a deep sleep, never to marry Angus." Aurora was quiet once more and Will waited for her to tell him the rest of the story.

Finally, he said, "It's okay, you don't have to tell me."

"Yes, I think I do," Aurora replied. She gazed up at him, her eyes moist with unshed tears. "I just feel so tired all of a sudden. Maybe I should lie down." She pulled back from Will's embrace. He rose to give her space, and she laid her head down on the mattress, using her arm as her pillow. "She told me I would fall asleep and that only one could wake me with loneliness...That makes no sense."

Will sat back down beside her and ran his hand along the curve of her cheek. Loneliness—he'd felt that emotion all of his life, especially when his mother died. When father left them, he was angry, but he had his mother beside him.

"I'm lonely." He voiced the thought unintentionally. For some reason, he felt the need to elaborate. "I live a life of solitude. A pirate doesn't have many friends for long. The day my mother died was the day I started my lonesome journey through this world. I left this island thinking the riches I sought would bring me all I needed. But, until tonight, I never realized just how worthless the treasures all are. No matter what riches I have, they will not bring back my mother's love." That was the most honest speech he'd ever made, and it felt good to get the words spoken. It didn't feel good to admit the emptiness though. In fact, most nights he drank himself to sleep when the memories became too much. Aurora placed her hand over his. Her touch was warmer still than before. "I'm sorry for ye loss. How long has she been gone?"

"Eleven years this winter." He found it hard to believe that much time had passed. It seemed just yesterday when he tended her sick bed.

"What year is this?" she asked.

"Seventeen sixty-four."

"My mother is long dead now too. How could almost four hundred years pass without me knowing?" He couldn't imagine the feelings she experienced—waking up one night and realizing that the world you knew no longer existed. "Will, dawn will be here in a few hours. What do ye think will happen to me?" Aurora stared at the moonbeam coming through the glass window.

"Have you seen anyone before I came to you?" He tried to rationalize some reason for all of this.

"No."

This was not promising. If the sun rose, would she disappear as she had that morning? "Where did you go this morning, after you saw me on the beach?"

Her brow knitted as she thought on his question. "I...I don't know. I remember turning to walk away from ye, and then...then nothing."

Nothing. That was very bad. "Nothing at all?"

"No. It was as if I fainted."

"Hummm." He really wanted to say damn, but that wouldn't do them any good. So instead, he asked, "Do you remember exactly what that old hag said? Maybe it holds a clue to end this?"

Aurora rolled over onto her back and stared at the ceiling. Silence stretched as she closed her eyes and then she spoke. "Fair lady, fall ye will, sleep will claim thee, wedded ye will not be. One could wake ye, but loneliness of his heart must not prevail. Then ye may rise, hale with the sun."

He thought on those words for a moment. Strange, but he knew he was the man she spoke of—Loneliness of his heart...Hale with the sun...

"Would you stay with me until the sun rises?" If he was right, this could all end for her tonight, and her life could begin again—with him.

"Aye." She took his hand into hers. "If this is the last night I have here, I'd like to lay in yer arms." Her cheeks turned pink with embarrassment. "I don't want to die without at least knowing what it feels like to be held by another."

It was a simple and genuine request. He'd hate to die alone, with no one to mourn him. Thinking about that, he realized that when he died, that was exactly how he'd leave this earth. There was not a soul who knew who he really was—well except for Aurora.

"Of course I will." He lay down beside here and pulled her close. She placed her head on his shoulder and sighed.

"Ye know, I thought I would go to Heaven. Instead, I know not where I am or where I will be tomorrow."

"Sure you do. You'll be with me." He hugged her tight to his chest and placed a gentle kiss to the crest of her head.

"Do ye ever think of what yer life will be? I mean to say, ye have all these chests piled up—what are ye going to do with it all?"

"Honestly, I don't know. There are a great deal many things I could do." She began to rub the palm of her hand on his chest. The subtle sensation distracted him. He could think of several things he'd like to do on the morrow if she remained in his life. "What would you do with it?"

"Me? I've never had more than a few coins to myself. If I were ye though, there is a great deal many things I could think to do. Look at this castle—ye own it, but do ye take any pride in it? I say I would repair it. That would require some craftsmen to live here on the island for a great deal of time. Offering them each a small parcel of land may temp them to work more diligently. Or at least the men of my time would have taken ye offer up." She nodded her head. "Aye, if I were ye, that's what I'd do—make this place honorable once more, make it a home to be proud of."

"But what good is a home without a family? That's why I left in the first place. Without loving people to keep you company, a home turns into a prison." Will ran his fingers through her long blonde hair. He inhaled her essence and considered a life with her. In his mind, he'd already decided it was the life he wanted.

"Ye should find a good woman and live out yer life to the fullest," she said in a low tone that mirrored a whisper.

"What if I said I'd already found a good woman to build my home with?"

Her breathing stilled. Did she understand his meaning? The movement of her hand slowed to a stop.

"The moonlight is fading," she whispered.

"Aurora," he reached down and titled her chin up so he could look into her glorious eyes. His nerves clenched his stomach with the words he longed to say, ready to spring forth, "Stay here with me. Forget the world you came from and start the day anew with me."

A lone tear slipped down her cheek as he spoke and he brushed it away with the pad of his thumb, hoping it was a tear of happiness. "Let me release you, my sleeping beauty."

"And if I disappear again?" Her bottom lip quivered.

"Say you'll stay, and I promise to never let you go into the day alone again."

"Those sound like vows, Will."

"Aye, they do. All we need now is for you to speak yours." He intertwined his fingers with hers. Everything about this was strangely right. He'd walked through life alone, missing something he never knew. Now, as he held her hand in his, he knew exactly what his life needed—her. *Aurora*—ironic that her name's meaning and her curse interrelated.

"Will, I will ever remain by yer side and warm yer nights."

They leaned into one another and sealed their vows with a kiss—one that spoke of their honest intent and flourishing love. The first fingers of dawn's rays came through the stained glass window and cast a rosy shadow upon the Celtic cross on the ceiling. A burst of golden glitter showered down up them, but they barely noticed anything beyond each other. The rest of their lives would start today, and forever would Will remember the night he found his sleeping booty.

About Ava James

Ava James is an avid writer and reader of everything romance. She lives near the 'Gateway to the West' with her husband, their English bulldog and two cats. Marrying her high school sweetheart, she is a hopeless romantic. Can't you tell already? You can find Ms. James at:

avajames.weebly.com and
avajamesromance.blogspot.com.

**If you enjoyed HAPPY EVER AFTER,
be sure to check out eXcessica's other anthologies!**

FOUR SEASONS: SPRING 2009
Selena Kitt, editor

Spring is a time of beginnings - after a gradual thaw, the melting of one season into next, comes a bright renewal - the exciting, passionate bloom of love, youth, new life, chances to begin again and all the rituals of re-birth. As the world blooms open again, so does the human longing for re-connection, both emotionally and physically. Come join your favorite eXcessica authors in this sensual, seasonal anthology, bringing you the best of all things sexy in the spring!

Night Owl Romance Review by Vee: 4/5 STARS!

FOUR SEASONS: SUMMER
Selena Kitt, editor

The heat of summer brings you the best in steamy erotica, a sultry collection to make you break into a wanton, feverish sweat. This one's a fiery scorcher, an exciting, wild ride, page after page. So come take a HOT vacation with your favorite eXcessica authors in this sexy, seasonal anthology, bringing you the best of all things summer!

FOUR SEASONS: AUTUMN
Selena Kitt, editor

The autumn weather might be cooling things off, but you won't need that sweater - we promise our erotica will warm you up! This time of year involves metamorphosis, from the changing of the fall colors to the places between, where the world wears thin and the strange and unusual happens. Join your favorite eXcessica authors in this sexy, sometimes spooky, seasonal anthology, bringing you the best of all things autumn!

FOUR SEASONS: WINTER
Selena Kitt, editor

If the spirit and magic of the winter season wasn't enough to keep you warm as the weather turns cold, you can count on the erotica in this spicy anthology to do the trick! So let it snow, and curl up with your favorite eXcessica authors and this sexy, seasonal anthology, bringing you the best of all things winter!

Stories included from: Sommer Marsden, Kiki Howell, Mallory Path, Phillip Sweeny, Paul McDermott, J.M. Snyder, Alessia Brio and Will Belegon, Giselle Renarde, Rachelle Le Monnier, Saskia Walker and Selena Kitt.

YOU'VE REACHED "THE END!"

BUY THIS AND MORE TITLES AT www.eXcessica.com

eXcessica's <u>YAHOO GROUP</u>
groups.yahoo.com/ group/eXcessica/

Check us out for updates about eXcessica books!

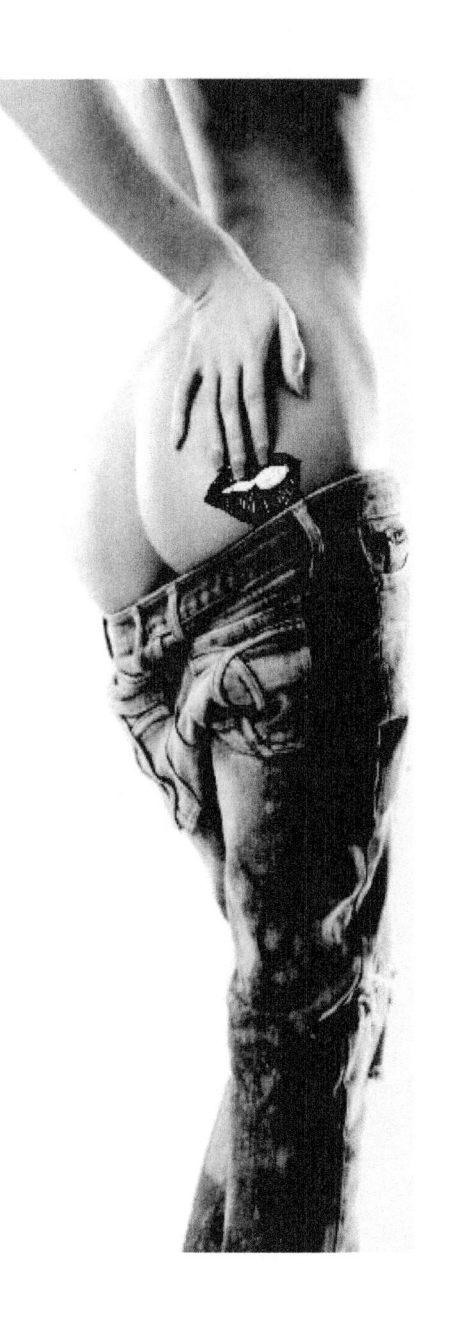

Happy Ever After
Selena Kitt, editor